The Corey Effect

Casey Dembowski

The Corey Effect
Red Adept Publishing, LLC
104 Bugenfield Court
Garner, NC 27529
https://RedAdeptPublishing.com/

This is a work of fiction. Names, characters, places, and incidents either are the product of the author's imagination or are used fictitiously, and any resemblance to locales, events, business establishments, or actual persons—living or dead—is entirely coincidental.

For my mom

Chapter 1

Now

The familiar eerie melody of a classic horror-movie theme shook the desk under me. I untangled my hands from Harry's hair and reached across my desk to ignore the call. My office returned to silence, the only sound Harry's shallow breathing as he kissed the crook of my neck. His hands worked the buttons of my blouse as mine undid the one on his pants. He'd had yet another mediation meeting with his soon-to-be-ex wife—if she would only sign the damn papers—that morning. He only dared to have sex in the office on the days he had to deal with her.

Harry pushed me farther back, and the pages of a marketing plan for our newest client crunched under my weight. He slid his hand slowly up my skirt, teasing me. I wrapped my leg around his torso, pulling him into me. I'd missed him over the weekend. My cell phone vibrated under me, and the theme from *Halloween* rang through the office again. I picked it up with one hand and pushed his pants down with the other. My gaze shifted to the cell phone. It was my mother. *Abso-fucking-lutely not*. My mother could wait a few—several—more minutes.

Getting Harry out of my office as soon as possible was paramount. Yes, we'd had the good sense to lock the door, but the last thing we needed was to arouse suspicion. We'd kept quiet for two years. There was no reason to blow it now.

Harry pressed up against me. My body sprang to life, waking up for the first time in days. Oh, how I wanted him. I dropped the phone back onto my desk and let my hands roam through his hair and down his back, settling under his boxers. And then I felt it again—that damn vibrating phone. The music returned. Michael Myers was coming to get us.

Harry pulled away, barely an inch but enough for me to notice. "Just answer it, Andi."

I grabbed the phone, my other hand still grasping Harry's bare ass. "What is it, Mom? I'm in a meeting."

"It's about Ryan," she said, her voice unusually low.

"Mom, I really don't have time—"

"He died, Andi."

I couldn't breathe. I clutched my desk to steady myself, but Harry didn't seem to notice or care. He lowered himself to his knees. His lips danced along my inner thigh, unaware that my world had started spinning. I placed a hand on his shoulder to pull his attention back to my face. My mother said my name again. She repeated herself with quick, succinct sentences, filling in more details, but the message was the same—my father had died.

"I'll call you back," I said.

The phone hadn't even hit my desk before I pulled Harry to his feet and found my way back into his boxers. Everything fell away except his lips on my lips. Our breaths intermingled and dissolved. I slipped out of my underwear and twined my legs around him. I pressed him closer to me. Pleasure washed over me and erased all coherent thought. A gasp escaped my lips as he let his tongue linger on my ear. He smiled at me disapprovingly and covered the noises I couldn't quiet with his mouth, swallowing my moans as he thrust deeper into me. Every extremity was piqued. My toes curled. I devoured him in another kiss as a scream worked its way up my throat. He shuddered and then collapsed against me with a laugh.

"Someone got a little carried away." He stepped back and pulled his pants up.

I was usually better at shielding my excitement, but everything had collided inside me. My father—Ryan—was dead. The monster who had haunted me for the last decade had been slain. Processing that fact had been impossible with Harry half-naked and at full mast between my legs. All I'd wanted in that moment was to feel everything and nothing. Harry was good for that. I straightened my skirt and fumbled with the last button on my shirt before sitting down at my desk.

"What did your mother want?" he asked, taking the seat across from me.

Harry knew I wasn't in contact with my father. He didn't know why, and he didn't ask. But if I explained my reasons out loud, they would become real. I wasn't sure I was ready to open that hermetically sealed door back up.

I straightened the crushed marketing plan against the edge of my desk. "Ry—my father died."

His brow furrowed, and he met my eyes. "How?"

I toggled a red pen between my fingers and focused on the pages again. My mom had sprinted through that part, but I'd heard her. "Cirrhosis."

"Are you okay?"

Anger and resentment threatened to break through the barriers I'd buried them under. An ache settled in my right wrist as vestiges of that time seeped into my mind. I shook them away. "Appearances, Harry. This is the longest meeting you've ever had." I smiled to lighten the dismissal, but our little tryst *had* taken a while. And everyone knew he held long meetings in his office because it was more comfortable than the windowless boxes the rest of us had.

He stood with a laugh. "You're right. I'm already going to have to go sit in Craig's office for at least fifteen minutes, listening to him drone on about his idea for the Nielsen campaign."

"Nielsen... organic..."

"Baby food." He groaned. "Trying to break into the baby bath products industry." He stopped at the door. "Andi, you know that... well, you can talk to me if you need to."

He was gone before I could muster up a response or a rejection. *Typical Harry.* I didn't have time for his sympathy. I needed to call my mother back before she called me. She wouldn't necessarily be upset about Ryan's death, but she would be worried for me. My parents had been separated practically my entire life. I didn't have a single memory of them together. The details of their marriage and divorce were a fuzzy tale I'd pieced together from relatives' stories, but she'd never said anything about it directly. And with the exception of my father's weekly arrival at my front door to pick me up when I was a kid, my parents had almost never interacted. *My* hands had passed letters and child-support checks between the two of them.

I needed to call her. But right then, I didn't want to deal with her or think about *him*. Fortunately, my computer dinged, signaling yet another email. With a wiggle of the mouse, my screen woke up, and my inboxes appeared. Unread emails had piled up—from potential clients and current clients and several from Harry about what he would need on his upcoming trip—but what I mainly noticed was the single read message in my personal email from Steve Alridge, a friend from college and the director of communications at Marathon Integrated Systems.

A year earlier, while Harry and I had been taking a break, I'd asked Steve if there were any openings at Marathon, wanting not only to be away from Harry but to have normal hours, a specific set of job parameters, and a real chance for growth. After a year of talking and working it out and waiting for a position to open, Steve had gotten permission to hire another communications manager, and he wanted me. That knowledge, combined with the fact that Harry's daughter was in town, had kept me avoiding Harry's texts all weekend. The decision was too much. It was a simple choice, but making it would change everything—and not only on a personal level. I couldn't be an associate project manager and Harry's part-time assistant forever. Corporate communications was a logical next step in my career path—and maybe, for once, I'd feel deserving of my position, confident that I'd earned it on merit.

I picked up the marketing plan again. It was still a draft, but it would help the client focus their marketing and embrace a much-needed social media strategy, thinking locally first before expanding and using advertising in the trades instead of commercials. The plan needed more work. I knew the level of excellence Harry expected from each of us, and it wasn't there yet. Revisiting the engineering journals and trade shows I'd listed, my mind turned away from everything not on the page—Harry, my mom, Ryan. And then the phone rang.

"Andrea Scott," I said without looking at the caller ID. It was probably Craig, calling to ask my opinion on a slogan for the baby lotion campaign, as if I knew about babies simply because I had ovaries.

"I hate when you answer the phone like that." Of course, it was my mother, calling me on my office line. She knew me too well. "Who exactly are you presenting yourself to?"

"Hello, Mom."

"You hung up on me."

I was tempted to do it again. Talking about my father was never high on my list of priorities, but discussing his death while I was at work was unacceptable. I had too much to do and needed to have my wits about me.

"I told you I was in a meeting."

This wasn't going to be a short conversation. My mother wasn't one of those people who could tell when it wasn't a good time to talk. We were meeting for yoga that night. She could have easily waited and told me then. She'd chosen to give me the news on the phone during the workday.

"Well, you're not in a meeting now, are you?"

"No, but I'm *working*. I do actually have to do work on occasion."

I typed the first name on my list of trades into my computer: *Engineering News*. Clicking through, I found their editorial calendar. Getting thought leaders in the news was always one of Harry's top priorities for B2B clients.

"You're avoiding me."

An immature and completely beneath me "Duh" stopped short of falling out of my mouth. "I'm not avoiding you. I'm just..." I trailed off, taking a second look at the calendar. Any theme that highlighted an understanding of regulatory changes would be a perfect issue to try to place an expert. Our client would want to submit a piece to this one. I scribbled *November* in the margin of the marketing plan.

"Busy? Everyone is always too busy for me."

That was a cheap shot, even for her. My stepfather, Sam, had died almost three years ago. It was hard to believe. And while my mom had dated a bit, no one seemed to stick. My return to New York had eased some of her pain, but I had a life, and Sam's kids were in Minnesota.

"I'm not too busy for you." I said it calmly, trying to relax my tone and my body. *Don't kill the messenger.*

"Have you really thought about what I told you, sweetie?" Just like that, she was back to being a worrisome mother. Sometimes, her mood swings gave me whiplash.

"I'm twenty-eight years old, Mom. I'm capable of comprehending death." The truth was I had never thought about him dying. Not once. He'd been dead to me for so long already.

"Being an adult doesn't make death any easier."

She couldn't be helped—my mother was a meddler. I rolled my eyes. "Am I supposed to break down and cry?"

My gaze flickered back to my computer and then the marketing plan. I added *February* to the margin. Earlier that year, *Engineering News* had done an article on the effects of site work on workers' health. If they did something similar next year, this client would be a good match.

"I just want you to do *something*. You're more concerned about me interrupting your business day than about your father dying."

Which was true. I didn't have a father—hadn't had one in a decade. Letting those memories in, that pain and anguish... I couldn't do it. I'd worked too hard for too long to fall apart at the mention of Ryan Scott. Except there was a difference between expelling someone from your life and them literally being off this earth. Something long buried stirred inside me.

No. I locked the doors around my heart. This wasn't happening.

I cleared my throat. "Who even called you?"

The question had been gnawing at me since she first called: *Who would have thought to call my mother, and how did they find her information?* When I'd cut my father out of my life, I'd done it so completely that I didn't even hear from him, not once. My mother had gotten me a new cell phone number, and she and I had moved across town. Only two people from that period of my life knew my information, and neither of them had spoken to me in years.

"I think you should go up there to the funeral—see Bethany and... your sister."

A shiver ran up my spine. My mother had never casually referred to my father's second wife and my half sister before. Not even when things had been "good" between all of us.

I started tapping my pen at a steady but rapid pace. "*Bethany* called you?"

"Will you go to the funeral?"

No, I wasn't going to go to the funeral. I didn't need to say good-bye or have some sort of postmortem closure. All the closure I needed had happened on the day I walked out of his house for the last time.

"Please go," she said. "Just trust me on this one. You will regret not going."

"I'll think about it. I really do have a lot of work to do." At least I wasn't intentionally avoiding her. Several emails had come through, two of them marked *high importance*. "I'll let you know what I decide."

"I love you, Andi. You know that, right?"

"Yeah, Mom. I love you too."

The phone hadn't even fully dropped onto its base before it was ringing again. A quick look told me it was Craig. I diverted his call to voicemail and switched off my monitor. I sat cross-legged on my desk chair, leaning my head back in a stress-relieving position. The cushions squeaked as they always did when I pushed the structure to its limits. But I could feel the stress draining from my body, out of my toes and through my fingers. I concentrated on relaxing specific parts of my body as I'd been taught in a meditation class my mom and I had taken together in an attempt to bond. Our personalities were so similar that we fought a lot. Most of my stress came from her, yet so did most of my laughter. Our breaking point had come right around the time I accepted Harry's invitation for drinks. My mom and I had both been heartbroken—she from her second husband's recent passing and I from the fallout with my fiancé. Telling her anything about my dating life had seemed cruel—her grief had been so heavy—but sharing that I was dating my much older, still technically married boss wasn't an option. But then, secret keeping was second nature for me when it came to my mother. It had become a necessity when I was younger and living under Ryan's roof and then in the mess that followed. But it frayed the connections between us, creating static where there'd once been clarity.

My office was quiet except for the monotonous buzz of white noise. The lack of distraction allowed me to take in what my mother had said without having to spout off an answer on the spot. It wasn't often that I wanted to sit in silence. Even when trying to concentrate on breathing and tuning out the world, I often listened to a carefully selected artist—usually Wilderness Weekend. Their music was a happy melancholy that I could lose myself in, relating to lyrics that I knew were completely unrelated to me. The right song at the right moment changed my mood, my perspective, even my life. The calm strumming of an acoustic guitar or the gentle flourish of piano keys that I'd fallen for when I was seventeen and making some of the hardest decisions of my life had lulled me into a love of music I'd never been able to let go of.

And I needed the courage that music gave me more than ever. It would take every ounce of strength I had to reenter Ryan's world and go back to Fairford, but my mother was right—if I didn't go, I might wind up regretting it. I couldn't afford to regret anything else.

My blood went cold, and the peace I'd reached just moments before vanished, replaced by hellish reminders and memories I'd long since banished. My heart ached, and the bad collided with the good as it had so often that year. I rubbed my wrist distractedly. I didn't usually allow myself to wonder about Corey, my first love—though that didn't even begin to describe what he'd been to me—but I couldn't help it now. *Is it possible that he's still in Fairford after all this time?* I hoped not, partially because we'd both wanted out of that town so badly and partially because I didn't know if I could survive seeing him again.

My phone buzzed, and I looked down, expecting a text from my mom, but it was Harry: *If you're going to the funeral, I'm coming.*

My fingers hovered over the keys as I thought of a million protests and all the consequences of bringing Harry to Fairford. He'd been separated from his wife for three years—long before we were ever involved—but until she signed the papers, we walked a fine line between right and wrong. Secret weekends away were one thing. A trip where members of my family—estranged or not—might be present was another. I glanced at his calendar, as if I didn't have it memorized.

It's the same day as your flight, I typed.

So, I'll push the flight to the next day. I'm not letting you go to your father's funeral alone.

I wasn't sure why he was pushing this, but I knew better than to argue with him.

Fine, you can meet me there Tuesday night.

I nodded at the calendar as I adjusted the dates, trying to reassure myself that this wasn't a colossal mistake. But the one hundred miles between Fairford and New York City might as well have been an ocean. I knew that better than anyone.

Maybe this trip would give me closure on more than just my father. Or maybe it would break me open again. Either way, Ryan was my cross to bear, and I was going back to Fairford.

Chapter 2

Now

I'd been standing under the awning of my apartment building for five minutes, but the rain only fell harder. I pushed the umbrella out into the open night and emerged from my cover cautiously. Water seeped into my sneakers. My socks stuck to the crevices between my toes, and the bottoms of my jeans dragged water weight with me across the street. I quickened my pace.

Once inside Emma and Charlie's building, I dropped the umbrella into a rack set up in the corner of the vestibule and pressed hard on the button for apartment 509—E. and C. Loughlin. The lock clicked open with a loud buzz, and I pushed into the open hallway, heading for the stairs.

Five flights later, I sucked in a deep breath to steady my frazzled nerves then knocked on the door. It opened almost immediately. Emma stood there expectantly, holding a twenty-dollar bill.

"You're not Chinese food." She stepped aside, letting me slip past her into the apartment.

"Ryan died." My voice—even to me—sounded flat and monotonous, an octave lower than usual.

Emma hugged me tightly, and I welcomed the comfort of her arms. When I'd left the office, I'd texted my mom that I wasn't up for yoga and then gone straight home to pack and figure out how I was going to get to Fairford the next day. But the silence had been deafening, dragging me from the warmth of my apartment to trudge the five blocks to my best friend. She was the only one who would understand.

"I know. Your mom called me." She led me into the kitchen. "Are you okay?"

"Why don't I smell kung pao chicken?" Charlie looked up from the book he was reading and noticed me standing there. "Hey."

A minute passed—I counted the seconds—before I lifted my eyes to meet either of theirs. I needed to steel myself for the looks of doubt and sympathy. Charlie and Emma had been at my mom's house the day I came home after my year in Fairford—skinnier than when I'd left, quieter, damaged, and clinging to a boy's hand like my life depended on it. And back then, it had.

"How do I go back there, Em?"

Her hand pressed into mine. "It'll be okay."

My wet shoes squeaked loudly on the tile floor as we passed into the living room. I fell onto the couch, grasping a throw pillow in my arms. Emma stood in the doorway. She picked up a photograph of the two of us off one of the bookcases, her eyes glazing over. We'd taken it the day I'd moved to Williamsburg. We had been sweaty and exhausted, but the smiles were real.

I looked up at her, my hands trembling against the pillow. "How do I go back to Fairford?"

"I can come with you." She shook her head and put the photograph back on the shelf. I wondered if she was remembering the story I'd finally shared, when I was safely back in my mother's home, about the year I'd spent with Ryan.

Emma couldn't come with me if Harry was going to be there. I squeezed the pillow against my chest. "No, that's okay. You have work."

"I can miss work."

I shook my head. "It's probably best if I go alone."

Which made no sense, but she didn't argue further. Fairford—and all it had brought to and taken from my life—was the one thing we couldn't share. And we both knew it.

She sat down, looping her arm through mine. Charlie sat down on the other side of me. A salty taste reached my lips—tears. My body shook as a waterfall of memories soaked my shirt—creaking stairs, shattered glass, pain, and a silence so loud it echoed. Emma's grip on me tightened, and I let her carry some of the weight for a while.

Chapter 3
Now

It was still raining the next morning when I drove my car out of my mother's garage. And after taking the subway into Manhattan and then the Metro-North to my mom's, I was done with the trip before it even started. Fortunately, an hour into the drive, the sky cleared. In the solitude of lightly trafficked Route 17, I bobbed and weaved, sang at the top of my lungs, and let the music drown out any thoughts I might have. I knew I was getting close to Fairford when my ears popped for the first time. It always happened right at exit 114, where the slope of the road was so slight that it was impossible to tell you were going up a hill until the car refused to accelerate. Pushing down on the gas only made the engine rev and the tachometer rocket above four. A few exits farther, signs for the Robinson Diner started to appear.

Less than thirty minutes later, the first sign for Fairford popped up. Fifteen miles to go. I pulled several CDs out of the visor, holding each one up to eye level. Who even knew what I'd left in this car—I'd hardly used it the last two years as it collected dust in my mother's garage. The last disc was an ancient mix CD that I hadn't seen in years, labeled *Jimmy Eat World mix (because I love you even if you still prefer CDs)*.

My breath caught at the boyish, messy handwriting. *Corey.* Everything Fairford had been purged from my life so long ago, but somehow, this had survived. My fingers shook as I slipped the disc into the player, the first song bringing back images of the boy who had made it for me and everything we'd gone through together. I pushed the memories away as best I could. But this music was undeniable. It was so intrinsically linked to the broken girl who loved a boy and tried—and failed—to keep him safe in their bubble.

I stabbed at the radio until the music cut off. What a stupid idea. As if dealing with Ryan and Bethany and my sister wasn't going to be hard enough.

Fairford didn't seem like much right off the highway. The exit was tucked away in the woods just outside of town. The area was filled with towering trees that, in full bloom, allowed only a few spots of light to escape through the foliage. Even in darkness, residents knew each dip in the road. After a couple of miles, the residential part of town started with a sprawling mansion. Another mile farther, the business district began. There were a few blocks of shops and apartments and the occasional house. It was the average downtown in a small town. The high school was at the next cross street, the elementary school just another block away, farther from the main road.

Cars—more luxury vehicles than I expected of Fairford—and school buses lined the streets. There wasn't an open spot in sight. Main Street now ended with an unfamiliar building that appeared to be a business of sorts. It was stately, newer than anything else in town, and landscaped to perfection with a garden and a few benches. The parking lot was nearly empty despite the hour being well past lunchtime. There wasn't a sign on the building, though some branding—illegible from the street—adorned the door. Stopping in front of this building was like standing at the crossroads of two different towns. Each road branching off from the end of Main showed travelers a different Fairford—left led to the rich district and private-school ilk, right to smaller houses and developments and acres of farmland. I was used to turning right, but Harry had booked us a room at the Cavanaugh Pond Bed & Breakfast, a staple of the rich district, so I turned left.

I'd only been to Cavanaugh Pond once. It had been the most beautiful place I'd ever seen. As I pulled onto the property, taking in the pond, gazebo, and cottages, it was still close to paradise. In a few more weeks, all these April showers would give life to the abundance of flowers I remembered covering the land. The lush green would be dotted with pinks, purples, whites. It seemed too cozy for a funeral visit, but that was what I got for letting Harry handle securing lodgings—he wasn't going to stay at the Howard Johnson. The welcome sign on the door was written in loopy cursive, inviting guests to *Come in and stay a while*. It was the only friendly welcome I'd ever received at Cavanaugh Pond. The woman who'd run the front desk back when I lived in Fairford had never taken kindly to me.

A little old lady sat at the registration desk, her gray hair short but thick, her eyes a faded shade of blue and neatly tucked into the folds of flesh on her face. Ten years later, same woman. She looked up over the rim of her glasses, giving me an aloof smile. I breathed a sigh of relief that she didn't seem to recognize me.

"I'm sorry to hear about your father, Andrea." She typed into her ancient computer without looking at me.

Screw this town and its long memory.

"Thank you," I managed to get out through a muffled breath. Apparently, ten years hadn't been long enough.

"It's about time you came back." She looked at me then. I didn't want to meet her eyes, but I couldn't stop myself. "That man's been waiting on you for a decade."

"Excuse me?"

She didn't even blink. "Just about time you showed your face."

For a moment, I wondered which man she was talking about—Ryan or Corey—but shook the thought from my mind. It didn't matter either way.

"Your reservation says two." She looked at my left hand—still void of a wedding ring.

"He'll be here tomorrow."

She handed me the key. "I see some things never change."

I let the door slam behind me despite the sign that cautioned care.

Chapter 4
Then

It was a Friday night near the end of the school year. I should have been out with my best friends, Emma and Charlie, but I was tired, and it was so close to summer I could smell it in the air. They could wait a few more days. And they probably didn't even miss me since whenever I wasn't around, they made out. So I was tucked into the cushions of my couch, reading *Les Misérables* for fun while the original Broadway soundtrack played in the background. My actual assigned reading—*Things Fall Apart*—sat half read in my backpack. As long as I finished it by finals week, I'd be fine. That book was unlikely to be on the Regents Exam anyway.

Halfway through the first-act finale, my mom walked into the room. She held an oversized mug in both hands, the logo for the company she worked for—Wellington Thorne—facing out. The floral scent of the tea she drank every night before bed wafted toward me. I gave her a wave and continued humming along with "One Day More" until she sat down next to me.

I took one earbud out. "Hey, Mom."

She gave me the slightest of smiles, but it barely reached her eyes. "Can we talk?"

I slipped my bookmark into place and closed the book. She never *asked* to talk. "What's up?"

"At work today..." She cleared her throat, and her fingers tapped against the mug. "I was offered an opportunity to oversee the opening of a new resort."

I nodded. This seemed like good news. She'd been waiting for a new opportunity to come her way for a few months. But that didn't explain why she was so nervous.

"And...?"

"It starts in three weeks."

I still didn't understand her dilemma. The only thing we had planned for the summer was a short trip to Wildwood in July. "You should take it. I'll survive one summer without the Jersey Shore."

"It's in Paris."

I almost laughed until I took in her expression. Worry lines creased her forehead, her eyes looked shadowed, and her hands were practically white knuckled. She was serious.

"My company would find us a place to live, and we'd enroll you in an American school there."

I could only nod. Mom's projects usually took at least a year. *A year in France?* And my junior year at that. Everyone knew eleventh grade was key to getting into a good college. A change in not only schools but continents as well could be really good or really bad for me.

"Do you want to go, Mom?" I asked even though I already knew the answer. If she didn't want to go, she'd never have mentioned it in the first place.

"Well, I've been waiting for this opportunity for a long time, and it might not come again," she said, her eyes downcast. "But it's a big change, and it's your junior year, so we need to decide this together."

I thought of all the summer plans I'd made with my friends, the varsity volleyball spot I'd earned for the fall, and prom. If I missed those moments, there'd be no getting them back. There was also no guarantee that the project wouldn't go on for more than a year. I'd seen that happen to my mom plenty of times, but none of those projects had required us to relocate.

"I could stay with Emma."

My mom shook her head. "Not for a year."

An idea popped into my mind then, a crazy idea but one she might agree to that wouldn't take me too far from my friends—I could deal with a highway between us but not an ocean. Just the thought of it started my heart racing. She wasn't going to like this plan.

"I could stay with Dad."

Three years ago, I'd never have made such a suggestion, but things had been better since he'd bought the Fairford house. Our visitation schedule had changed from once a week to once a month, but the weekend trip gave me a lot more time with my sister, and he hadn't missed picking me up once.

"That doesn't sound like the greatest idea." She wrung her hands. "Is that really something you would want?"

Want? Not exactly. But at least I would be able to see my friends outside of a computer screen.

I shrugged. "I think it could be good for me, Mom. I don't spend nearly enough time with Nicole." An image popped into my mind—my sister playing with her dolls on the deck while my dad grilled. I usually sat nearby, reading a book, together but apart, never quite fitting into their lives. "I'm her big sister. She should know me."

It wasn't the ideal situation. I would still have to switch school districts and try out for the varsity squad and make new friends, but at least I'd only be two hours from home. I could come back for homecoming and Christmas and prom.

"Can I at least ask him?"

My mom closed her eyes, her chest rising and falling as she considered the idea. When her hands unclasped, I knew she'd decided. "We'll talk to him tomorrow when he comes to pick you up."

Three weeks later, I was in Fairford.

Chapter 5
Then

The sun blazed overhead. I rolled onto my stomach, propping my book up on the back of the lounger. Days like this were the worst. All I wanted was to eat the ice cream I had brought home from work earlier, but my stepmom had told Nicole she had to wait until after dinner, and I assumed that applied to me as well. Plus, I'd already had way too much ice cream at work. A summer job at an ice cream shop had seemed like a great idea. A few of my soon-to-be classmates were my coworkers, and in a small town, my arrival was news, so too many teenagers were stopping in each day to get a glimpse of the new girl. It was awkward but nice, I supposed.

I glanced over at Nicole, who'd climbed up onto the chair next to me and had been sitting there for thirty minutes. She'd stared longingly at the pool before picking up a book from the stack she'd carried over. She was the calmest six-year-old ever. And with my frequent babysitting gigs back home, I'd been around a lot of six-year-olds.

Moments like this were exactly why'd I'd told my mom I wanted to stay with my dad. I maybe hadn't meant it at the time, but not being an only child anymore was nice. I still felt outside the family most of the time, even after a month in Fairford, which was to be expected since I'd never spent more than forty hours straight in their presence before. But that night, I felt included, which made me miss my mom less. The truth was, it had been just me and my mom for so long that

I didn't know how to be part of a larger unit. But I was trying, and so were they. Maybe this year *would* be good for me.

"You want to move this show inside?" I asked my sister. "I feel like I'm melting."

"Me too." Nicole popped up before I'd even closed my book and ran into the house, her stack of books weighing her down.

"I'm going to order a pizza," Bethany said as I dropped into a chair at the breakfast nook. "Any requests?"

My mom would have known I only liked cheese on my pizza. No extra seasonings, no toppings. Just gooey, gooey cheese. But honestly, I wasn't sure we'd ever ordered pizza before at my dad's house. Bethany generally cooked when I came up for weekends, and before they'd moved to Fairford, I hadn't been around for many meals.

"Actually," I said bouncing in my seat, "Krystal, my coworker at What a Scoop, invited me to hang out tonight with her friends."

"Well, look at you—making friends before the school year starts."

"Yeah. She's on the volleyball team, so *hopefully*, we'll be teammates." I blushed. Making friends had never been hard, but Fairford was spread out. It was small in population but huge in mileage. My drive into town for work each morning took nearly fifteen minutes. But at least I'd gotten a car out of the situation.

Official preseason practice started a few weeks before the school year, but the team had unofficial practice at the park, which Krystal had promised to get me an invite to.

"As if there are any doubts." Bethany picked up the landline and passed the receiver between her hands as she read through the menu. "Who are you going out with?"

I shrugged. "Krystal, her boyfriend, umm, some girls who also play volleyball, and I think Brian, you know, my other coworker. We're just going to the mall."

Bethany's eyes met mine, and she smiled. "Sounds fun. Do you need cash?"

"No, I got paid today, and I still have most of what you gave me at the start of the week." My allowance was huge compared to back home, but then, I hadn't had to drive a million miles to do anything there. Gas was not cheap.

"Be home by midnight, okay?" Her gaze shifted to the living room, where my dad sat watching something that could only be ES-PN, with Nicole at his side. "And be quiet when you come in. You know how light a sleeper your sister is."

Chapter 6
Then

It was nearly midnight when I pulled into the driveway. I hadn't missed curfew all summer, but everyone was sound asleep each time I got in. Back home, my mom was always waiting up for me. But I wasn't complaining. Summer was winding down, and now that I officially had my spot on the volleyball team, nights out would be relegated to actual weekends. I could already tell my busy schedule was going to cause issues with Emma. She'd been blocking out dates on the joint calendar she'd set up for us for weeks without care for my volleyball or work schedules.

I swung open the car door and nearly jumped out of my skin. Bethany stood in the dim light of the front stairs. There was a bag at her feet. In the car next to mine, Nicole was buckled into her booster seat, the puppy we'd gotten only three weeks ago next to her.

"What's wrong?" I gave Bethany a once-over as I approached her. Even in the darkness, I could see that she'd been crying. She clasped her hands in front of her—her wedding ring notably absent. I should have felt surprised, but a sinking inevitability took up root in my chest instead.

That was the thing about staying with someone for longer than a weekend—the rosy, happy life they feigned for the eight to thirty-six hours spent with them wasn't real. And the Scott household was no different. Things were a mess. They'd been able to put up a good act for the first few weeks, but slowly, the situation had devolved. My dad drank *a lot*. He yelled a lot, too, about stupid things. He slammed doors and sent Nicole to bed without dinner. I always brought her something, not caring if he noticed. There was punishment, and then there was being unnecessarily cruel. For whatever reason, he mostly ignored me. But then, that had been true my whole life.

He'd been even worse that week, and considering I hadn't been home much, it was saying a lot that I'd noticed. The day before had been particularly bad after the puppy peed on the carpet again. When the fighting started, I locked myself, Nicole, and Chance upstairs with *Cars* playing on the highest volume. It had drowned out the worst of the noise, but my sister had kept looking at the door.

"What's wrong?" I asked again.

Bethany's eyes darted toward the house, and I realized we were standing awfully near their bedroom window. I stepped closer to her.

"We're leaving," Bethany said, her voice a whisper but steady. "I can't take it any longer."

I nodded and started past her. "Okay, let me just pack a bag."

"You can't come with us." She looked pained, but her tone was firm and final.

I stood at the base of the stairs, unable to move. She couldn't seriously leave me alone with him. Maybe her priority was her biological child, but she'd always treated me as her own. Then again, it had never mattered much before. Bethany had been half the reason I thought living with my dad for a year would be enjoyable. And if she couldn't—I prayed it was *couldn't* because *wouldn't* was unbearable—take me with her, I didn't understand why she'd waited for me to come home.

She placed a hand on my arm. "You'll be okay. He'll be okay."

Her hand was warm against my skin, yet all the hair on my arm stood on end. A cold vibration shook me. "Don't leave me here."

"I'm sorry." Her voice shook. "I can't take you with us. You aren't my daughter. If he went to the police, he'd just get you back, and that... that would be worse."

Part of me knew she was right. If my dad cared enough to get me back, there would be no more ignoring me—of that I was certain. But the other part didn't want to stay here without her. She was the only buffer I had against a man who looked just like me but knew nothing about me.

"Bethany, please."

She held up her hands in a frantic shushing motion. Her eyes darted to the window a few feet away and back to me. "Listen, I'll call your mother. I'll explain what's happening. If she gives me permission, I'll put you on a plane, or you could—"

I walked down the two porch steps and stood face-to-face with her. Our eyes locked. "Don't call my mother."

That was the last thing I wanted. My mom wouldn't even think about putting me on a plane. She'd come home in an instant, and she'd see right through all my happy texts and emails. And then she'd drive to Fairford and kick my dad's ass. And the past two months would be for nothing. My mom *had* to stay in Paris. This was her shot—I'd heard her telling her best friend that on the phone the night before she'd left.

"I can't stay, Andi." Bethany's voice pleaded for me to understand.

I stood up straighter and took a breath. My answer needed to be firm. "I understand, and you're right—I'll be fine."

She waited a second longer and then pulled me into a hug. I didn't reciprocate. I couldn't hug her goodbye. She looked at me again, her eyes fearful, as if this would be the last time we'd see each other. "I'm sorry. Be safe."

I ran up the front steps and into the house, unable to watch her leave me. I shut the door behind me as quietly as I could and then sat on the second stair, my feet resting on the step below, chin on my knees, and hands covering my face. Blood rushed through my veins. My heartbeat was loud enough that I could hear it. Stretching out my legs and then my arms, I forced my body to relax.

The car started in the driveway. The gravel under its wheels was the only noise besides the ticking of the grandfather clock in the dining room. I watched my dad's door until I could no longer hear Bethany's car on the drive. I considered getting in my car and driving home, but there was no way to get reenrolled there without involving my mom. My options were to stay and deal with him or go home and call my mom and ruin everything. It wasn't even a choice.

Before half a minute had passed, I took the stairs two at a time and shut myself in my bedroom. I looked around the small space, my home for the foreseeable future and the only place I knew I'd be safe. I turned the lock, tested the knob, and then crawled into bed, pulling an old stuffed animal into my arms. The silence was peaceful yet ominous.

Chapter 7

Now

I parked my car in the back corner of Clementine Funeral Home's parking lot and watched a parade of people I didn't recognize enter the building. With each brown-haired mourner, my heart stopped as I equally wished for them to be Corey—waiting for me because he knew on this day, of all days, I would need him—and prayed he was nowhere near this town or Ryan anymore.

After a few more minutes, the stream of cars entering the parking lot slowed. I stepped out of the car, straightening my pants, and glanced quickly around. Everyone was inside. There was no one I could sneak in with. It should have occurred to me that waiting until the wake had started would only make my arrival that much more noticeable. A few blond strands of hair lingered on my outfit, and I stopped to pick them off. After the tenth piece, I finally gave up. I needed to go in.

I crossed the lot, continuing to scan for other latecomers, but I was the last one. With a fortifying breath, I reached for the door just as it opened. A woman stood in front of me, looking down at her phone. I jumped back as if scalded. *Bethany.*

She looked up as I backed away from the door, her eyes focusing on mine, trapping me in place. "You came."

I nodded as too many emotions tore through me. I'd trusted this woman wholeheartedly once. Loved her like family. But she'd left me, left *him,* and Fairford. She hadn't looked back.

"So did you."

She typed something into her phone and then pocketed it. Her eyes bored into me, an emotion I didn't recognize flashing in them. "If you'll excuse me, I need to get something from my car before the service officially starts."

Inside, the hall was crowded. Small groups sat across the two rooms. Snippets of conversation hit me, but I couldn't catch any of them. My head buzzed with tension. Plaques and poster boards lined the hallway, all filled with photos of Ryan's life. A few stragglers remained in the hallway, taking in the pictures. I walked up to the first board, which was dedicated to a young Ryan. I bypassed it and moved onto the next. And there I was—a bundled-up newborn in her proud father's arms, a wailing postbaptism baby, an infant walking toward Daddy. After that, the locales changed, and the time between photos grew longer, an effect of my parents' divorce. I ran my finger over one in particular—Ryan with his arms wrapped loosely around me. I was little, probably four or five, my arm in a bright-pink sling. A floppy straw hat with a bow covered my head and fell into my eyes. I'd been laughing, though I couldn't say at what—maybe at the nurse who had taken the shot. It was a cute enough picture to the lay observer. Anyone could have put it up there—it was before Bethany's time. But on close inspection, tearstains covered my cheeks, the hat still had a tag on it, and we stood in front of the doors to the emergency room. I hadn't seen Ryan for six months after that day.

"Who is that?"

In my peripheral vision, I saw two women, maybe in their sixties, staring at a photo on the board next to me.

"That's his oldest," the woman closest to me said. Her voice wasn't overly loud, but it wasn't quiet either. The way they stood, it was unlikely they would see me if I didn't want them to.

I turned slowly toward the board. One of the ladies still pointed at a photo of me and Nicole in a leaf pile outside the Fairford house.

I'd been about fourteen, but if they glanced my way, they were sure to recognize me. I returned my attention to the board to hide my face.

"He had another daughter?"

"Oh, honey, yes. This girl—Andrea, I think her name is—she came here for one year, lived with the man. Now, this was before... he was still..." She lifted her hand to her mouth, her pinky finger sticking out just slightly, the universal sign for drinking. "She comes into the hospital all bloodied and bruised one night and says she fell down the stairs."

"How do you know all this, Stella?"

"I was there. It was while I was still nursing over at County."

"You think it was him?"

I clenched my hands in front of me. Though I'd hoped otherwise, what had happened during my time in Fairford was clearly not a secret. I wondered how much of the town knew—or assumed they knew—about that night.

"Who else, honey? I know he cleaned up, but do you blame that girl for never coming back? I remember the old Ryan Scott, even if this younger generation only sees the company."

The company? My eyes went misty and unfocused. Their conversation was bothering me more than I liked. I headed toward the back of the room, needing a moment to breathe—to make sense of the bits of knowledge that were coming through.

Across the room, Bethany reentered the fray. She was quickly stopped by a couple offering condolences, which seemed odd. I couldn't imagine my mother getting the same treatment, and she was an ex-wife, same as Bethany. But my mother would never come here. For all her talk about how this was important for me, she hadn't offered to accompany me. Watching my stepmother so obviously embraced by this community, I felt more alone than I had in a long time. Bethany's eyes found mine for the briefest of moments, but this time, she couldn't hold my gaze.

"Andi?" The young, high-pitched voice was hopeful.

I knew who it must be, because if I was here, and Bethany was here, then certainly, Nicole was here too. Longing and dread waged a war inside me. I wasn't ready to see her. Not yet. But anticipation came off my sister in waves. Steeling my nerves, I turned to face her. Recognition and awe hit me hard. My stomach roiled, and my chest clenched as an unbearable sense of loss rocked me back on my heels. My six-year-old sister was now a bubbly blond teenager.

"Nicole?"

"It's Nikki now." Her face twisted into a sad smile, and she closed her hand around mine. The touch was so unexpected that I almost jerked away. I reined in my emotions and forced myself to close my fingers around hers. Nikki tugged me forward. "Come on."

I followed my sister through the room. People were staring. My entrance might have gone unnoticed in the crowd, but Nikki and I walking side by side were a spectacle. I thought I recognized a person or two from my time in Fairford—a kid I went to high school with, one of our neighbors—but overwhelmingly, I saw a sea of anonymous mourners. Ryan hadn't had friends. Our life in that house had been disturbingly silent—except for the times when it hadn't been, and I didn't think about those days.

Nikki stopped a few feet away from the casket. "I have to go up there." She pointed to the front of the room and the line of people waiting to pay their respects. "Do you want to go up to the casket?"

The hand she wasn't holding shook at my side. Seeing Ryan wouldn't have been easy under any circumstances, but seeing him and my sister and Bethany was too much. My emotions felt ready to boil over. I took a breath. I needed to go up to the casket for any of this to be real—to know he was really gone—and for this part of my life to finally be over.

"Do you want me to go with you?" she asked quietly. "They'll wait."

I looked at this young girl, amazed at how much she'd grown up while I was away. She was so collected, as if it was every day that a family reunion occurred at a funeral. She watched me, her gaze steady, her expression open. But I couldn't focus on her question. All I could do was stare at that coffin and mull over the fact that Nikki was part of the receiving line. Which only led to more questions, the biggest one being: *How well did she know Ryan?*

"Did you know he was going to die?" The question tumbled out before I could stop it. And of all the things to ask, this information was so low on my priority list.

Nikki fixed her gaze on her feet and nodded. "He was sick for a while."

A while. She'd known him *for a while.* "I think I'll go up now."

Goose bumps sprouted on my arms, and ice ran through my veins. It was time to see my father. I unfurled my hand from Nikki's and walked up to the casket. I knelt down, as was the custom. In death, Ryan appeared calm and contented, with none of the rage that had hardened his face or the sadness that had aged him before his time. An image of him opening his eyes and reaching out to me played in my mind. Even in death, the sight of him incited fear. A prickle rose on the back of my neck, and another shiver passed through me. He couldn't hurt me anymore, but still I recoiled from the casket. I stood up abruptly and backed away.

I watched Nikki accept a hug from a woman and a handshake from a man. She gave them her full attention. Next to her, Bethany had taken a spot on the receiving line. Questions ricocheted around my mind, but I couldn't ask them. Not here. Nikki's eyes met mine as the couple moved to Bethany, and she gave me a small smile, motioning to the spot next to her. But I couldn't go to her. I couldn't be on that line.

I slipped into the crowd and made my way back to the vestibule. Tears pricked at my eyes, and a tremor shook my body. Nikki seemed to be a kind, well-put-together person. And I didn't even know her. I'd had nothing to do with shaping the person she had become. I inhaled deeply, forcing myself to pull it together. I had to get out of there.

The brisk April air was a balm to the heat in my cheeks. I walked to my car, my head down. If I made it to my car, I would be fine. I would be free. But it couldn't be that easy. My car was in sight when I heard the footsteps behind me, followed by my name in a voice that I knew would haunt me after I left town—Nikki. If it had been anyone else, I would have kept going. *But my sister...*

I turned, expecting to find her standing with her hands on her hips or some semblance of annoyance. Instead, she greeted me with a compassion I wasn't sure I deserved. "I can't stay in there."

"It's okay. I just wanted to give you this." She held out a single key on a bare ring.

No. Absolutely not. I was never going back to that house. Still, I took the key. "Thank you."

"I hope we'll see you tomorrow," she said before turning and walking back toward the funeral home.

I crossed the remaining distance to my car and got in before anything else could happen. Panic inched its way from my stomach to my chest and finally to my throat. It would be fine. *Just breathe.* I dropped the key into the cupholder, unable to bear its weight for another second. My hands shook on the steering wheel. I inhaled and exhaled, counting the seconds between each breath the way I'd learned so long ago to control these panicked moments. One more breath, and then I'd go. I filled my lungs and then breathed out in a whoosh. The shaking in my hands stilled, and I shifted the car into drive.

By the time I got back to Cavanagh Pond, my mind was racing. None of that had been what I was expecting, and the key felt like it was burning a hole in my pocket. Fortunately, Harry was already there. I pushed through the door, dropped my purse on the table, and closed the space between us.

Harry looked up at me from his perch at the edge of the bed. He wore a bathrobe, and his hair was still wet. The smell of his soap permeated the air. Harry studied me, concern clouding his eyes. But concern wasn't what I needed. I slipped out of my heels, worked my way out of my pants, and climbed onto his lap. His grip on me tightened as I brought my mouth to his. He knew better than to ask questions.

Chapter 8
Now

The quiet drawl of whatever news station Harry had on the radio was almost enough to calm me. Almost. The incessant tapping of my foot against the floorboard and the white-knuckled grip on my purse spoke otherwise.

Harry reached across the center console and covered my hand with his. "We should probably get inside."

He was right. We'd been sitting in this spot near the church for ten minutes. The bustle outside hadn't died down, though. People entered and exited the building—mourners going in, family and loved ones coming back out. Most of the pallbearers were there already, though the sixth one seemed to be missing. I didn't recognize any of them. Nikki had come and gone, though Bethany hadn't made an appearance, which meant she must be inside, probably seated in the front row.

Cool air brushed across my skin, and I slid my eyes away from the crowd to Harry's tall form. I hadn't even heard him exit the car. With a steeling breath, I accepted his hand. This was why I wanted *him* here rather than Emma, who might have let me stay at the hotel, or my mother, who would have dragged me into the church already.

"Thank you," I said.

"Of course, babe."

I can do this. I scanned the group across the street, my eyes stopping on the one familiar face. But it couldn't be.

Time and distance were clearly playing a game on me. But then she spoke. I would have recognized Krystal Rivera's voice anywhere. It was almost as ingrained in my memory as Corey's and for good reason: Krystal had been my best friend in Fairford. She looked so much like the teenager I'd known but older and somehow wiser. The tremble started in my hand, but soon, my whole arm was tingling and shaking. There were any number of reasons she could be at Ryan's funeral. It looked like the whole town had shown up, only not in the good-riddance way I'd expected. Krystal stood with a man in a well-fitting but clearly off-the-rack suit. I could only see the back of him, but there was something familiar in the set of those shoulders and that cowlick. He leaned down and kissed Krystal, and my heart fell to my stomach. Corey couldn't have ended up with Krystal. He wouldn't do that to me. Except why not? Nine years was a long time to remain loyal to someone who didn't want you.

I stepped back toward the car. "I don't think I can do this."

"Babe," Harry said, bracing himself against the car, "we're already here."

The man who might be Corey turned, and ice encapsulated me even as anticipation zinged through my chest. My eyes stayed locked on these people who were practically strangers yet were so alive in my memory. *Don't be him.* Another second passed. The man's profile came fully into view, and my breath stuck in my throat. It wasn't him. Those weren't his eyes or his nose or any of the contours I'd memorized in our years together. Those weren't his fingers gently stroking my best friend's cheek. Tears sprang to my eyes, disappointment and relief and too many other conflicting emotions torturing me.

"Please, Harry." I pulled open the door. "Let's go back."

He grimaced but relented, helping me into the car. I tried to control the panic like I had the day before, but it raged. I closed my eyes, refusing to bear any further witness to the morning's events. The wake would have to be enough. Even with my eyes closed, Harry's gaze was palpable. His worry filled the car. He'd never seen me like this. I had sworn he never would.

I counted backward from ten once and then did it again. Finally, my breathing regulated. I opened my eyes, letting the world return to focus. Harry tentatively reached for my hand, and I accepted the offer, entwining our fingers. As we made our way back to Cavanaugh Pond, I watched the trees and houses go by. They didn't whiz by like people always said. I could make out the nuances of the houses and the color of the leaves on the trees. Watching the ordinary lives of these people from behind the tinted window of my car, I became the outsider I always thought myself to be.

"Babe?" Harry's voice shook me from my reverie. I tried to smile, but even that little effort hurt. "Since we're not going to the service, I really should leave within the hour."

"What?" I asked, tears again pricking my eyes. Hurt cracked through everything else I felt. It wasn't that I planned on staying longer than necessary—though we had the room until the next morning—but I *needed* him to stay if only as a distraction.

"I wasn't able to move my flight."

"Did you try?" It was a cruel question, but I'd been handling Harry's travel for years, and he hadn't asked me to move it for him. And he certainly couldn't have asked anyone else to do it.

He brought our entwined hands to his lips, kissing my knuckles. "Yes. The only flight I could get tomorrow would've gotten me in too late for the meeting."

He meant the only business-class flight. Harry didn't fly coach. But he could have moved the meeting. Harry Stengel was a name that warranted moving meetings. It had been stupid to believe he'd do that for me.

"You asked me if you could come, Harry."

"I know I did. And I drove all the way up here, and you didn't even walk into the church." Annoyance tinged his tone, but he tried to cover it with a sigh. "It's business, babe. You know that."

"Right, business."

The car slid to a slow stop, and I opened the door and climbed out before he'd even shut off the engine. It was a perfect April day. The sun beat down, but a little breeze kept it from being too warm. The grass was crisp beneath my weight. The fountain by the lake spouted water, and a light mist formed. I walked to a stone bench just to the side of the lake, far enough away from the fountain to protect myself from any splash, and sat with my head in my hands. I never should have let him come. I'd known it was a bad idea, but *dammit,* I had wanted him with me.

"Don't be upset. I can stay for a bit if you need me."

If? Clearly, he hadn't been paying attention at all. "Just go, Harry. I'll be fine." *Once my hands stop shaking long enough to let me drive.*

He sat down next to me on the bench. He was so warm. I wanted to melt into him. It was all I'd wanted since I saw him on that bed the night before. It had kept me occupied all night and that morning, and I'd planned on it enveloping me until we left the cozy confines of our cottage the next day. But I couldn't. I stiffened against him.

He kissed my temple. "One more thing before I go..."

"What?" My exasperation clung to the single word, but I didn't care. He was deserting me after forcing himself onto my trip.

"Darlene signed the papers."

"When?" I asked in disbelief. When we'd "talked" on Monday, that had not been the direction things were going.

"Yesterday." He cupped my cheek. "I guess she met someone, and that was more important to her than the house." Their house on Long Island had been her sticking point in the latest round of proceedings and the one thing Harry wouldn't give up.

Holy shit.

He kissed me, and I let him. He'd been waiting for this moment for too long. "I'm a free man."

I knew what he meant, but the words still stung. "What are you going to do first?"

He laughed. "I don't know, but second, we're going away."

And there it was. We could finally *not* go away. We could stay in or go to a restaurant where we might run into people we knew or walk into work hand in hand. But according to Harry, we were still going somewhere no one could see us.

"You should probably go."

He nodded and stood. "Right. What would I do without you?"

"Miss a lot of meetings?"

"Probably true." He kissed my forehead. "Take all the time you need. I'll see you when I'm back in the city."

I stayed put until his car faded into the distance, too frazzled to move. Harry was a single man. Technically. For all intents and purposes, he was mine now. I couldn't even fathom what that meant.

The breeze picked up, and I moved inside. Sitting down on the edge of the overly fluffy bed, I held my head in my hands. The room was too big, too pink, too couple-y for one. Shutting the world out—or even driving home—seemed like the best course of action. His news had at least steadied my hands. If it hadn't been Harry, I would have suspected that was his intention. I felt in my pocket for the key, which had hardly left my person since Nikki had handed it to me as if I was afraid that if left alone, it would disappear.

My visit to Fairford had passed with little fallout. It was time to leave, yet I couldn't bring myself to pack my bags. There were so many questions and almost no answers. Nikki had given me the key for a reason, and I had to find out what that reason was. I picked my purse up off the floor—hesitation would only help change my mind.

TEN YEARS GONE, AND I still knew the way. My breathing hitched as I turned the corner, and the pale-blue house came into view. It was a two-story tract house, though Ryan had given it some customizations, including a porch that had been one of my favorite spots to sit in the morning. Especially *after*. He wouldn't bother me if I was outside. There'd been good memories in that house once. But now all I saw was the monster it had become.

I would never be prepared for this, so I didn't even try. I rode out the terror as I pulled up the long driveway. He was gone. It was just a house. I parked beside an old Civic, and my heart jumped—it was my Civic. I couldn't remember my current license plate number, but the old number was burned into my memory.

Breathe, Andi. I was perfectly safe. Still, my feet took root on the floorboards. From the radio, the dulcet tones of a classic Wilderness Weekend song reached me. I turned up the volume, letting the music wash over me. Ryan was gone. The song faded out, and I turned the car off and forced myself to step outside.

The Civic was caked with spring pollen. The tires were brown with dried dirt. Inside, the detritus of a long life filled the car. So, he'd used it in the last decade. That made sense—there wasn't another car in the drive. He'd been sick for a while—that was what Nikki had said. Did that mean he couldn't drive? This was more than a week of disuse. I tried the handle, and the driver's-side door pulled open easily. Sitting down in the driver's seat, leaving one leg outside on the ground, I examined the car. Dirty soda cans, cigarette butts, and candy wrappers lined the floor. I didn't want to touch anything, afraid of what it might be coated in, but a gleam off the windshield caught my attention. Hanging from the rearview mirror was a silver crucifix. My father had never been religious. He'd always picked me up after Sunday services and hadn't even acknowledged my confirmation. The few times I'd been to church in Fairford had been holidays, and Bethany had taken us. I cupped the crucifix in my hands and examined it. As I ran my finger across the back, I felt the grooves of an en-graving. It was a date eight years ago.

I looked into the back seat, and my eyes fell on a small stuffed fal-con. And there was the proof. This car had been mine once. I'd aban-doned it in my retreat, but I remembered that falcon. I'd looked for it among my things when I got home. It was a relic—one of the good things, a gift from my teammates after I'd hurt my wrist, to show that I was still a part of the team.

I stepped out of the car and looked up at the house. In a few steps, I would be inside the house of my nightmares. My pulse rock-eted into a gallop as I took the first steps toward the house. I bound-ed up the porch steps, knowing if I hesitated, I'd turn back. And then I was at the door, the key burning my palm. I unlocked the door, pushed it open, and entered. It was like stepping into a memory.

I shut the door and sped through the foyer, ignoring the closed door of the master bedroom on my left and the dining room to the right. There was this house, and then there was the dining room. And I was not ready for it. I walked quickly to the kitchen, keeping my eyes forward. The appliances had been updated, but it was still the same kitchen. The sink sat against the back wall with a window view of the pool. The stove and refrigerator took up one side, and a long counter ran along the other, separating the space from the living room. Barstools lined the far side. The biggest difference was that the cabinets that had once sat above the nook had been taken out, giving the space an open-concept feel.

I'd forgotten how nice this house was. It wasn't grand, but it was well put together and designed. No part of it had been over-looked. But then, Ryan had known what he wanted and had always had enough money. He'd been a contractor at an architectural firm for much of my life. After living with him and experiencing the depth of his alcoholism, I found his ability to go to work every day—and to be successful—to be somewhat of a wonder. His client list at River-walk Architecture had extended far beyond Fairford.

I moved into the living room. It was painted light green. Last time I'd been here, it had been blue. I knew because on the hottest days of summer, I still had nightmares about the house, each room perfectly preserved in my memory. The couches had also been re-arranged and the television moved to the back wall. The new layout opened up the space and made the room look bigger.

I slipped out of my heels and sat down in front of the entertain-ment center. The bottom cabinet door was already partially opened. I nudged it farther and pulled out a stack of CDs. I sifted through them—*The Passion*, *Mercy Me, Lauren Daigle*. More religion. I dropped the pile back into the cabinet and stood up. My eyes unwit-tingly landed on the entryway to the dining room. I couldn't see into the room itself, but it was enough. A chill ran through me. A phan-tom ache started in my wrist, but I stepped closer. It was just a room. I took another step and then another until I stood in the doorway. I willed my legs to move into the space. They refused. But it didn't matter. The grandfather clock stood where it always had, in the cor-ner near the front window. The clock door had been replaced. *Again.*

Chapter 9
Then

Bethany and Nicole had been gone for a few days, and the house that had been so noisy and full of life had gone quiet. My dad and I danced silently around each other, surrounded by the sounds that had become so familiar to me in only six weeks—the fridge opening, beer cans hissing, and the hourly chime of the grandfather clock. He seemed okay—not good or bad, just okay. He drank more than usual. It wasn't easy to tell, but I heard him walk the short distance from the couch to the refrigerator more often, and the recycling piled up at a faster rate despite there only being two of us.

I sat at the dining room table, working on my summer reading assignment due the first day of classes. We needed to create a storyboard for a chapter of *The Great Gatsby*. A few pieces of printer paper were laid out in front of me with scribbled notes and badly sketched humans—stick figures really. I'd taken to working outside, sometimes by the pool, more often on the porch swing, but it was too hot to venture outdoors for long. Krystal and I were planning on meeting the team at the ice rink soon. It would be crowded, but it was hard to argue with hanging out at the coldest place in town. We'd inevitably end up at the diner, eating our weight in fries and ice cream, but we'd work it off at practice.

A beer banged loudly on the table in my peripheral vision. I jumped to attention. My dad stood behind my right shoulder. I turned to look at him as an envelope dropped down onto the table.

"Put this in the mailbox, would ya?" His breath was rancid with the smell of too much beer.

I almost said no. He could walk to the mailbox just as well as I could. Especially to pay the freaking electric bill. But the fight wasn't worth it.

"No problem, Dad," I said, forcing a smile.

Being nice to him was the smart thing to do. But he'd brought all of this on himself, and I was honestly pissed off. This was not the year I'd signed up for. These last few days, he hadn't been his usual casual drunk—fully functional and personable. He was actively staying drunk and almost never left the house, as far as I could tell. Though he must have somehow gotten to the store for more beer, unless he had a stockpile in the basement.

As soon as I stepped out of my chair, he plopped down into it, missing landing on my leg by an inch. His eyes scanned the papers in front of him, but I doubted he was taking any of it in. A moment later, he closed his eyes, his chin resting on his hand. I wouldn't have been surprised if he passed out on the couch before Krystal picked me up.

I padded upstairs to grab my sneakers and then headed outside. It was like walking through mud—sticky and musky and gross. I could handle heat, but this humidity was awful. I patted my hair, feeling it go frizzy in the short walk across the lawn. After returning inside, I grabbed a water bottle from the kitchen and made my way back to the dining room. My dad sat where I'd left him, his chin in his hand and his eyes closed.

"Dad?"

"What?" He jumped awake from his half-asleep state at the dining room table. The beer he'd been holding toppled over onto my book and my project.

"God, seriously?" I scrambled to pick up the book, holding it out as beer dripped from its pages.

My dad mopped at the mess with the bottom of his shirt, hardly caring about the project he'd just ruined. "Not like it was anything to look at."

Anger roiled inside of me. We had the whole house to ourselves. There was no reason for him to be in the dining room. *Or to be awake for that matter.* "Yeah, just my homework."

"It's summer," he said with a shrug.

I spaced out the papers on the dry half of the table. They were unsalvageable, but at least I'd be able to tell what I was going for when I had to recreate them. "Would you just like go to bed or something? God, Dad, you're so drunk. It's embarrassing."

"Don't you talk to me like that." He wobbled out of the dining room, and I heard the fridge open, presumably for another beer. "I'm your father."

"As if that *means* anything," I muttered low enough that he wouldn't be able to hear me in the kitchen. "No wonder you can't keep a wife."

"What did you just say?"

Fuck. I scrambled for an apology, but nothing came fast enough. He popped open his beer and closed the space between us. He up-ended the can on my project. The table was bathed in cheap beer. The can crunched in his fist.

"Do you think I even wanted you here?" He threw the crushed can onto the table next to me. Tears pricked my eyes. "Just what I need—a freakin' smart-ass teenager under my roof for a fucking year. Disrespectful little bitch, just like your mother."

I felt the blood drain from my face as fear clouded my vision.

He grabbed my arm, his fingers cutting into my bicep. "Your mother's always telling me I'm the selfish one. Well, who ran away from you this time? Not me."

Tears flooded my eyes, salty against my tongue. Any calm I'd had fled, and a current of adrenaline seized control of my limbs. I pulled away, but his grip was too tight to break. My brain went fuzzy, and the back of my head tingled with stress.

I pulled my arm futilely. "Let go of me."

"This is my house! My house." He was so close I could smell the beer on his breath and the potato chips he'd eaten earlier. His blood-shot eyes were even with mine, his teeth gritted. His usually pale face was a bright red. I leaned as far away from him as his grip would allow, but it wasn't far enough. "You'll show me some respect."

As suddenly as he'd pulled me in, he let go. My attempt to create distance had left me off balance, and there was no time to catch my footing or brace myself for the fall I knew was coming. How close was I to the wall? Would I miss it? I barely had time for these thoughts before I hit something hollow. Glass shattered, and the grandfather clock chimed with the force of my weight. Blood dripped down my cheek, and the taste of rust reached my lips. Pain shot through my right wrist. I bit down to keep from crying out.

My dad stared at me, glassy-eyed. "Clean up this fucking mess."

Only after the door to his bedroom slammed shut did I dare move. Glass covered the floor. I checked my body one part at a time—legs, neck, left shoulder, and wrist. My right wrist hurt from landing on it, but I could move it. I'd had enough sports-related sprains to know that was a good thing. My head pounded as I gingerly touched the gash in it. I was going to need stitches, but it could have been worse. I tried to sit up. The room passed in a blur, nothing focused. With my chin on my chest, I waited for everything to stop spinning. As the world righted itself, sound came back to me, first the ticking of the clock above my head and then the muted sounds of the television from my dad's room and finally the blaring of a car horn—Krystal.

Chapter 10

Then

"What took you so long?" Krystal's eyes were trained on her phone, which I supposed was good. At least she wasn't freaking out about the blood-soaked paper towel I held to my forehead. Yet.

"Krystal?" My voice came out scratchy and shaky. I cleared my throat. "I need you to drive me to the hospital."

Her head shot up, and her eyes went wide as she focused on my forehead and then at the way I braced my wrist against my chest. "Oh my god. Is your dad home? Shouldn't he take you? What happened?"

"Krystal," I said evenly. "Breathe."

"Right. Sorry."

"Can you take me to the hospital?"

"Yes, of course, but isn't that your dad's car?"

Damn. "He can't drive right now."

She pulled a box of tissues from her center console and then pulled back onto the road. "What do you mean, he can't drive right now?"

I hadn't thought this night could get any more complicated. "He's passed out."

"Like drunk?"

I nodded and then wished I hadn't. "My stepmom moved out. She took my sister. My dad's just not in a good place."

"Okay." She turned onto the road leading to the hospital. Except everything in this town was so spread out that it would take us another fifteen minutes at least. "And your head?"

"I fell down the stairs." The lie came easily. Too easily. "And into the grandfather clock."

"Oh my god."

"You said that already."

She laughed, and I hoped I'd distracted her from the heavy part of the conversation. "Only you would fall down the stairs and into a clock. What were you doing?"

I closed my eyes and leaned back against the headrest. So many questions. And there were only going to be more. I needed to come up with the answers. Unless I told the truth. But then I might as well have let Bethany call my mom. Because if my mom would have been pissed before, she was going to be a nuclear bomb now. And it would ruin everything. All because I'd said something stupid when I knew better.

"Andi?"

"Sorry, my head's kind of pounding. Can we talk after we get to the hospital?"

"Yes, of course." The engine revved. "We're almost there."

Ten minutes later, we pulled into the hospital parking lot. Krystal drove right up to the emergency entrance, ignoring the signs that indicated she should park first.

"I'll meet you inside," she said, practically shoving me out of the door.

"Thank you, Krys. I'll be fine if you want to go."

She stared at me as if I was insane. And at the moment, maybe I was. "I'll see you inside."

DESPITE THE NURSE'S reassurance of privacy, I knew she'd called my dad. I'd seen enough medical dramas to know what happened when a minor showed up at the hospital without a parent. My wrist was already strapped into a brace—a bad sprain, limited mobility for at least four weeks. My volleyball coach was going to be thrilled.

I heard my dad before I saw him. His gait had a particular beat to it. He walked on the off beats, an unsteady but patterned series of footfalls. In the hall, my dad laughed, joking with my doctor. He sounded sober enough—an impossibility. The hair on my arms stood up as if an electric current had passed through my body. My heart rate quickened, and blood rushed to my cheeks. My dad stepped into the small space, the doctor behind him. Dr. Greenwald had a stern and skeptical look on his face. His eyes settled on me, sad and resigned, as the smell of old alcohol invaded my nostrils.

Dr. Greenwald knows.

"So, like I was saying, Mr. Scott, we just need to stitch up that gash on Andi's forehead, and then she'll be good to go home."

My dad stepped closer to the bed and put a hand on my shoulder. I flinched noticeably. This was bad. I eyed Dr. Greenwald as he wrote something on my chart. If he hadn't known then, he definitely knew now.

I exhaled and tried to relax, despite the fear-induced bile rising in my throat. "Hi, Dad."

"Doctor here says you fell down the stairs?" I nodded, unable to speak, as his breath washed over me. "You always were a clumsy one." My dad's voice was gruff, but he was doing an impeccable job of keeping the drunkenness hidden. "Wish you'd woken me."

I clenched my jaw to keep it from dropping open, at least until I realized both he and Dr. Greenwald were waiting for a response from me. "Well, Krystal was there. It seemed easier to just have her drive me over."

"Krystal—right. That friend of yours in the waiting room?" My dad had never laid eyes on Krystal, but there weren't many teenage girls sitting out there. "Weren't you two going somewhere tonight?"

He had to be hedging his bets that I would go along with whatever he said. I clearly had lied about what happened before he arrived. "Yeah, we were supposed to go ice skating, but I think that's probably not going to happen."

"Still..." He rummaged in his pockets and dropped a few twenties on my lap. "You should take her out for coffee or ice cream or whatever you kids like, for her trouble."

It clicked then. He wanted Krystal to take me home. He wanted to be out of this room and away from my presence. I understood the first but not the second. I turned to him for the first time since he'd arrived, taking in the crinkle near his eyes and the set of his jaw. His hand, where it sat on the bed next to me, trembled.

Is he scared?

"Sure, Dad. Thanks."

"Should we go get her?" Dr. Greenwald asked from his perch near the head of the bed. "Make sure she can take you home?"

"No, it's fine." I organized the money in my lap with my good hand. Anything to keep from looking up. "She said she was going to wait, so I'm sure she'll bring me home."

"Great." My dad stepped away from me, and my shoulders came down from my ears. He directed his next words to the doctor. "Well, I'm going to get back to bed and hope this bug is gone in the morning."

And then he left without looking back. I held my breath until the sound of my dad's footsteps faded into the bustle of the ER. With the room to ourselves, Dr. Greenwald went about doing my stitches. It wasn't the first time I'd had stitches, but it didn't make getting them any easier. I grasped the edge of the bed, losing the battle against tears.

When he pulled back, he locked me in his gaze. "Do you want me to call your mother? I know she's overseas, but we can figure it out."

I glanced over at him, careful not to move my head too quickly. He was younger than any of the other doctors I'd seen in the hospital. He wasn't an intern but was probably in his early residency and trying to decide the best course of action without involving his attending. It wasn't surprising that he knew about my mom. Fairford was *that* small. I had a feeling he would follow my lead.

"No, don't call my mother."

Chapter 11

Now

I needed to get out of the dining room and away from that clock. Memories bombarded me, and standing at the literal scene of the crime, I couldn't push them away. I hugged myself. The familiar pangs in my stomach and the shortness of breath of a panic attack came upon me. I took a step, trying to fight through the dizziness. The foyer was as far as I made it. I slouched against the front door. My head dropped down, my chin resting on my chest. I took several long breaths. With my eyesight blurred, the floor swirled beneath me. I stayed doubled over until my body could hold its own weight.

It had been ludicrous to think that I could just walk back into this world. Feelings I had long since reached some sort of closure on were thrown to the surface, old wounds ripped open. My stomach constricted. I stared up the stairs. There was a bathroom at the top. Sucking in my breath and sealing my lips, I took the stairs two at a time. The dry heaving began as I threw the lid off the toilet. Nothing came up. Leaning against the edge of the bathtub, I rested my head on my arm and closed my eyes, imagining that I was anywhere but here.

It was past time to go home, but I still couldn't bring myself to leave. I stepped out of the bathroom and into the hallway that connected the two bedrooms. My old room—the smallest of the three—was to the left. I still remembered the joy that had filled me the morning Ryan and Bethany showed me the space that would be mine. Mine, even though I would only be there three days a month. I stepped closer. The door was ajar.

I hesitated with my hand on the door. It wouldn't still be mine. Certainly, it had become an office or a true guest room. I bit what was left of the nail of my ring finger as my foot tapped a quick beat against the carpet. *Now or never.* I pushed open the door. It was too dark to see anything. I blindly scrambled for the light switch and flipped it. Light bounced off the same pale-blue walls. The first weekend I'd spent in the house, we'd painted it and bought a roomful of furniture because Bethany wanted me to feel at home. All of it was still there.

The room seemed bigger than it had when I was seventeen. The space was filled with all the usual furniture—a bed, a desk, a dresser. A bay window next to the bed looked out over the front yard. I sat down on the edge of the bed, just far enough back that my feet dangled above the floor. When I'd lived here, the walls had been covered in photographs of my friends, band posters, and one of the banners from the pep rally before we left for the state championship. I'd covered the walls with the good and tried so hard to bury the bad.

I'd taken the pictures and posters home with me when I left Fairford. Now framed photos lined the walls. First, there was a large portrait of the Scott family—me included—over the bed. We'd taken it just before Bethany walked out the door. We'd driven out to this campground about thirty minutes away and spent an hour in the summer sun, getting our pictures taken. Posed candid shots. Cheesy photos of me and Nikki. It had been a fun afternoon at a beautiful place. With our matching outfits and similar features, there had been no doubt that we were a unit. We'd been a family that day, nothing more, nothing less. I'd never actually seen any of the pictures before. And seeing them in *this* room—I wasn't sure what it meant or what this room was even supposed to be. A hideaway? An homage? A memory of a life that might have been?

I turned from the photo, focusing on the back wall, where a series of certificates hung. I couldn't read them from where I stood. On the dresser, next to the television, a few framed photographs were lined up. I opened the top drawer, delaying having to look at the collection of photos my father had decided to keep displayed. Inside, a smattering of clothing I'd left behind sat, collecting dust. I pulled the jacket off the top of the pile—Fairford Volleyball. I'd thought I'd lost it. My team had made it to the Section 4 finals that year for the first time in a decade. I refolded the jacket, the familiar crinkling of nylon sending me back to the days when I wore it no matter the weather, and placed it gently in the drawer. Fairford hadn't been all bad. There was the proof. I shut the drawer. I hadn't wanted to find anything. I thought it would be full of stuff that had nothing to do with me. But though my father had cleaned up and organized my room, and clearly used it as *something*, he'd left it alone. My room was still waiting for me. *But why?*

With nothing else to distract me, I turned to the pictures. Many of them were of Nikki throughout the years. I picked each one up, dusting it off as I did. Whatever this room was, no one had been in it for a while. The final picture in the back was one I hadn't seen in maybe eight years, showing Corey and me at junior formal. I'd taken my copy with me. It was currently buried in the bottom of a box under my bed at my mother's, along with probably two hundred more pictures from that era of my life.

Where did this copy come from?

I walked over to the bay window, the photo clutched to my chest. The day it had been taken had been bittersweet. Yet the girl in the photo seemed happy—happier than I remember being in Fairford. But then, I'd always been content in Corey's arms.

I sat down in the window seat and surveyed the room, my gaze landing on those frames again. I blinked rapidly, forcing back unexpected tears. They were Alcoholics Anonymous coins framed with certificates—seven of them. It wasn't possible. Seven years of sobriety.

I walked toward the wall, my hands clenched. Anger, unfettered and overwhelming, blasted through me. My body temperature rose, and a small tremor shook my arms. The top frame was year one. I didn't know much about AA, but I knew that one of the steps was asking forgiveness. But there'd never been any apologies for me. There hadn't even been an acknowledgment that I existed in the last decade.

My eyes trailed down the years and then back up. Seven years of sobriety. Seven years of silence. I ripped the first frame off the wall.

THE SOUND OF THE SHATTERING glass made me smile, and a little of the weight I'd been carrying since I pulled off the exit ramp lifted. I pulled two more off the wall. Glass shards scattered. My temples throbbed with adrenaline and rage. A scream, high-pitched and raw, ripped from my throat as I tore the final frames from the wall. I should have been pretty high up on his list of people to apologize to. All those people at the wake came before me—they were a part of his sober life. But me, he'd tortured with drunkenness and cutting silence. In his seven years of sobriety, he had said nothing to me.

Why? Why didn't I ever matter to him?

I leaned against the wall, focusing on my breathing and hoping to stave off another panic attack. My body relaxed with each breath. The anger faded, taking my energy with it, and I looked at what I'd done. Only one frame survived the wreckage. I picked it up. The certificate was not from the program, as I'd suspected, but ordered off the web. I read it more closely. His sponsor had signed it. I couldn't make out the name. The second name, however, was easy to read in its school script—Nicole Scott. *Shit.* I started to pick up the coins, careful not to cut myself on the glass. I found five, plus the one still in its frame. The last one, I would have to find after I cleaned.

The opening cords of a Lifehouse song broke the silence in the room. I jumped back from the bay window in shock. My phone flashed and vibrated on the bed. *Emma*.

"Are you okay?" she asked, her voice pitchy with concern. "You sound out of breath."

I smiled at Emma's voice and her lack of a greeting. I lay back on the bed, using my free arm as a pillow. "Sorry, I'm fine. I'm just exploring Ryan's house."

"Wait, you're in the *house*?" There was trepidation in her voice. "Alone?"

I started to answer her but stopped at the sound of the front door slamming. I gasped, and it came out as a squeak. Emma shot worried questions my way.

"Someone just got here," I said quickly in hushed tones.

"Who is it?" she whispered back even though she was sitting in her own apartment.

As if I had any idea who it could be. There'd been a whole town at the wake, not to mention all the people I'd watched enter the church that morning. I hoped against hope it wasn't Bethany. I could not deal with *her* in this house.

"I'll let you know." I hung up and walked toward the bedroom door on tiptoes, tucking my phone into my pocket.

I froze after one of the floorboards creaked. Not that it mattered—my car was parked outside. Whoever had come in knew someone was here. A voice I could hardly decipher called out my name. I pulled the bedroom door closed behind me, and it barely clicked, but the metered sound of footfalls downstairs stopped. The voice had been male.

I was halfway down the stairs when I saw *him*. I stopped so fast my legs nearly buckled.

Corey.

Anticipation, confusion, and a little excitement bubbled in me as I took in his profile. Corey stood in the foyer, facing the dining room, his hands in the pockets of his perfectly tailored suit. How had I ever mistaken that man beside Krystal for him? The muscles in his jaw tightened. Maybe he was reconstructing the same memory I'd worked through, remembering the story I'd told him at the Robinson Diner the night we'd gone from being friends to so much more.

I took another tentative step, and a creaking filled the house. *Dammit.* I didn't move. He didn't turn around. But he knew I was here. He'd called my name.

I wished he'd face me and give me a complete view. It had been so long since I'd laid eyes on him. I wanted to know what the last nine years had done to him. Was he still that same boy who'd held me when the rest of my world crumbled, or had time turned his gaze hard?

I crept one step closer, and though there was no sound, he finally turned to face me. His blue eyes, the same ones I used to get lost in, met mine. Those eyes had seen beyond the broken girl I'd been. They'd been my safest haven. I gripped the banister, afraid to move or blink or breathe. A decade of shadows and regrets twisted inside of me, unfurling from the deepest parts of my soul. They wound their way through my body, not stopping until they surrounded the fortress I'd built around my heart.

Chapter 12

Now

"Hi, Andi."

That voice. I hadn't heard his voice in years, but it had been the one in my head, telling me when I was doing something stupid all this time. It was a voice I tended to ignore, one that was so embedded in me that I'd forgotten it was his.

The rest of the stairs came fast under my feet, and then he was there in front of me. He looked *good*. Tired and sad and overwhelmed, but good. Too good. Every nerve in my body was on alert as his familiar scent washed over me. Corey. My first love. My biggest regret. The one familiar face in a sea of familiar faces who could possibly understand everything I felt being here again.

I hugged him, unable—or unwilling—to stop myself. After a moment, he hugged me back. Those arms closed around me, and I clung to him. I breathed him in. After all the pain and distance and time apart, we still fit. Warmth spread through me, even as the subtle ache in my heart that I'd lived with for so long turned into a throb.

"It's good to see you," he said, pulling back after indulging my longer-than-average hug. The words sounded like the truth, which did nothing to help curb the adrenaline coursing through me.

"What are you doing here?" I asked.

"I could ask you the same thing," he said evenly, though the corner of his mouth twitched.

His eyes tracked every movement I made—from tucking my hair behind my ears to stepping back before I hugged him again to wetting my dry lips. A flush worked its way up my neck—from the scrutiny or the fact that his body had just been pressed against mine or both. I forced myself to focus on his face and not the breadth of his shoulders or the perfect fit of his pants or the way his eyes didn't quite meet mine but still swept across me.

"I came for the funeral."

He met my gaze finally. The softness was buried beneath something else, but it was there. "Yeah, I figured. I wasn't sure you would." He motioned toward the kitchen. "Come on—let's sit."

The fact that he'd somehow become the host didn't go unnoticed. I felt my hand start to tremble and closed it into a fist as I followed him into the kitchen. I sat down on a barstool, and he jumped up onto the counter despite what I guessed—based on my knowledge of Harry's closet—was a thousand-dollar suit. The dichotomy between this man and the boy I'd loved pierced my armor. The army was breeching the walls of my heart fortress. This had been how we'd always sat while we snacked in the kitchen, waiting for water to boil, ice to freeze, or Ryan to come banging in.

"Why are you here, Corey?" I kept my tone neutral, but my insides turned at the thought of his inevitable answer.

"Well, the neighbors called and said a strange woman was over here. I figured it was you since Nikki told me she gave you the key. She couldn't really leave all the guests."

I trembled at his casual use of my sister's name and the fact that the neighbor had called him. An ominous feeling settled inside me, taking up more residence the longer we sat there. "You know Nikki?"

Because he hadn't known her. My stepmom had fled *before* I met Corey.

"Going on six years now." He picked up a copy of *Architectural Digest* off the counter and flipped through it.

"Corey, why are you *here*?" I asked again, agitation rattling my words.

The look he gave me was direct and resigned and pained. He'd known I would have questions. He'd maybe even *chosen* to come here instead of Nikki. And whatever came next, he wasn't about to sugarcoat it. "I'm Ryan's business partner."

I choked on the breath I'd just taken. This couldn't be real life. I stood up and took a few nervous steps toward the living room and then back again. "What exactly does that mean?"

"It's a long story."

Neither of us said anything. I kept pacing, tugging at the ends of my hair. My heart raced, and any calm I'd felt in his embrace dissolved. My hands shook. Corey was the one person I could trust unconditionally. He couldn't be Ryan's *anything*.

When I spoke again, the words were frantic and frazzled. "Business partner?"

He ran a hand through his hair, a tangled mess of brown that needed a cut. "I never thought I'd see you in Fairford again."

I stopped my pacing and looked at him, my heart pounding in my ears. "Is that supposed to make this somehow okay?"

"I told you, it's a long story." He jumped down from the counter, placing the magazine under his arm. He was comfortable in here. Too comfortable.

"Why weren't you at the wake or the funeral?"

"We had a private viewing earlier in the day, but I was there last night after you left. And this morning, had you stayed, you would've seen me. I was a pallbearer. I gave a eulogy."

Gave a eulogy.

He swallowed, and a hint of something akin to mischief glinted in his expression. "But I saw you and..."

"Harry."

Any other name would have been better—I'd spent years actively *not* saying Harry's name. But Corey's presence had me off-balance. I'd never thought that Corey would still be in Fairford, that he would know Ryan, that he would find me.

Corey met my gaze. "I know."

"Excuse me?"

"You are googleable, Andi. I know you work at Harry's firm." He paused. He clearly knew the truth. It was written all over his face. I could practically see the glib comment formulating in his mind. "So, uh, how'd you two wind up together?"

"It's compli—you googled me?"

In all the years we'd been apart, I'd resisted the urge to look up Corey. Sure, I might have typed his name into a search bar or ten, but I'd never hit Enter, not once. I hadn't found him on Facebook or stalked his Twitter or even looked at his LinkedIn profile on private. Though I regretted that last one now.

"Once or twice over the years. Anyway, you were saying, about you and Harry?"

I'd forgotten his tenacious nature and ability to push people's most vulnerable buttons. I sat down again, keeping my hands in my lap so he wouldn't see them shaking. "We spent a lot of late nights together. I was his assistant. We got to talking..." Sweat beaded at my temples. I never had to give answers about Harry, and this off-the-cuff story could easily go wrong. "You know how these things happen. No one was more surprised than me when our feelings turned romantic. But then, I guess *you* know plenty about strange bedfellows."

His eyes narrowed, but then he laughed. "I guess that's fair."

"You swore you'd never be a townie."

He shrugged. "I wouldn't say I'm a townie, but that's another long story."

"Maybe you could tell me sometime." I squirmed in my seat, feeling as if I'd just asked him on a date.

Corey's glance shifted from the floor to my face. An openness that hadn't been there before played across his features, making him look more like the boy I used to know. "How about dinner tomorrow?"

I bit my bottom lip. I had no intention of staying in Fairford any longer than necessary. Coming to the house had already pushed my limits, and another full day here... I didn't think I could survive it.

"I'm leaving tonight."

"They're reading the will on Saturday. You need to be here." It was a statement, with no hint of question or request. I needed to be here. End of story.

My mouth went dry. There was no way I could spend three more days in Fairford with everyone apparently Stepford-wived into liking Ryan. But we both knew that if I left now, I was never ever coming back. God, I was going to need a drink or several to survive this. I hopped down from my stool, crossed to the refrigerator, and swung the door open. Not that a recovering alcoholic would have alcohol, but I'd take anything at this point. I scanned the contents of the fridge—milk, water, orange juice... and there it was, proof it had all been a sham: a beer.

"You don't want to drink that," Corey said from just over my shoulder as if he'd known what I would find and what my reaction would be.

I turned the bottle in my hand. "Sober for seven years, my ass."

"Look at the expiration date."

He was close enough that I could smell his cologne again. I took a breath to settle my nerves. The beer was six years old, according to the expiration date. I didn't even want to think about what bacteria might be living in it. "Why is that still in there?"

"He used to say it tested him every time he opened the door."

"Gross." The outside of the bottle had been perfectly clean, but I still felt dirty. I flipped on the sink faucet and washed my hands.

Corey didn't say anything, but I could feel him watching me and hear him breathing a little too fast behind me. Tension weighted the air. He was as nervous as I was.

I dropped my hand into a paper towel and turned around, leaning against the sink. "Do you want me to stay?"

The openness that had been there before faded. "I—" His phone buzzed. "Sorry." He pulled it out of his pocket and glanced at it, a line forming on his forehead as he read whatever was on his screen. When he looked up, his expression was carefully blank. "I've got to get back. People are asking after me."

"But..." *But what?* This was his life, his loss. It was not mine. Of course, he couldn't stay. *But does he want* me *to?*

He handed me a business card with a logo for Scott and Johnson Home Design printed in the same colors I'd seen on that building at the end of Main. The reality of their—our—names side by side made my heart sink. It was real. This wasn't some elaborate hoax designed to mess with my head. Our fingers brushed as I took the card. A tingle of excitement ran from my hand all the way through my arm. I wanted to reach out and touch him again—to reclaim what we'd shared in that hug. Instead, I stepped back.

The touch had affected him too—he bit at his bottom lip, and pink spots dotted his cheeks. His hands were back in his pockets. "My cell is on there. Call me if you want to get dinner tomorrow."

He was out the door before I could think to say goodbye or ask any of the questions running through my mind. But it didn't matter. The one thing I needed to know was clear—Corey wanted me to stay.

Chapter 13

Then

An hour after I'd finally let myself fall asleep, convinced that my dad had passed out and I was safe, a door slammed downstairs. The front door. A moment later, a second door slammed—my dad's bedroom. Krystal had parked behind his car when she dropped me off. I'd sat staring at his license plate as she tried to get me to sleep at her house or let her come inside and make sure I got settled. It dawned on me that he hadn't driven himself to the hospital. That was why he'd made such a big deal about me going out with Krystal. I couldn't imagine who might have taken him to the hospital and where he'd disappeared to after, but it didn't matter really—he was here now.

I squeezed my eyes shut, but there would be no going back to sleep. My heart raced, and my head throbbed. I waited five, ten, fifteen minutes, but there was no further movement from downstairs. Still, I couldn't sleep, and sitting there all night, awake and terrified, wasn't going to help anything. My stomach growled, loud and insistent. I hadn't eaten since lunch. Unhooking the chair from under the doorknob, I pulled the door open and listened. I heard only the undertones of snoring.

I slipped into my shoes and crept downstairs—avoiding the creaking plank—and out the back door. Leaving through the backyard made for a longer walk to my car, but it also kept me from having to pass by his bedroom, which felt safer. Once in the car, I fumbled the keys in my left hand, clumsily grasping the key and turning it. *If I'm not ambidextrous by the time this brace comes off... am I supposed to be driving?* I didn't know how long the pain meds lasted, but I felt like crap. That would have to be enough of a sign that I was ready to drive.

The roads were nearly empty—just me and the creatures of the night, which I hoped didn't include bears this far north. I flipped on my brights and drove slowly. I stopped at the entrance ramp to Route 17. East would take me home to Westchester, to an empty house. I'd never driven west of Fairford, but I'd heard about a diner up the road. Not that anyone I'd met went there, since Fairford had its own diner that was cheaper and supposedly had better food.

A car pulled up behind me close enough to let me know they didn't like my dawdling. *West, it is.*

Ten minutes later, I reached the exit for the diner. I took it, realizing too late that I hadn't thought to check if it was an all-night diner. But as I pulled off the ramp and onto the back road, it was lit up. Three cars and one precarious-looking motorcycle waited in the parking lot. I checked my face in the mirror. The bruising around my gash hadn't gotten any better, but it also hadn't gotten any worse. I wiped my hand on my jeans and stepped out of the car then walked slowly into the diner. The waitress called for me to take a menu from the stack on the hostess stand and waved toward the back section of the diner from behind the counter, where she was making a pot of coffee. I held a hand up in thanks and walked over to where she had pointed. I hadn't spoken a word since leaving Krystal's car. I'd ignored two calls from Emma, knowing that if I said anything and confirmed what had happened, it would all become too real.

It's real.

Bethany had left because it was real. She took her daughter and moved across state lines. She'd never looked back. Our denial—my denial, my willingness to be left behind—had caused this.

Crap. I couldn't go down a rabbit hole of blame in the middle of a diner. I sat down at a table close to the only other patron in this section of the diner to make it easier on the waitress. The guy wore a green-and-white windbreaker like the one I'd just ordered for volleyball. The WR on the arm confirmed my suspicions that it was a Fairford Football warm-up. *Corey* was embroidered in neat cursive above his heart. Based on the way he sprawled out at his table, he was tall and moderately lanky. I glanced at the book in his hand—*The Great Gatsby.* He was a junior too. He alternated between scribbling furiously in a notebook to his right and reaching around everything he had on the table to take a bite of a half-eaten cheeseburger. It seemed impossible that his book and notebook were not full of food splatter.

The waitress walked over to the table with a surprisingly real smile, an order pad in her hand. She was friendly enough though clearly preoccupied. She took my order—a grilled cheese with fries—then returned to the front. She took a seat at the counter and opened a giant textbook. Only a few minutes passed before a bell rang through the quiet of the diner. A moment later, the waitress placed a plate heaping with fries in front of me. My stomach growled as the smell of cheese and grease mixed in the air.

"Thank you," I said, my voice sounding stilted even to me.

"You need anything else?"

"No. Maybe just leave the check?"

She scribbled something on her notepad and dropped the paper next to the napkins. She paused, her face pinched in concern, but then gave one last smile and turned. "Have a good night, hon."

I lifted my hand to my cheek to find it wet. *Perfect.* I wiped away the tears and took a few shallow breaths. They kept falling. Since I apparently couldn't stop them, I ate. At least eating a sandwich with the wrong hand was fairly easy. I would have to order not-messy food for a while and nothing that I had to cut.

"You go to Fairford, right? On the volleyball team?"

The voice startled me. I looked up to find the guy at the next table over looking at me. I hadn't even thought he'd noticed my arrival.

"Well, I guess I used to be." A laugh escaped my throat. Laughing—I couldn't believe I was able to do that.

"Yeah." He motioned in my general direction. "What happened?"

I opened my mouth to give the story I'd told Krystal and Dr. Greenwald another try. Nothing came out.

"I'm Corey, by the way. You're Ryan Scott's daughter, right?"

It was creepy how in a small town where I knew almost no one, they knew me. I nodded.

He stood up and walked over to my table. "The guys on the team have mentioned you. You work with Brian, right?"

That made sense. I'd only met a few football players. In fact, now that I thought about it, I'd heard the name Corey before. He'd never joined in on any of our adventures thus far. Perhaps he'd been too busy hanging out at the out-of-town diner.

"Andi Scott," I said, extending my left hand.

He took it and gave my hand a quick shake. "Corey Johnson." He motioned to the seat across from me. I nodded only slightly, but he took it as an affirmation. I checked my cheeks. They were finally dry.

"So, what happened?" he asked again. "That gash looks gnarly."

"It's really embarrassing." I dropped my head. To him, it probably looked like I was hiding a blush, but I was trying to compose my answer. It needed to sound natural, organic. It needed to sound believable. And if the way Krystal had looked at me when I stepped out of her car was any indication, it was not yet believable. "I was taking my sheets down to be washed and I got tangled up... me, stairs, glass clock..."

"Oh man. I feel your pain. See this tooth?" He pulled back his upper lip and pointed to a tooth just two away from the front two.

"I did the same thing but with basement stairs. Knocked this tooth right out of me. There was so much blood. My mom was screaming and freaking out."

"You're lying." I was laughing again. My wrist didn't hurt either.

"Actually, I'm not." He smiled, and it was big and toothy and adorable. It brightened his face and made his eyes crinkle "But it was a baby tooth, so all's well that ends well."

"Best tooth fairy present ever?"

"You have no idea." His eyes drifted to my plate. "Do you mind if I bring my food over?"

I shook my head. "Not at all."

Chapter 14

Then

"Come on," Krystal said from her perch at the edge of my desk in homeroom. "There's no way you two haven't kissed."

I rolled my eyes. This was our new daily conversation. According to Krystal, both the volleyball and football teams were placing bets on when exactly Corey and I were going to make it official. "There's been no kissing."

It had been over a month since our first meeting at the Robinson Diner, and Corey and I had become friends. It was an inadequate phrase but all I had. We weren't dating, and we *hadn't* kissed, despite what Krystal thought. But having Krystal and Corey by my side had made my transition into the Fairford junior class seamless. With my brace finally gone—three weeks after I "fell down the stairs"—life had fallen into the familiar pattern of school, practice, work, and homework.

Krystal sighed. "At least you don't sound happy about it." She grinned, and I knew whatever was about to come out of her mouth was going to be an awful idea. "Have you tried to kiss him?"

I palmed my face. "Krys. Really. No."

"Morning, ladies." Corey approached, smiling like he did every time he saw me. He placed a cranberry muffin from S&R Deli on my desk. I flushed as Krystal's eyes practically turned into little hearts. "What are we talking about?"

I fiddled with the plastic container, knowing Krystal was about to tell him *exactly* what we'd been talking about. The bell rang. *Thank God.* Corey slid into the desk next to me, and Krystal moved off my desk and into the chair in front of me.

Homeroom was short, but those fifteen minutes felt like an eternity. Krystal's words had wormed their way into my brain. I *hadn't* tried to kiss Corey. I wasn't even sure I'd given him any sign that he could kiss me if he wanted—aside from not hiding the fact that I liked him. *He must want to, right?* Teenage boys didn't show up with muffins for no reason. And the other day, after practice, he'd been waiting outside the gym with coffees.

The bell rang again. I shot out of my desk, sliding my backpack on, so that I was standing before Corey had even put away his copy of *Catch-22*. We'd been reading it the night before at Robinson, but as usual, we'd gotten distracted, this time playing French fry Jenga. It was time to make my intentions known. Krystal was right. Corey and I weren't *just friends*.

"Hey." I slipped my hand into his, entwining our fingers. For all the coffees and late-night conversations and hands on the small of my back as he walked with me to class, we hadn't ever held hands. My fingers slid between his, and electricity shot up my arm. A shiver worked its way through me as he closed his hand around mine.

He glanced down at our hands and then back at me. Pink spots appeared on his cheeks, and his smile was bashful. He squeezed my hand. "Hey."

Behind us, Krystal tried and failed to cover a squeal. Brian called out "It's about time," and I swear I heard a slow clap—which had to be Dustin.

Corey ignored them, tugging me toward the exit. "Can I walk you to class?"

He'd been walking me to class since the first day of school, but just as he'd understood my gesture, I understood his. This was the beginning. This was official. And we both knew that by lunchtime, the whole grade—if not the whole school—would know that Corey Johnson and Andi Scott were a couple. I wondered who would win the bet—*probably Krystal*—and how high the winnings had gotten.

I squeezed his hand. "I would love that."

"HEY, YOU TWO." THE waitress at Robinson, Peggy, hadn't even asked our order after shooing us to our usual booth in the back. She dropped a plate of fries on the table along with two waters. Her smile made it clear she noticed that we were sitting on the same side of the booth and that Corey's arm hadn't left my shoulder.

It had been such a perfect day. And we hadn't even kissed yet. I'd thought maybe it would happen as we stood outside, waiting for our respective buses to take us to away games, but he'd only pressed his forehead to mine and said he'd see me that night. I didn't know what he was waiting for. I would gladly have taken a first kiss pressed up against the side of the high school or in the blocked-off stairway that everyone knew how to get into. Even though we hadn't kissed yet, I was clearly his *something*.

When Peggy left, giving us one last wink, Corey moved his arm from across my shoulder and held my hand. His eyes were serious and not in the heavy-lidded, *I'm finally going to kiss you* way I'd hoped for.

His thumb ran a circle across my palm. "Tell me what happened that night, Andi."

My eyes widened as his fingers brushed over my wrist, and his gaze shifted to my forehead, where a thin scar remained. I tried to keep my expression neutral, but I could tell by the discerning look in his eye that I'd failed. "Corey, you already know..."

I didn't want to lie to him, especially not with him looking at me with those open, trusting eyes. There was nowhere to go in this small space. It was just me and him and the truth. But I couldn't—not after a month of carefully crafted lies. My mother hadn't been happy to hear Bethany was gone, and she'd been more than angry when I told her I fell and sprained my wrist, mostly because I'd mentioned it about a week after it happened, which was as long as I assumed I could wait before she got some sort of notification that I'd used her insurance. My social media post with my brace had been wry and sarcastic. The injury had kept me from keeping my promise to go home and go to the beach with Emma, as I'd thought it would. Because the truth was, if I left Fairford, I wasn't sure I'd come back. I knew my forced isolation was a temporary reprieve—I would have to face my best friend eventually.

Corey's fingers lightly rubbed at the sensitive skin of my wrist. "You can tell me the truth."

There had to be some alternate version of my story that would appease him. But I couldn't think of one. I lived with one person. So, either I'd fallen down the stairs and hurt myself, or my dad had hurt me. Corey didn't deserve a lie. The first time he'd asked, we hadn't known each other, but now, he was one of the few things holding my life together.

I stilled his hand and forced myself to meet his imploring gaze. "It was my dad."

"Dammit." He ran a hand through his hair. "We have to tell someone."

I shook my head. "It was my fault. I knew better than—"

"Than what? Nothing you would've said or done could've warranted a sprained wrist and a head laceration."

"He was drinking and upset. It wouldn't even have been anything if the grandfather clock hadn't been there." I'd played out these justifications so often in my own mind that I almost believed them. But Corey's expression hardened. "Please, Corey. Please just let it go."

"Let it go?" His voice rose. I watched him force his emotions back. "You can't stay in a house with someone who physically hurt you."

"It's just until the end of the school year."

"That's nine months from now!" He rubbed at his temples. "This is too big. You can't expect me to—"

"I can handle this. I can," I reiterated when he started shaking his head. "You have to trust me."

He looked up at me, his face resigned but also determined. "Are you safe in the house?"

I shifted so I could rest my head on his shoulder. He wrapped me in his arms and ran his fingers through my hair.

"He doesn't talk to me," I said, speaking the truth of the last month for the first time. My house had become a silent prison. "He doesn't even look at me." I lifted my head and looked into Corey's eyes, our faces only inches apart. "So yeah, I'm fine in the house."

He didn't look like he believed me, but he didn't push it. He wiped a rogue tear from my cheek. "If you're not okay there, Andi, you need to tell me."

I met his eyes and forced myself to hold his gaze. "I'm fine in the house. If that changes..." Whatever promise I made next, I'd have to keep. "If that changes, you will be the first one to know."

"Promise?" His shoulders relaxed slightly.

"I promise, Corey." At those words, a weight lifted. I wasn't alone in this anymore. Someone else knew the truth, from my own lips. There was one person I didn't have to lie to. The one person I never wanted to lie to again. I leaned my head on his shoulder. "How long have you known?"

He lifted my chin. "For a while."

"Then why did you ask now?" I asked, placing a hand on his chest.

He covered it with one hand and lifted my chin with the other. "I had to know the truth before I did this..."

He kissed me then. His lips were soft against mine, tentative. But I didn't have hesitations. Not about Corey. I leaned into him, opening myself up. He cupped my face and deepened the kiss. Beneath my hand, his heart pounded just as mine did. We pulled apart only to come together again.

The next time we broke apart, his gaze was heavy and dazed and his lips swollen. He smiled. "Andi Scott, will you be my girlfriend?"

All these weeks fell together. In a world where nothing made sense, everything became clear—Corey was why I was here. I wrapped my arms around his neck and hugged him as best I could in the small booth. "Yes," I whispered against his neck. "I would love to be your girlfriend."

Chapter 15

Then

The bleachers quaked. Everyone on the Fairford Central side was on their feet. With thirty seconds left in the fourth quarter of the homecoming game, we were down by four and on the fifteen-yard line. Third down. I cupped my hands around my mouth and screamed. Krystal hooked her arm around mine and bounced on her toes. Her boyfriend, Dustin, took the snap and backed up into the pocket. Corey broke to the right and outran his coverage. Dustin found him wide open in the end zone. Corey went up for the catch and came down in bounds, the ball cradled carefully in his arms.

The bleachers shook as the crowd roared with delight and flooded the field. We hadn't beaten Liberty at homecoming in a decade. The crowd surged forward, surrounding the team. Green and white confetti floated down on top of them. Krystal tugged my arm. We ran down the bleachers together, screaming at the top of our lungs. Krystal grinned at me before running straight into the crowd. Dustin was somewhere in the middle.

Like Dustin, Corey was encircled by teammates. They chanted and howled. But somehow, our eyes connected through the madness. He pushed his way through the crowd until he was free. Dropping his helmet, he jogged toward me. I opened my arms to his embrace, and he twirled me around, kissing me intensely.

"My girl." He placed me back on my feet. "I know just how we're celebrating."

I entwined my fingers with his. "You don't want to go out with the team?"

He scrunched up his nose and narrowed his eyes at me. "Hang out with a bunch of sweaty jocks or spend the night with my hot girlfriend? That's an easy choice."

I kissed him, tasting salt and Gatorade and Corey, and tugged at the sweaty hair at the base of his neck, not caring that we probably—most definitely—had an audience. The school hadn't stopped talking about us for three weeks. But it didn't matter. Corey had become home. It was terrifying and electrifying in equal measure. He deepened the kiss, his hand warm against the sliver of exposed skin at the small of my back.

"Get a room!" Brian called, his voice hoarse from the game.

We pulled apart, but Corey didn't let me go. He rarely did anymore. I leaned into his chest, and he nuzzled into my neck, his chin on my shoulder. He was sweaty and muddy, but I couldn't have been happier to be in his arms. I linked our fingers and kissed his cheek. Across the field, Dustin and Brian gave Krystal and Bella—Brian's girlfriend—piggyback rides. They came barreling toward us, stopping only inches before crashing into the bleachers.

Righting himself, Dustin held up his hand, and Corey took it in that way guys do. Had I not been in his arms, they probably would have bumped chests.

"Nice throw, man!"

"Nice catch." Dustin grinned and motioned toward the rest of the team, who were slowly retreating to the locker rooms. Fans still loitered on the field, which was littered with confetti. "Are you coming to Tim's?"

"Nah. I have other plans tonight." Corey nudged me with his shoulder as if he could be talking about anyone else. "But tomorrow at the dance, it's so on."

Dustin nodded in approval. The team's win would add to the excitement at the homecoming dance and the after-parties. Krystal waggled her eyebrows at me because I knew her plans for later that night, which did not involve staying at Tim's very long. I was certain Dustin would be on board once he realized exactly how his girlfriend intended to celebrate his game-winning throw.

Behind us, I heard Bella laugh and turned to find Brian tossing her over his shoulder as they walked toward the school. I stepped out of Corey's embrace and linked hands with him again as the four of us headed inside. Krystal nudged me with her hip as she passed and whispered a not so covert "I'll call you in the morning" before jumping on Dustin's back again.

"So," I asked, swinging our hands between us, "what are we doing?"

"Anything that doesn't involve listening to Dustin replay that throw all night at Tim's."

I rolled my eyes. "You know you want to be part of that replay."

"It can wait until tomorrow. Tonight, I just want to spend some time with you. Maybe we can go get some hot chocolate at S&R and make a pit stop over at that little park on Elm or maybe..." He cleared his throat. "The Peak?"

The Peak, I'd learned from Krystal, was where everyone went to make out. But tonight, everyone was going to be at Tim's.

"The Peak?"

He flushed. "To hang out without Peggy interrupting us with more water or extra fries or my dad so obviously clomping up the stairs even though my door is wide open." He stopped at the door to the school and gave me a sheepish look. "We don't have to if you don't want to."

Did I want to make out with my boyfriend in the privacy of his car? Yes, I did. But I'd heard many a story about what happened at the Peak. "I've never been to the Peak before."

Which was an idiotic thing to say. Obviously, I'd never been there unless I'd had some clandestine summer romance no one knew about.

"Me neither." He smiled. "Well, at least not for the reason everyone else our age goes there. There's a killer view."

"All right," I said, following him into the school, "let's go get some hot chocolate and then check out the view."

A blast of warm air hit me, and I had never been so grateful for our overheated high school. Wearing only my volleyball jacket hadn't been the smartest idea for the coldest day in October, but that was what you did when you were on a varsity team. Those letters were hard-earned. I would wear that thing through Thanksgiving if our team made it that far into the playoffs.

We stopped outside the locker room, and Corey gave me a quick kiss. "I'm gonna take a shower. Meet you at your locker in ten?"

Ten minutes became fifteen, but I used the time to call Emma. Even though we texted nearly all day, every day, we still tried to connect on the phone at least once a week because, as she'd put it, "I miss your voice, Scott." And I had to agree. Hearing Emma's voice made her feel closer and farther away all at once.

"So, I was thinking maybe I could come up to you one weekend?" Emma ended nearly every call with this request or a similar one. I'd been able to hold her off, claiming practice and work and games and weekend tournaments. But it wouldn't last forever. If I didn't see her soon, she was just going to show up in Fairford one day.

"Maybe," I said halfheartedly. "We made the playoffs, so things are hopefully going to be a bit crazy for a while."

Down the hall from where I sat, I heard Corey laugh. Peeking over there, I saw him talking to a group of what looked like freshmen girls. He had his new letterman jacket on and looked every bit the high school football star he was. And he was mine.

"Anyway, I gotta go. Corey's back. Talk next week?"

"Yeah. Send me pictures tomorrow."

"I will." I hung up and stood, folding my arms as Corey crossed the hallway. I glared at him in mock anger. "How's your fan club?"

He shrugged. "What can I say? The people love me."

"Yeah, yeah."

He looped his arm through mine as we walked back toward the exit. "How's Emma?"

"She's good. She keeps asking to come visit, and I'm running out of excuses."

Outside, the night had only gotten cooler. I zipped my jacket up to my neck and snuggled in closer to Corey.

"Well, what if we meet her halfway or something? There's an outlet mall about an hour south of here."

"Yeah. Maybe."

The thing was, I didn't want to see Emma. Seeing her would only make the distance between us real. It would force me to lie to her face instead of sidestepping questions I didn't want to answer. With my friends in Fairford and now Corey, life here felt almost normal. But every time I talked to Emma, I was reminded how *not* normal it really was and how next year, I'd be back to Emma and Charlie and the life I'd left behind. I wasn't ready to deal with any of those issues. It was easier to stay in my Fairford bubble with the good and the bad than to try to balance my two homes.

We were almost to his car when Corey stopped short. I followed his line of sight. Someone had confetti bombed the car. It had definitely been Dustin and Brian. They'd even drawn two birds inside a heart on the back window.

"Lovebirds." Corey said, shaking his head. "Subtle."

By the time we pulled into a spot near S&R Deli, most of the confetti had fallen off the car. But the sheer amount that had gotten inside—Corey was going to be finding football confetti for the next year. S&R usually closed early, but on game nights, they reopened at halftime. Half the town usually showed up after a game. As we got closer, I could see that the crowd had already overflowed. I waved at a few sophomores I knew from the newspaper, who were huddled outside the door. Through the window, we could see Dustin reenacting his game-winning pass. Corey groaned. "They're supposed to be at Tim's."

Inside, we were met with cheers. The line wound through the tables and back to the pinball machines. I offered to wait for the drinks since he was being beckoned by half his team. Krystal took his place at my side. We whispered about her plans with Dustin that night. Across the room, Corey was already pretending to go long for a catch from Dustin. The crowd went wild as if we were back on the field. Football in Fairford was something else. It had never been like this in Pinewood. After several more minutes and yet another replay, our hot chocolates were ready.

Krystal leaned in close as we made our way back to the guys. "Wish me luck."

"Luck," I whispered back. I knew I'd hear all about it in the morning. She'd been talking about losing her virginity for weeks. And the win was just icing on the cake.

Corey and I freed ourselves from the crowd and worked our way back outside. I turned at the door to give Krystal one last thumbs-up for luck, but she was already perched on Dustin's lap, lost in a far-too-public display of affection.

"You looked like you were having fun," I said as we moved away from the store and back toward his car. "We can stay. Go to Tim's. The Peak will wait."

Corey stopped and pulled me in for a kiss. When we broke apart, he kept me close, our bodies still aligned in all the right places. This part of the street was quiet, the businesses long since closed, and I considered pulling him back into me. Before I could, he motioned to the bench in front of the stationery store. We sat and drank our hot chocolate, a heated silence between us.

He took my hand in his and traced the lines on the inside of my palm. "You're amazing, you know that?"

The intensity of his gaze sent a shiver through me. I sipped my hot chocolate, averting my eyes. Three small words fluttered to the edge of my lips, but I held them back, afraid it was too soon for such proclamations.

He lifted my chin, pulling my gaze back to him. His blue eyes were bright and open and full of emotion. "I love you, Andi."

Tears welled in my eyes. It wasn't too soon. Corey was on this ride with me. He felt what I felt. He *loved* me.

I cupped his face and pulled him close. "I love you too."

Chapter 16

Now

My hotel room seemed to be getting smaller by the second. I was sprawled out on the bed, counting the cracks in the ceiling. I'd told Corey I was going home. And I'd meant it at the time. Except I hadn't been able to convince myself to grab my bag and go. After Corey's abrupt departure, I'd cleaned up the mess in my old bedroom and then left Ryan's house. I found all seven of the coins and salvaged the certificates then made sure everything was in a safe spot.

My time in Fairford was over, but the pull of seeing Corey again had kept me coming up with excuses to stay until long after dark. First, I needed to get the frames and fix the mess I'd left at Ryan's—something I still hadn't done. Then I figured I should eat before hitting the road. Finally, I'd decided that I shouldn't waste Harry's money—he had paid for the room through the night.

Now it was nearly eleven. Fairford would be shut down, and only the 7-Eleven and the diner just outside the city limits would still be open. The houses in town would be dark, only a few upstairs bedrooms lit. It was such a far cry from my city life, where the party started at eleven. Williamsburg seemed farther away than one hundred miles, and it was too easy to forget the woman I'd become away from Fairford. Which was exactly why I should have left already.

But those few minutes with Corey had released a long-buried yearning to be in his presence. He'd always been a balm for my soul, and even with his unexpected connection to Ryan, he still was. Emma and Krystal had called it "the Corey effect." Any bad day could be fixed by his voice, and when I had been one hundred miles from the guy I loved, there had been a lot of bad days. Being in his presence was better—chiseled cheekbones and abs for days amplified the effect.

His business card taunted me from its spot on the bedside table. For nine years, I hadn't allowed myself to know how to contact him, and now I'd already committed the ten digits of his cell phone number to memory. I couldn't give him three days, but I could give him twenty-four hours.

My cell phone buzzed, and I sat up, scrambling for it. Too late, I realized it couldn't be Corey. I had his number, but he didn't have mine.

"Hey, Mom."

"How are you, sweetie?" Her voice, which two days ago had irked me to no end, brought a smile to my face. She was exactly what I needed. Corey might have been a balm, but my mom was my rock.

I reached for a pillow and propped my head up. "I'm okay, Mom. It'll all be over soon enough."

"I thought it was already over. I figured you'd be halfway down 87 by now."

I opened my mouth to respond, but nothing came. Everything from the day jumbled together into a mess of questions I desperately wanted answered. I needed to know how Nikki and Corey and Krystal fit into this new reality of Fairford and how they fit with Ryan. But to do that, I needed to stay for another day.

I closed my eyes, and all I saw was Corey. He was eighteen again. His letterman jacket hung loosely off his body. An acceptance letter rested in one hand, car keys in the other. He stood in front of a silver sedan, his hand held out to me.

"Andi?"

All at once, the room rushed back into focus. The flower design on the curtains fluttered against the wind from the open window. Drops of water sounded on the ground outside. The vase of fake flowers on the table tipped over. I draped the blanket over my shoulders and tucked the phone between my ear and my shoulder. With one hand, I shut the window and straightened the vase and its flowers.

"Andi?" My mother said again, annoyed. "What is that racket?"

I dropped down into one of the chairs. It was comfortable, padded on the seat but sturdy enough not to distract from the goal at hand—eating and relaxing were not to be confused. I'd have to buy one.

"Sorry. It started to rain."

The flowers in the vase were made of that fabric easily mistaken for real. I pulled a purple one out. They even smelled real.

"That was rain?" she asked. "I thought a tractor trailer had just driven past you. When are you coming home? I don't like you being up there all alone."

"I ran into Corey today."

I shouldn't have said it. My mother would blow it out of proportion. There'd always been a sense of relief around her whenever Corey and I had a fight or broke up, and when it finally stuck—when that final Fairford cord snapped—she'd accepted it with a simple "It's for the best," even though I cried for weeks.

"Get in your car. Come home." They were commands, but there was also panic in her voice.

I tugged at the fake petals. They pulled off easily. *He loves me... not.* Corey had asked me to stay before, and I'd left. Losing the love of my life. Losing the last nine years of my life. I couldn't lose nine more. A girl needed closure.

"I think I might stay just for a few more days."

She sighed heavily. "Oh, Andi."

"Listen, Mom, I need to go." I hung up before she could protest any further.

My stomach turned and then growled. There were only two places open this late—the Fairford Diner and the Robinson Diner. I was not staying in Fairford. It was inevitable that I would run into someone I once knew. But the Robinson Diner would only make my confusion blurrier. I picked up my keys.

WALKING INTO THE ROBINSON Diner was like walking into a memory. It looked like any other diner, with its neon lights and uncomfortable booths. When the waitress motioned toward the nearly empty front half of the restaurant, I picked up an overstuffed laminated menu from the stack by the door. My eyes lingered on the back wall and the booth where Corey and I had spent so many nights. High school team photos from several area schools covered the walls, each one dated and autographed by the players who frequented the diner. It was a Sullivan County rite of passage. Corey was up there somewhere. I was too. Back then, I'd walk through the diner to see all the names and pictures signifying hope and dreams and escape.

I slid into a booth by the window, away from the photos and memories. A minute later, the waitress placed a glass of water in front of me. She waited expectantly. I hadn't opened the menu, but I still knew it by heart. Plus, my diner order rarely changed. It consisted of one of three items: cheeseburger deluxe, chocolate chip pancakes, or eggs and corned beef hash. It was definitely a pancake night. Stress, sleep deprivation, and love troubles always equaled pancakes and chocolate.

Harry's departure had shaken me. When he'd asked to come, and I allowed it, I hadn't thought that I'd need him. But with him gone, I felt off-balance. Or maybe it was Corey. Absence or presence? I couldn't tell. I wanted to believe it was absence—I needed that to be the truth. But my heart hadn't skipped a beat for Harry in months—a year, if I was being honest. My heart had only ached for what I knew love could be. It was a dull pain I'd learned to ignore enough to function in dating society—or at least to hide out with Harry.

"You need a minute?" the waitress asked.

"Oh, no. Sorry." I handed her the menu. "Chocolate chip pancakes and a decaf coffee, please."

I pulled my iPad out of my bag as she went to put in the order. With me being out of the office for two full days, my inbox had to be brimming with messages. Normally, I would check in at least once a day. Working at an agency didn't give me much leeway to ignore my email. But I didn't open the application. Instead, I navigated to the Scott and Johnson Home Design website. It was well put together—sleek and bold and everything an architectural firm's website should be. Scott and Johnson. The names should have looked weird side by side, but they didn't—maybe because I'd spent two years putting my name and Corey's together. I zoomed in on the logo. Scott and Johnson. They really were partners. Two names, equal footing. On the About page, a picture of the two of them side by side appeared next to a brief history. I didn't read it. The public history mattered little. It was the personal story that I needed, and I wanted to hear that straight from the source.

Before I could snoop further, my phone buzzed. I fished it out of my purse, knowing who it would be. Only one person would call me this late. I stared down at the photo of Harry, a professional one in case anyone else saw it. I wasn't sure I was ready to talk to Harry. The idea that Darlene would divorce her husband was so farfetched—she'd once even told him she would never give him the satisfaction—but she'd finally caved, and he was free. Free to be with me. That had never really seemed a possibility, so I hadn't thought about what it would mean. The repercussions of our relationship be-

ing out in the open felt too big. I didn't want to deal with the questions and the looks and the perpetual doubt that would come from
people knowing I was dating my boss. I liked the secret, romantic
whirlwind of the relationship we had. It worked, in part, because it
was illicit.

With a sigh, I picked up the call. "Hey, Harry."

"Hey, babe. How are you holding up?"

The waitress placed a plate of pancakes in front of me with a
smile and a nod. Unlike most things, the portions at the Robinson
Diner had gotten bigger. "I'm fine. Just eating dinner."

"It's midnight."

I shrugged, even though he couldn't see me and poured maple
syrup over my pancakes. "I was hungry."

Harry had never understood my strange eating habits. I could
go a whole workday without eating and then hit up some overpriced
diner that was open late. He didn't understand, but he loved the ability to come for a late-night booty call. Without a doubt, if I were
going for late-night food, I would almost always want late-night sex.
Even now, staring down at my pancakes, making small talk between
bites of chocolate and dripping maple syrup, I wished Harry wasn't
several states away. I wished I was at home and could cajole him into
taking a car all the way to Williamsburg.

"How was your flight?" I asked.

Muffled voices sounded on the line followed by Harry's laugh.
Knowing him, he was at the hotel bar and hadn't even bothered to
look at his room yet. "I can't talk long. Did you get home safely?"

"Oh, I actually decided to stay until tomorrow."

"Really?"

"Yeah, something came up after you left."

I knew better than to mention Corey. Harry might be technically married, and there were most certainly female voices in those
muffled sounds in the background, but he was the jealous type. And

telling him I was staying in town to have dinner with the former love of my life wouldn't go over well. However, I couldn't pinpoint why I didn't want to mention the reading of the will. Harry was a father—if anything, he might understand Ryan better than I could. He might even be able to provide some insight into what Ryan could possibly bequeath to me because I couldn't think of a single thing I would accept. But as with my mom earlier, I just couldn't.

"Okay, well, when do you think you'll be back to work? Craig could really use help on this baby campaign, and Hansen is looking for the monthly report, and I don't trust that new assistant to do it well."

I rolled my eyes. That "new" assistant had started a year ago and was more than capable of handling the monthly report. And helping Craig—who was two positions higher than me and paid vastly more—was not my job. Not to mention that Harry had told me not twelve hours earlier to take all the time I needed.

"The funeral was this morning, Harry."

"The funeral you didn't go to?"

I pulled my phone away from my ear and stared at it. *Did he really just say that?* "There are other ways to find closure than sitting in a church."

He cleared his throat, and the background noise behind him quieted. "You're right, babe. I'm sorry. It's just, you know, the office can't function without one of us there."

There was a compliment in there somewhere, but I wasn't in the mood to find it. "I'll be back on Monday."

I hung up. *Men.* He'd ruined my pancakes. Even if I was binging on self-pity and bordering on pathetic, there was no way I'd be able to enjoy them now. I shoved my phone back in my purse, tempted to shut it off. As I reached for my wallet to pay for my uneaten food, my fingers landed on the piece of card stock I'd snuck back into my purse before leaving—Corey's business card. He'd always been a night person. Uncertain if it was a good idea, I pulled out my phone and dialed his number.

While it rang, I took a few more bites of my pancakes and connected my iPad to the wireless. His voicemail picked up. *Great.* I hung up without saying anything. Surely, Corey hadn't meant that I could call him anytime when he'd handed me the card. *And what would I have even said?*

My phone rang almost immediately. No picture appeared. No name glared at me. Just the same numbers I'd just dialed, warning me I was in uncharted waters.

"Hi," I said quietly.

"I figured it had to be you." His voice was low and his words amused yet annoyed. I swore I heard him sigh, though it was hard to tell. When he spoke again, he sounded closer. "Do you know what time it is?"

"Were you sleeping?"

"No, I'm awake. Most people don't call so late unless something's wrong."

I laughed a little. "It's barely past midnight, old man."

"Why did you call? Did you just get home?" A door closed in the background, and there was a slight echo to his words. He hadn't been wearing a wedding ring, but that didn't mean anything. The possibility that there was a woman behind whatever door he'd closed hurt more than it should, and the panic I'd felt outside the church when I thought I'd seen him with Krystal crashed back into me.

"I'm at the Robinson Diner," I said, my words too quick and my voice too high. "Come join me?"

My request was met with silence and some more shuffling. I imagined him tossing in bed, his eyes focused on the ceiling, his hair mussed from running his hands through it in frustration as he considered the ramifications of accepting my request—the same ones I'd ignored when I'd asked him to come.

"I can't," he said finally, his voice shaky. "My parents need me at home."

Parents? That was unexpected. I pictured Paul, strong and determined and loyal, and Maya, petite and sweet and kind, and hoped they were both okay.

The waitress came to fill my water and coffee. She picked up my plate and then placed the check facedown on the table. I left it where it was.

"You still live with your parents?"

"It's..."

"A long story?" I asked, trying to keep an edge out of my voice. That phrase was starting to grate on my nerves.

"One for another time," he said with finality.

"There might not be another time." I'd more than decided to stay, but he didn't need to know that. He needed to tell me how nine years had turned into Scott and Johnson. And he wanted to. I felt it in my bones. Something was holding him back. Or someone. I hated that thought. "Just come meet me. I'll order you cheese fries."

"I don't... it's not a good idea." This time, he did sigh, loud and long and, if I was reading him correctly, pained. "Just call me before you leave town."

The click of the phone disconnecting rang loud in my ear. Shock coursed through me. Corey had never refused to meet me—late at night or otherwise. Not once in the whole time I'd known him. He'd even once driven to Pinewood in the middle of the night on a school night because I'd asked him to.

My heart ached, and one question kept volleying around my mind: *Who is on the other side of that door?*

Chapter 17

Now

E ven in the darkness of the unlit Fairford streets, I was able to find my way from the Robinson Diner to Corey's parents' house. It was a medium-sized two-story brick home. It had a widow's walk over the entryway that I'd always loved. In the back was a first-floor sunroom with a balcony over it. The balcony could only be accessed from the master bedroom or the windows in the other rooms. Too many times, I'd had to crawl out Corey's bedroom window when we were hanging out late at night. It was a great place to hide when his parents would come to check and make sure I'd left and had made for some interesting eavesdropping, especially the sex talk his father had given him one night. It had been one of the coldest nights of the year, and I'd been sitting outside with just a hoodie on, shivering, my teeth chattering, for nearly a half hour.

There was an outline of gravel stones around the side of the house. I'd done this once before, and even then, I'd been terrified of breaking the window. The first few stones I picked up were too heavy. I turned the flashlight on my phone toward a pile of smaller, rounder stones a step closer to the house. The light in what had been—or maybe still was—Corey's room was the only one on in the house. I threw the first stone and hit the siding. I tried again and almost reached the window.

Dammit. The feeling of being seventeen came back to me. Throwing rocks at Corey's window to get his attention, even when he said he couldn't give it, was something that had already happened. Standing outside his house now, ten years older, I wondered if he was really home. I'd already thrown four rocks at the window, and no one was responding. Maybe I'd caught him in the bathroom. I dropped the rest of the rocks I'd gathered and rubbed my shoulder. This was ridiculous. I stood on the grass, looking up at his window. Calling him would make the most sense—or simply going back to my hotel instead of acting like a stalker. But I wasn't going to do that. Not after driving all the way here. So that left me to stand out here all night and possibly freeze to death or call him and own up to my insanity. I opened my recent calls.

The sound of a door opening broke the silence of the night. I jumped back and switched off the flashlight on my phone, wondering if there was a place to hide in this yard. I couldn't remember any. In the dim light of the porch stood Corey in loose-fitting sweatpants and a white tank top.

He leaned against the porch rail and stared in my general direction. "Why are you throwing rocks at my window?"

Though I could see him clearly enough, I wasn't sure how well he could see me shrouded in the darkness of the yard. Maybe he didn't. Maybe he was only guessing. I stayed quiet.

"Andi?" He walked down the two steps and over to where I was standing.

Or not.

"You wouldn't come meet me." I wished I could take it back before I'd even finished saying it. Obviously, he had reasons for not meeting me in the middle of the night at our old haunt. But not knowing what they were gnawed at my stomach.

He reached out and took my hand. Heat sparked between us, and I almost pulled away from the shock. His grip tightened. "Come on, then."

Inside, it was dark, but I let my memory guide me through his house and up the stairs. He stopped two doors to the left of the staircase, where his room had always been, and swung open the door. The space had changed though not drastically but more in the way bedrooms became spaces to sleep instead of lifelines as you got older. The desk that had always been partially buried under sports uniforms and padding was gone and, with it, the computer. The television—though upgraded—remained atop his dresser, which was still adorned with the punk rock band stickers of our youth. It was still his and his alone. My frazzled nerves settled slightly.

I sat down at the edge of the bed—now a queen-sized one. Corey stood in front of me like he had many times before in this exact room on nights exactly like this one. For more than one weekend and countless weeknights, it had been a haven for us, an escape from the complicated world we'd lived in during junior year and the separate ones we'd suffered through senior year. He sat down next to me but didn't say anything.

We stayed like that, surrounded by the past but stuck in an uncomfortable present. The silence was suffocating, and the awkward distance between us felt like a chasm.

"Why couldn't you just come to Robinson?" I asked, unable to stand another moment of quiet. "If there's any place we should be able to talk about *this*, it's there."

He shifted, and his familiar scent washed over me. Next to me, his hand gripped the comforter. "Because I can't just drop everything for you anymore."

Ouch.

He ran a hand through his hair, making his tousled hair even messier. "A lot happened in the last decade, and you need to understand—"

"How can I understand if you won't tell me the whole story?" I couldn't keep the petulance out of my voice. All I wanted was to understand, but he kept walking away and hanging up and stalling. *I wasn't the one who'd teamed up with the enemy.*

He bit his bottom lip. It made him look young, like the boy I'd once known. He ran a nervous hand through his hair—I still knew his tells, and this was his biggest one. He fell back against the bed, a hand covering his eyes. "We buried someone really close to us today, Andi. I know it's confusing for you, but I promise—"

"I'm sorry." I put a hand on his leg. He flinched under my touch.

My stepfather's funeral had been the last one I'd attended, and it had been horrible. The mere thought of it made my eyes misty. I hadn't taken a moment to consider what Corey—or Nikki or anyone who'd been at that funeral—must be feeling.

He stared at my hand on his leg with a look I couldn't decipher. "What did you think would happen if you threw rocks at my window?"

It was a simple question, but I couldn't find the words to answer it. Nothing. I didn't think—that was the whole problem. He'd hung up, and I'd stared at that phone, urging it to ring again. But it hadn't, and I'd gotten in my car and driven to his house. I returned my hand to my lap and glanced over at him.

He met my eyes with a sheepish smile. "I mean, last time that happened we, uh, lost our virginities."

"Well, I didn't expect *that* to happen again."

He laughed lightly. "Good to know."

People said you never forgot your first love, and it was true—I had never forgotten Corey, though the memories were fuzzy around the edges. But sitting with him now, I could feel the warmth of that memory and the security that had come with loving someone so intensely and having that love returned. I remembered him leading me up the stairs, his hand in my hand for the first time in a month. I remembered him gently tucking a loose strand of hair behind my ear before leaning down and kissing me. I remembered how our eyes met, and his had been filled with a passion I'd never seen in anyone else's eyes.

I smiled back at him. "Thank you for letting me come in. I know it's late."

He sat up. His feet rested flat on the floor even though he sat farther back on the bed than I did. "So, what *did* you want?"

"I don't know. I just wanted to see you," I said without thinking. I cleared my throat, focusing on chipping away at an uneven piece of nail. I stood up, needing some distance from him and everything that being back in this room—back on this bed—conjured in my mind. I leaned against the dresser. "I really wasn't expecting you to be here, and then you were and..."

He glanced up at me, his expression guarded. "Do you want to know why I couldn't meet you tonight?"

He motioned toward the door, and I followed him into the hallway. We walked past his parents' room to what used to be the guest room—where I was *supposed* to sleep when I visited. I didn't understand. He opened the door and stepped back. I knew before I even looked what would be beyond that door. Part of me didn't want to see it—didn't want to entertain what that would mean. But curiosity propelled me forward. In the dim light from the hallway, I could see the outline of a little girl.

My hand flew to my mouth, silencing a gasp. "Is that...?"

"My daughter."

I looked at him and then back at the girl in the bed. Though I couldn't make out much in the dark room, I knew that she couldn't have been anyone other than his daughter—her features were so much like his, down to the way she slept with the blankets tossed off and her pillow balled up under her head.

I took a step into the room and waited for my eyes to adjust to the darkness. From the bookshelf next to her bed, I could tell she was smart. Old Illustrated Classics lined the shelves as well as a few of my favorites from when I was a kid. She was athletic too—the perfect future scholar-athlete. Lacrosse sticks were piled in a corner, and a volleyball hid under her desk. I expected nothing less from Corey's daughter.

After a minute, Corey nudged me back out and closed the door behind him.

"What's her name?" I asked as we moved back down the hall.

"Emily."

There were so many questions running through my mind, and I didn't know which one to ask first, so I settled on something simple. "How old is she?"

"Seven."

"And her..." It would be rude to ask about her mother. What if she was dead?

"Sharon's gone," he said. "She bolted around the time Emily turned one. Emily doesn't remember her."

"I'm sorry." And I meant it. The thought of Corey with someone else was heart-wrenching, but the idea of that little girl without a mother—and by the woman's own choice—was worse. I knew what it was like to have only one parent, and even though the choice had been mine, that didn't make it any better.

I'd always thought Corey would be a good father, in that way teenagers do when they don't know anything of the world, but I'd never actually imagined him with a kid. Now there was this beautiful little girl sleeping a few feet away whom he was responsible for. Of course, he couldn't meet me for late-night conversations at the Robinson Diner. His lack of visibility at the wake, his running out of the house earlier in the day, and his reluctance to just come out and tell me the reasons I should stay all started to make sense. We weren't kids anymore. He had everything to lose.

A yawn wracked my body as we reentered Corey's room. I looked at my watch. It was after two. The hotel wasn't far away, but at this time of night, in this darkness, the winding, unlit roads of Fairford could be perilous. "I should get going."

"It's late. You can just sleep here." Uncertainty must have colored my face because Corey laughed. "I'll sleep on the floor."

Thirty minutes later, safely tucked into Corey's bed, wearing a pair of his sweatpants and a Fairford Central T-shirt, I still couldn't sleep. His smell was intoxicating. He had to have the strongest pheromones known to mankind. Sleep loomed close by but wouldn't settle. I'd spent so many nights in Corey's bed. Back then, it had been a twin bed, and we'd just fit, finding the right way to arrange our arms and legs together to be comfortable. The first few times, Corey had slept on the floor, certain his parents would come in at some point and we would both be in trouble. And the very first time I'd stayed over, after having escaped a raging Ryan, his father *had* found me in Corey's bed. Corey had been on the floor in front of the bed, wrapped in two comforters, a pillow covering his face, but we'd been in enough trouble that Corey had told them a partial truth—that things with Ryan were sometimes bad, and occasionally, I would need to stay over.

The bed was lonely now. He lay perpendicular to me in a sleeping bag. I felt guilty depriving him of his own bed, but it would be all sorts of wrong to ask him to sleep next to me. I squeezed my eyes shut. If I could just sleep, I'd be that much closer to getting more of the truth, and maybe after that, I'd stay for the reading of the will. The thought turned my stomach, but it felt like another one of those things I'd regret if I missed it, especially since technically, I hadn't gone to the funeral. But staying meant facing more than the boy I'd once loved. There was Nikki and Bethany and this entirely new version of Ryan I hadn't even begun to understand.

From the floor, I could hear Corey's slow and even breaths. I tried to time my own to them, but with him so close yet so very far away, sleep was impossible.

"Corey," I said into the darkness, "did you ever miss me?"

I curled onto my side, hugging the pillow close. Corey's bed used to be the only place I got a truly good night's sleep. He shifted in his sleeping bag. I waited for his answer. Just when I thought one wasn't going to come, his voice reached me.

"Every day."

Chapter 18

Now

The clothes racks soar above my head. I can hardly see any of the adults in the store. The floppy straw hat in my hand hangs loosely at my side. There's a mirror a few steps ahead of me. I look back at him, walking down the aisle in the opposite direction. It has to be quick so I won't lose him. One, two, three steps. I stare at my reflection. My hair falls in straight blond strands down past my shoulders. It looks raggedy all the time. My arms are too long, and my legs extend far past the bottom of my shorts. The hat covers my eyes once it's on my head. I tilt it back onto my forehead and lean my head back toward the ceiling. I pretend to curtsy in my faded denim shorts. The hat falls back over my eyes. I yank it off and hold it between my two hands, examining the bow tied across the brim.

"Daddy!" I spin around to face where he'd been standing just a minute ago. He's gone. "Daddy!" I yell again, louder. I suck in a deep breath and run a few steps forward. On all sides are clothes racks. No people, no aisles. Just clothes. I keep running, my eyes blurry with tears. I fall to my knees as I clear the last rack. I can't see, I can't hear, and my breathing comes in gulps. "Daddy, where are you?"

A soft hand touches my shoulder. A gentle, motherly-looking figure leans down close to my face. She hands me a tissue. "Are you okay, dear?" She helps me to my feet.

I sniffle, unable to completely shake the lost feeling.

"Is that him?" she asks, pointing behind me.

I turn slowly. My breathing relaxes. "Daddy."

He turns briskly in my direction. He's in front of me in three large steps. I shrink back into the folds of the lady's skirt.

"Andi, get over here." His voice is heavy, his eyes bloodshot. He grabs my arm, yanking me out of the comfort of the stranger and down the aisle.

"Daddy, no, stop. Daddy, you're hurting me."

He yanks me again. My feet are barely coordinated enough to keep up with him. The pop of my elbow stops me. An uncontrollable scream shakes my body as the pain becomes all I can understand.

"DADDY, DADDY, STOP, Daddy, that tickles." The hushed voice shook me from my nightmare.

I rolled over in bed, uncertain of where I was. I sat up quickly. Blood rushed to my head, and the room spun. I inhaled, rubbing my eyes. *Corey's room.*

"Daddy, she's awake."

Corey's daughter. *Emily.* My eyes focused after a moment. She was sitting on the end of the bed. Corey stood at the foot, watching her watch me. He looked at ease. I wondered how many women she'd found in his bed. He yawned and lifted a foot to scratch an itch on his lower leg. I glanced at the clock—it was only six thirty in the morning, but it was Thursday, a school day.

I looked back down at Emily. Awake, she looked even more like Corey than she had asleep. Their eye color was nearly identical, except for golden flecks splattered across her blue. Her smile, barely showing her teeth, mirrored the one on Corey's face as he watched her.

"Say hi, Emily." His voice was filled with the warmth reserved for sacred loved ones. It was the same tone he used to use with me. He placed a hand on her shoulder and gently squeezed.

She looked at him over her shoulder and rested her head on his arm. "Is she really Uncle Ryan's daughter?"

Uncle. Ryan. I bit my lip hard against the sting of those two words coming from Corey's daughter's mouth.

Corey caught my eye and grimaced before nodding at his daughter.

Her nose scrunched in disbelief. "How come she's never been here before?"

"You know how Alex lives with just a mommy and his dad lives far away?"

"In Califor-ni-a." Her elongated pronunciation of the word made me smile.

Corey bit down on his bottom lip, hiding a laugh. "Right, in California." It was a gentle correction. "Well, Andi grew up living with just her mommy. She didn't get to see Uncle Ryan for a long time. Now, say hi, honey."

She scooted forward on her knees, till our legs were almost touching, and then leaned in for a closer look. I could only imagine what I looked like with my hair in a ponytail pushed to one side like a battered, disheveled eighties child.

"You look like Nikki." She sat back on her knees, her eyes still on me.

Another name I wasn't ready to hear quite so early. I swallowed and offered her a smile. "Yes, I do."

Emily placed her small hand on top of mine. "I'm sorry about Uncle Ryan."

Tears welled in my eyes, and I forced them back. I would not cry. Not in front of her. "Thank you, Emily."

I shifted my focus to the room around me, trying to rein in my tear ducts. In the daylight, everything seemed different. The room, which had felt so familiar four hours before, was not what I thought. Stacked under the television were Disney movies, and sticking out of the dresser was the frilly end of a pink shirt. A copy of *Ramona the Great* peeked out from under the bed. The clues had all been there, but I hadn't wanted to see them.

She twirled a loose strand of hair around her finger and flattened herself into a more comfortable sitting position, her toes resting on my calf. "So, why are you in my daddy's bed?" She turned to Corey, indignation on her face. "You said sleepovers were only for weekends."

"They are, pumpkin. This was a special circumstance because Andi's only here for a few days to say goodbye, remember?"

She nodded and then looked between the two of us. A mischievous glint came into her eyes, and her lips quirked. She looked so much like Corey in that moment that my insides wanted to burst. "Were you Daddy's *girlfriend*?"

I laughed at the excitement behind that single word. The question sank in. This was clearly a new experience for her. A girl in her dad's bed wasn't normal at all, and the idea of a girlfriend made her giddy. I glanced at Corey, but he only had eyes for Emily.

"All right, that's enough from you. Breakfast is almost ready—get your butt down there."

As he said it, a gut-wrenchingly good smell hit my senses—buttermilk, maple syrup, bacon. Corey's dad had made the best breakfasts every morning, no matter what time the earliest person had to be out or who he found in his son's bed. My stomach growled despite the midnight snack I'd had.

Emily jumped down from the bed and hugged Corey before skipping out of the room. She turned at the door, sneaking a look back at me, and then she was out of sight. Her small feet were loud on the stairs in the silence of morning.

I stood up, glancing around the room for my clothes. "I guess I should probably—"

"Come have breakfast, Andi," Corey said, cutting off my attempt at escape. "My parents will be happy to see you."

"Happy to see me stumbling down the stairs in their son's clothing, looking a hot mess?" I couldn't help but laugh. The way this town worked, anything was possible. My mother, even now, would kill me if I had a man stay over in my bedroom at her house.

"It'll be just like old times." He turned to walk out of the room but stopped in the doorway. "Plus, you have a no-questions-asked invite, remember?"

Yes, I did remember. It was the kindness of Corey's dad that had helped me through my last months in Fairford. "The rule was I slept in the guest room."

He grinned. "We don't have a guest room anymore."

I rolled my eyes and tried to fix my bedhead. When I pulled out my hair tie, my hair fell in one big knot at the back of my head. Running my fingers through it didn't help. I pulled it all back up and retied it straight this time.

"You look fine—let's go." He extended his hand. Then, as if realizing that wasn't the right thing to do, he let it drop.

My steps were short and quick behind his retreating frame. A grand entrance wasn't on my agenda for the morning. Enough of my actions the last few days had been off the cuff. It was time to get back on track. Whatever that meant. Some semblance of a plan, something to latch onto. *Ouch*—a misaligned step sent me tumbling down one step. I planted my foot, happy to feel only a nagging pain, and caught my balance before he noticed. My eyes landed on the photos lining the staircase. Emily had been one of the cute babies, all pink cheeks and bangs, no bigger than the oversized teddy bear sitting in the picture with her. Another photo showed a first ponytail for the little girl tucked into her father's safe arms, sucking her thumb. There was a picture of the first annual Scott and Johnson summer cookout, with people wearing matching T-shirts and a young Emily surrounded by a gaggle of other children. Uncle Ryan was hidden in the back behind the kids, his arm resting comfortably across Corey's shoulders.

There was a lifetime laid out on that wall. But Corey stood two steps down, waiting. With a last look at the man who was both my father and not, I pulled myself away from that life and all I wanted to understand. I followed Corey into the kitchen. Paul and Maya were sitting with Emily, their backs to the doorway, with stacks of pancakes too big for even an enthusiast like me. Corey moved behind me and nudged me into the kitchen.

"Mom, Dad," Corey said. Emily was dousing her stack in maple syrup. Her plate looked about to overflow. "You remember Andi."

Maya looked up first, pancake dangling from her fork. Her eyes lit up. She clutched her husband's arm. I waved.

"My goodness, Andi," Paul said. "You don't look a day older than the last time I saw you stumble out of my son's bed."

The heat rushed to my cheeks before a response could even formulate in my brain. Paul was always the brazen one. He said what he meant, and he meant what he said. Despite everything, Paul had loved the weekends when I'd stayed in Fairford. I would drive up and get there before Corey was done with practice. Maya would be humming away in the kitchen, washing dishes and catching up on her prime-time shows on a television they kept hidden in a cupboard. Paul would pick out a movie just for these occasions. He kept a pile near the television—movies reserved for Andi's visits.

"Grandpa?" Emily asked, her mouth full of pancake.

Corey walked past me into the kitchen. A warm tingle started where his bare arm brushed mine. It flowed to my fingertips.

He took a seat on the other side of his daughter. "You know not to talk with your mouth full, sweetie." He handed Emily a napkin.

She chewed large, with her mouth closed, making a point. She swallowed with her whole body then opened wide and showed him the recesses of her mouth. She ran the napkin across her face. Corey motioned to the chair next to him, where a place was already set for me—not surprising, since I doubted any seven-year-old could keep a girl in her dad's bed a secret for longer than it took her to find an adult. I scooted behind Maya's chair, fitting with ease between her pushed-back seat and the kitchen counter. They had a dining room, but breakfast was always eaten at the small round table that took up most of the kitchen.

"Grandpa," Emily started again. She pushed a few leftover pieces of pancake around her plate. Syrup soup, mush, with a soggy bit of bacon that added another color. "Was Andi Daddy's girlfriend?"

The heat that had just left my cheeks returned with a vengeance. We turned to look at Paul. He met Corey's eyes. No decision was made that I could see. Paul's eyes shifted to mine and then back to Emily's. Corey dropped a short stack of pancakes onto my plate, followed by two slices of bacon. He remembered my breakfast rituals. My flush grew even hotter. I still knew how Corey took his coffee—two sugars and milk—and that he would eat no less than four slices of bacon with his pancakes, but I hadn't expected him to remember mine. An urge to grab hold of the hand that rested next to mine on the table shot through me. I turned my attention back to my dish. Though I'd cut bacon out of my diet, I picked up a piece. It smelled like a memory. A small bite brought back all the pleasures of a good, crisp slice.

"Well, honey," Paul said with another quick glance at Corey. "She was his girlfriend a long time ago, before you were even born."

I ate my pancakes. This was awkward. I should have left. Breakfast was a stupid idea. Emily's laugh shattered the hard shell I was trying to create around myself.

"Ha ha, Daddy. You're old!"

Corey leaned over and began to tickle her. She squirmed, giggling. Paul and Maya had the same look—it was the one I saw in Harry's eyes when he talked about his daughter.

"Yeah, Corey, you're old," I said through a laugh that came so deep from my belly I wasn't sure I'd ever laughed like that. The simple happiness of this family surged through my blood.

"Really?" Corey's laugh was one of my favorite sounds, especially this one, when it caught him unexpectedly. "Really, Andi? Because that makes you old too."

I grinned at him. "I call 'em like I see 'em."

"Andi?" Emily's voice silenced the table. I swallowed a piece of pancake and waited for her to continue. Her eyes met mine, looking into me. I wondered what she saw. "Were you *in love* with my daddy?"

Corey shuffled in his seat. He exhaled audibly. I knew those sighs. It was the sound I made whenever anyone asked me about my father. He was about to deny her an answer. I placed a hand on his arm. He met my eyes and nodded slowly.

"Well, Emily, I was in love with your daddy, but that was a long time ago."

She nodded without another question. Her focus shifted to the piece of bacon left on her plate. Everyone turned back to their breakfasts. Maya began clearing the dishes one at a time. The ticking of the clock was the only interruption of our silence. I never left a pancake behind—it was the same policy I kept for fries—but there was no way I could stomach the rest of the food.

"Go get dressed, honey." Corey stood up and took the plate from her.

Emily crept down off her chair. Even at seven, she could distinguish an awkward silence. "Can you drive me to school today, Daddy?"

"What's wrong with the bus?" He dropped her plate into the sink. It clattered against the others.

My body shook with a chill. My wrist ached. The sound of clattering plates hadn't bothered me for some time, but being back here was reviving haunting reactions that had taken years to overcome.

"What's wrong with Andi?" Emily asked, walking over to me. Her hand felt warm on mine.

"Honey, go upstairs, please." Corey crossed the kitchen in a step and a half.

Through the haze, I saw Emily hiding on the stairs, watching us between the rungs. Corey knelt down in front of me. He took both my hands in his.

"I'm sorry. I forgot. Are you okay?" The concern in his eyes was real.

Once, we'd had a system that kept the plates from crashing into each other. The panic attacks the sound had incited had nearly caused me to be hospitalized with an ulcer in the first years after Fairford. But it hadn't bothered me in a long time.

All the muscles in my right shoulder rippled and made the knots in my back stretch. The left shoulder muscles weren't as bad, but they were still tight, and the muscles popped as one when I rotated my shoulder. I set my shoulders straight and pushed myself up in my chair, fixing my posture just so. I wasn't that girl anymore. And Ryan was gone.

"I'm fine." I stood, letting Corey's hands slip out of mine. Emily scampered up the stairs once she saw me stand. "Really, Corey, I should go." I turned to Maya and Paul, who were now carefully washing the dishes. "Thank you so much for breakfast."

Maya smiled with a soapy wave. Paul embraced me. It took me a moment to adjust to the unexpected contact, but then I sank into his hug like I always had.

"I'm sorry that you didn't get to know him." He squeezed me tight again. The air rushed out of my lungs. Behind him, Corey hid a smile.

I stepped back, gasping for air. "Thank you."

"Let me get your stuff." Corey walked out of the kitchen. I followed closely behind. "Listen, I'm sorry about Emily. She's a little nosy. She's never really seen me with anybody."

It took effort to keep walking. I'd assumed as much from Emily's inquisition, but to hear it from his own mouth was different. We reached his room, and I rested my hand on the door. "She's adorable, really."

He leaned back on his heels. "Listen, let's have dinner tonight. I'll have Krystal move some of my day around."

"Krystal?"

He flushed. "Yeah, she's our executive assistant."

Right. Apparently, Ryan had to hire all my friends. "What time should I meet you?"

"I'll text you once I see what I can shift around." He glanced at his watch. "Anyway, I should go check on Emily. The bus will be here soon."

As soon as he turned away, I closed the door behind me and leaned back against it. The vestiges of the chill from downstairs clung to my skin, but I shook them off. In Corey's room, everything seemed clearer than it had the night before. There'd been a plate for me at breakfast. My clothes were draped across the back of a chair like they belonged there. I could fit back into this world. Each person would move to make room, and eventually, they'd fold me into the fabric. I blinked back tears. That wasn't my life, and even if everyone would allow it, I couldn't.

Chapter 19

Then

I unlocked the front door and shoved it open. Behind me, Krystal laughed so hard she snorted. We shucked off our winter coats and hung them on the rack by the door.

"I can't believe they did that," I said, her laughter infecting me. "I thought Coach Killian was going to kill them."

We'd transitioned from volleyball to basketball season without a break, thanks to our run at the state title. We'd lost, but it had been an adventure. I didn't generally play a winter sport, but Krystal and Bella had insisted I participate until I finally showed up the first day of practice. I was decent but would still be riding the bench. At least it kept me out of the house. Today, Dustin, Brian, and Corey had come in during practice and done some silly cheer that ended up with them ripping off their warm-up jackets to reveal handmade fan shirts for the three of us. My cheeks still went hot at the thought of it.

"Evening, girls." My dad stepped into the foyer from the living room. His voice sounded strange to my ears after so long of rarely hearing it. He didn't look right at us, more at some spot behind our heads. He appeared to be not sober—I wasn't sure my dad was ever sober these days—but clearheaded. Like he'd been before Bethany left.

I held out a bag to him. "I got you a sandwich from S&R."

He took it with a nod, careful not to touch me. Then he moved toward the dining room. I didn't go in there. Ever. After weeks of skirting the proof of that night, one day I'd come home to find the wooden plank that covered the door gone and a new glass pane in its place. Now if I could avoid even looking in that direction, I did.

"Come on, Krys. We should start on that assignment."

She met my eyes across the foyer. There was no assignment. We were completely about to talk about her last escapade with Dustin at the Peak, and then we were doing something else. No one would tell me what it was—not Krystal or Corey or Dustin. And Dustin was awful with secret keeping. Which meant I wasn't going to like what my friends had planned, and if I knew about it, I would probably try to stay in the house.

Krystal bounded up the stairs with me on her heels. We didn't hang out here too often. Usually once a week was enough to keep her questions about how my dad was doing at bay. I also tried to make it the same day each week, and the regularity had helped. My dad might be in a constant state of inebriation, but he'd caught on to the schedule, evidenced by his less-than-drunk appearance. We all had a part to play until June. Even him.

Thirty minutes later, I knew more about Dustin's skill with his tongue than I ever wanted to. Emma and I had never really talked about boys in this way, but then, there'd never really been boys to talk about. We were playing spin the bottle at parties, not parking at the Peak. But Krystal talked, and I listened since I didn't have much to share in return.

Krystal lay on my bed, flipping through the latest *Cosmopolitan*. She turned the page but was clearly not reading, as her eyes were locked on mine. "When are you two going to do it already?"

The question wasn't unexpected. If she'd been surprised that it took us so long to officially start dating, she was even more surprised that we hadn't immediately run through the bases. Corey and I had our fair share of pit stops at the Peak and in the parking lot behind the high school and in that locked stairwell. And the few times we'd ventured to my house, where no one made us leave the door open or loudly came upstairs, the tension between us had been electric. It would have been easy to skip ahead. But we'd quickly given our hearts to each other, so we were taking the rest of it slowly. Things were complicated enough.

I rolled my eyes. "We've been dating for, like, two months."

She shrugged. "So? You're star-crossed. The rules don't apply. Plus, I mean, you have a countdown. You totally have to do it before the end of the school year."

"That's months from now," I said defensively. She wasn't wrong—things would be a lot more difficult when my mom got back—but it was only December. June might as well have been a lifetime away.

"Exactly—months that you could be having sex without risk of parental interference."

Right, because normal teens have parents who know they exist.

Krystal waggled her eyebrows. "I think after junior formal would be perfect."

Formal was a few months away, but still... "You are not planning my sex life, Krys."

"Of course not," she said, a goofy grin forming on her face as she read whatever message had come through on her phone. "The boys are here."

"What are we doing again?"

Krystal jumped off my bed and headed for the door. "Just wear your boots."

After a long drive through the winding dark roads of Fairford's rural side, I was staring at a tractor. Not one of those small ones that the people who tended our lawn used but a real tractor on a real farm. And we were about to take it for a joy ride.

"Come on," Dustin said, "we're just borrowing it. Langen won't care."

Langen was apparently the man who owned the tractor. And something told me he would mind. I glanced at Corey, but he was too busy sizing up the beast we were about to ride. He climbed onto the wheel and reached down to pull me up.

"We're going to get arrested!" I whispered loudly as Corey turned the key, kicking the tractor into gear.

Krystal had climbed up behind me and leaned over our shoulders, her arms wrapped around me. I clung to Corey as we inched forward, safely sandwiched between the two of them. This was such a bad idea. Dustin had been charged with manning the camera and stood a few feet away from us.

"It'll be fine," Corey said, his words coming out on a white puff of air. "Mr. Langen would never press charges." Which, in Fairford, was code for *he'd never dream of getting the star wide receiver and quarterback in trouble even if the season was over.*

I glanced around the large field. The night, like the house in the distance, was still and dark. The air was crisp and heavy, like snow was on the way. I did not need to be on a tractor in the snow. I did not need to be on a tractor at all. Yet here I was.

"Where are we going?" I buried my hat-covered head in Corey's neck and stuck my hands in his pockets as the tractor bumped along. "Why do you know how to drive this thing?"

Corey laughed. Beside me, Krystal giggled. "Relax, we're just going to get closer so Dustin can get a picture," she said.

"Why are we *documenting* this?"

Before either of them could rein in their laughter enough to answer, lights flashed in the distance. My heart practically broke out of my chest, it pounded so hard. "Is that Mr. Langen?"

"Hey! What are you kids doing?" The voice was deep and theatrical and kind of familiar.

I wondered if I'd met Mr. Langen at some point. *Maybe at the ice cream shop?*

"Shit." Corey turned to me, his eyes wide. "He wasn't supposed to be home."

"What?"

Behind me, Krystal broke into a fit of laughter. Corey was grinning.

I crossed my arms. "Is this a prank?"

"Dustin!" Krystal half yelled, her hands waving in the air. "Please tell me you got that on video."

Corey parked the tractor, letting the engine idle. Dustin hopped up on the wheel, still snapping photos. The lights down the field were getting closer until a familiar face appeared—Brian. I was going to kill him next time we shared a shift.

He climbed up onto the tractor and gave me a half hug. "You're officially a Fairford Falcon now."

"Smile!" Krystal said.

The flash on her camera practically blinded me. "What just happened?"

Corey squeezed me tight. "It's a football tradition. The freshmen on the team have to steal Mr. Langen's tractor before the first game."

"Mr. Langen always 'catches' them," Brian added. "Scares them senseless. Until they get to his house, and we're all there."

"Langen was a football legend back in his day," Corey said with the reverence given to an alum of a small-town football program.

"Like myself," Dustin said without a hint of irony.

"We thought you should be initiated as well." Corey kissed my cheek. "And one more thing..." He took his letterman jacket off and put it around my shoulders, the first time he'd done so in all these months. My hometown wasn't as small as Fairford, but I knew what giving someone your letterman jacket meant. Krystal didn't even have Dustin's jacket, much to her chagrin.

"Oh man." Dustin whistled. "You are going to get so much shit tomorrow."

Corey shrugged. "Worth it."

I flushed and kissed him sloppily despite all our friends watching.

Corey pulled back but kept me close. "You'll wear it?"

I nodded, pressing my lips to his again. He would be lucky if I ever let him wear it again. "I love you." I turned to my friends and wrapped them in a hug. "All of you."

"Awww!" Dustin said, his face scrunched in an imitation of cutesiness. "We love you too."

Krystal pulled me to her and snapped another picture and then motioned for the boys to join. We squeezed together, our cheeks red, our eyes watering from the cold but smiles plastered on our faces. Normal teenagers doing normal teenager things. I held on to them after the flash went off. After all these months in Fairford, I'd finally found where I belonged.

Chapter 20

Then

Home. The word had meant something different for so long that the single-story ranch I'd grown up in felt like a stranger's house. I stared at it from the passenger seat of Corey's car, unable to get out and walk through that red door I'd insisted on when I was seven.

When I'd first moved to Fairford, I'd dreamed about the day I would return to my room and my life and my friends. But it hadn't been that way for months—not since Corey had become the biggest part of my world and my friends had adopted me as their own. Now I spent my days wondering how I could avoid going home—how I could keep my mom in Paris without hurting her feelings and how I would be able to manage my two lives in a few months. I tried not to think too hard on that last one. Because even a hypothetical day without Corey hurt to the core, and after this school year, there would be too many real days apart.

"I think I'm the one who's supposed to be nervous." Corey reached for my hand and gently rubbed a circle on my palm.

I smiled, his words cracking the anxiety that kept me in place. "You're right. She's going to have many a question for you. And there will probably be threats. I mean, she lives thousands of miles away, and who knows what you're doing to my virtue."

Corey snickered and pulled my face to his, his lips brushing mine. "One last kiss, then."

It was not a kiss we should be having outside my mother's house, but that was how I was with Corey—sappy and in love and full of PDA. I unbuckled my seat belt, leaned farther into the kiss, and pulled him as close as we could get with the gear shift between us. He clutched my waist inside my jacket, his touch sending sparks through me, even through my shirt. I pulled back, reminding myself we were not at the Peak, and it was broad daylight, and my mother was probably spying on us through the curtains.

He tucked a strand of hair behind my ears and planted a quick kiss on my lips. "Ready?"

"Knock, knock." We jumped apart at the muffled voice, but it was only Emma.

She stood on the sidewalk, arms crossed, a grin on her face. When I stepped out of the car, she enveloped me in a hug so big I almost fell over. "Oh my god, I can't believe you're here!"

"Me either!" At least that was the truth.

"Are you three trying to catch pneumonia? Get inside!"

Mom. Tears flooded my eyes, and all that worry from the car vanished. I was across the yard and in her arms before she'd even finished yelling at us.

"Hey, honey." She soothed me, brushing my hair back. "Merry Christmas."

We stayed like that until the cold seeped in beneath Corey's letterman jacket that I wore like protective armor.

My mom let go first with a shiver. Her hand was cold yet so warm against my cheek. "You look so grown up."

I rolled my eyes as we followed her into the house. "It's been six months, Mom."

"Must be all the green and white." Her eyes traveled to Corey, whose presence I could feel behind me.

I pulled the coat tighter around me, even as a wave of self-consciousness ran through me, and reached for Corey's hand. "Mom, this is Corey."

She knew about Corey—had met him on a video call—but this was different. Her gaze felt heavy and judgmental as she took in the two of us in person for the first time. I was hyperaware of how close we stood, of the way my hand gripped his, of the small heart necklace he'd given me before we left, and of the letterman jacket she'd already commented on. It all screamed that I was his. And I was. Behind her placid smile, I could feel her trying to figure out exactly how much I was his. But I didn't move away.

"My boyfriend."

"Yes, I know." Her expression froze somewhere between a smile and a grimace. "It's nice to meet you in person, Corey."

Corey smiled in a way that was so genuine compared to my mom. "You as well, Ms. Martin. Thanks for having me."

"Of course." She pulled Emma—who had been so quiet I almost forgot she was standing right next to me—into a hug. "Merry Christmas, dear." My mom motioned toward the kitchen. "Come on. Sam is dying to meet you."

Sam was my mom's boyfriend. I knew about him in the same way she knew about Corey. Except in all the years that it had just been me and my mom, she'd never brought a guy home. She must have dated, but no one had been formally introduced. No one had stayed the night. And now Sam was in our house for Christmas Eve.

"Right." I glanced at the bag at Corey's feet. "Let me just bring my bag to my room."

She eyed the two of us, still bound together. "Door open."

"Mom!" I said, a flush rising up my cheeks.

She draped an arm around Emma's shoulders and started toward the kitchen. "Don't make me come get you."

I palmed my face. There were going to be condoms in my stocking tomorrow. One hundred percent.

"Hey." Corey brushed a hand across my cheek. "You okay over there?"

I leaned into him, wrapping my arms around his waist. "That was embarrassing."

He grinned and hefted my duffle onto his shoulder. "No worse than my parents."

I giggled, thinking of the clomping steps of Mr. Johnson that always had us jumping apart and rearranging our clothing. We walked the short hallway lined with photos of me throughout the years. At my bedroom, I paused with my hand on the door. Corey had been in my room at my dad's house plenty of times over the last few months, but the girl who had lived in this room had been a different person. I thought of the myriad posters I'd had on the walls when I left for Fairford—the Jonas Brothers, Fall Out Boy, Zac Efron, James Lafferty, and so many other celebrities.

"Don't laugh."

Corey stepped inside, a big smile on his face. He scanned the space, his eyes falling on the polka-dot comforter on my bed and the Pinewood Soccer sweater draped over my desk chair. He spun in a circle, taking in the posters. "I feel like this is a whole new side of you."

"Shut up."

He pulled me close, his lips finding mine. "Thanks for letting me see this part of your life."

A cough sounded behind us, and I turned to find a man I'd only seen in photos standing in my doorway. "Not to interrupt, but Linda is going to be back in about thirty seconds, so you might want to wrap it up."

Oh. My. God. "Uh, thanks."

He winked. "I'll stall her if I can." Sam inched the door farther closed and called out loudly to my mom as he walked down the hallway.

Corey grinned. "Best. Christmas. Ever."

I SAT ON THE COUCH, trying to read a Sarah Dessen book. I kept getting distracted by the flurries outside the living room window. Across from me in the armchair, Sam was snoring, having dozed off thirty minutes before. He seemed nice enough and clearly made my mom happy. I could hear her tinkering in the kitchen. We didn't go to Mass like Emma and her family, but we had Christmas Eve traditions all our own—like eating pumpkin pie right out of the tin and exchanging one of our presents. It had been my mom's way of giving me a gift when I'd still believed in Santa.

I closed my book and pulled her present onto my lap, drumming my fingers against it. We usually exchanged books and would spend that night and next day reading them, side by side, but I'd gone for something more sentimental to help pass the time apart. I scrolled through my text messages, smiling at the novel Krystal had sent me about her evening with Dustin's family. Corey also messaged that he'd gotten home safe. He'd left after dinner, as his parents had expressly stated that he was not to spend the night. The urge to call him hit me hard. Most nights, I fell asleep to the sound of his voice.

"Hey, honey." My mom sat down and placed the pie on the coffee table. She handed me a fork. "Let me send Sam to bed, and then we'll eat and talk."

I tried not to think about the fact that she must be sending him to bed in *her* bed, as we were sitting on the only unclaimed bed in the house. This whole us-having-significant-others thing was going to take some getting used to.

When she returned, she held a very large gift. She leaned it against the coffee table and turned to me, pie in hand. "So, tell me about your life."

I took a bite of pie. "What do you want to know? I tell you about my friends all the time."

"So, tell me more." She pushed the present toward me.

"Tonight's is supposed to be small," I said, eyeing rows of snowmen.

"It is small in cost, just big in size." She nudged it closer to me. "Seeing your life in Fairford has been hard for me. I guess I thought you'd just still spend all your weekends here with Emma and Charlie and want to come to Paris on school breaks, but you're so busy with friends and Corey and now basketball."

"Mom..." I ripped the wrapping paper off, revealing the collage frame underneath.

Each picture was connected by a black frame, making it one cohesive piece that looked like several separate photos. At the bottom was one of Emma and me at the beach last summer. Next to it was a photo of me and my mom in front of the Wildwoods sign at the boardwalk, taken right before she'd left for Paris. Then there was a team photo from the regional championships, a picture of me and Corey on the bleachers, and one of me and my friends huddled together on Mr. Langen's tractor.

"Where did you get these?"

She smiled. "Emma had Corey's number."

"I love it, Mom."

"I'm glad you're happy there, Andi. I hate that you have a basketball tournament this weekend and I'm losing out on a whole extra day with you, but it makes me so happy to see you thriving. I worried after you told me Bethany left, but things seem good?"

I nodded, afraid to speak. Things were good everywhere except in the house—though I had to admit my dad had leveled out lately.

He still didn't talk to me, but at least I didn't have to sneak out of the house and stay at Corey's until all hours of the night.

"Andi?"

I met her gaze and realized she wanted an actual answer. Which meant I'd have to lie. "Yeah. Dad's sad, but we manage."

"And you haven't heard from her at all?"

I shook my head. "Not that he's told me."

"I'm sorry, honey. I know you wanted the time with your sister."

"It is what it is, Mom." I handed her the present I'd gotten her, hoping to distract her from this line of conversation. "Your turn."

She smiled and peeled back the paper, revealing the wooden frame with Mom written on it. Inside was the same photo she'd put in the collage. Our last one together. She ran her fingers over the photo. "Thank you. I know just where I'm going to put this."

On the table, my phone chimed, and I looked down at the screen to see Corey's name. I rejected the call and typed out a quick text, adding far too many hearts and a promise to call him before I went to bed. When I looked back up, my mom was staring at me, a frown on her face.

"You and Corey seem quite serious." She fiddled with the frame in her lap. "Are you being safe?"

"Mom, we're not doing that... yet."

"But you're in love with him."

"Yes. I am."

"Have you thought about next year?" Her voice shook at the end of the question. She was worried for me, but she also saw what I knew in my heart: Corey and I were the real deal. Our relationship wasn't going anywhere. "You know you can't stay in Fairford senior year."

Her words knocked the wind out of me, both because of how much I didn't want to leave Corey and my friends and because after the loud and loving household I'd spend the day in, I couldn't imagine six more months under my dad's roof, much less another whole school year. I would bear it, like I'd borne everything else, because my mom was happy. She practically glowed all day under Sam's gaze. And while she was annoyed by my basketball tournament, she was excited to go to Minnesota and meet Sam's family next week before returning to Paris. This wasn't some workplace romance. Just as she'd sensed the truth about me and Corey, I knew that when she came home in June, Sam would be with her.

"I know that," I said. "And he knows that. We're going to make it work."

"I hope you do." She patted my leg. "You need to call him back?"

I snuggled into her, taking the last bite of pie. "Not right now."

She wrapped her arm around my shoulder and kissed the top of my head. "Merry Christmas, honey."

I closed my eyes, soaking in her warmth. "Merry Christmas, Mom."

Chapter 21

Now

I looked up from the book on my lap, the coffee shop slowly coming into focus. A cliffhanger. *As if I don't have enough of those in my real life right now.* I skimmed the last lines again, frustration eating away at me. I didn't have the third book. And I hadn't seen the movies. *Damn.* I closed the book and picked up my latte, which was mercifully still warm even though I'd neglected it for the last several chapters.

The coffee was good here. Dorthea's hadn't been in Fairford ten years ago, and lattes had been something we could only get at the mall. But it was a good addition to the usual spots on Main. There'd been a steady stream of customers despite it being midmorning, and the barista knew everyone by name. I should have been at Ryan's, fixing my mess. But after the morning at Corey's and checking out of Cavanaugh Pond, I needed a moment. I could have stayed on the hotel grounds—it was a nice enough morning to sit outside—but not with the front desk lady's judgmental stare following me. At least in Dorthea's, no one seemed to notice me. Or if they did, they didn't care to say so.

As I sat in this new-to-me coffee shop with my book, it was almost possible to forget I was in Fairford. Almost. I sighed and pulled out my laptop. I needed to head over to the mall to pick up replacement frames for the ones I'd smashed—and some more clothes now that I was staying for the week—and then I needed to find a new hotel. Cavanaugh Pond wasn't in my budget, and though I knew Harry would foot the bill for my extended stay, I couldn't ask him—not when my clothes still smelled faintly of Corey.

I glanced down at my watch. For once, time was something I had in abundance. Corey hadn't told me an exact time for dinner, but that meal was still hours away. The book in my lap taunted me with its incomplete ending. Checking my inbox would probably be the smart idea—Harry wasn't lying when he said the office fell to pieces without one of us there—but instead, I downloaded the sample of the third and final book. There would be no cliffhangers for me.

"What are you reading?" Corey stood in front of me, a to-go cup and a pastry bag in hand, as though he hadn't eaten all those pancakes at breakfast.

"Hungry already?"

He shook his head. "Groveling after making Krystal rearrange half my day."

"Right. Your executive assistant." I shifted in my seat. It was hard enough coming to terms with Corey and Ryan. Figuring out how Krystal fit in made my head hurt.

He sat down in the seat next to me and reached for my book. He tilted it so he could get a better look at the cover. "Is that the one about vampires?"

I shook my head. "Dystopian love story."

He nodded. "Spoiler alert—she picks the baker."

"Wrong dystopian," I said dryly.

He shrugged. "Was it good? You had the same look my daughter gets when she reaches the end of a book—half-content, half-devastated, and all 'If you interrupt me right now, I will hurt you.'"

I laughed because that summed up my adventures in reading. "Always wait for the chapter break."

"So I'm learning," he said with a warm smile. "She's only seven, but you do not want to unleash her wrath if you stop her in the middle of a chapter. She loves those Junie B. Jones books. But we've been reading *A Wrinkle in Time* together. Aim high."

An image of Corey with Emily on his lap, reading *A Wrinkle in Time* aloud, popped into my mind. It was at once adorable and incomprehensible. Even though I'd seen them together only hours earlier and watched them interact, the idea of Corey's daughter still felt surreal.

He held out his hand. "I'm Corey, by the way. You're Ryan Scott's daughter, right?" He winked when I stared at him incredulously, and his voice dropped to a stage whisper. "I thought maybe we should start over."

I took his hand. "Andi Scott."

"I'm sorry about your father."

"Oh. Thank you." This was weird, but Corey was making an effort. So I would too. "Did you know him?"

He settled back into his chair, holding his coffee with both hands. "Yeah, we've worked together for a while now. I'm his lead architect."

I nodded again, unsure what to say. His business card had said *founding principal*, but I knew enough of corporate America to know that could mean anything. "What does a lead architect do exactly?"

As Corey told me about his job—from the basics, like schematics, to the nitty-gritty of project management and vendor selection—a mock marketing plan took form in my mind. He was the perfect spokesperson, and he hadn't even really said anything about the company yet. I found myself laughing with him, enjoying his presence without all the pressure and tension that had been the last few days. And the best part was that I liked him. He was funny and contrite and self-deprecating. He laughed easily and often and went off on tangents.

"Sounds like a dream job," I said.

I knew it was. He'd gone to school for architecture. But in our current roles, we were meant to be strangers. Weird game or not, this was the most Corey had told me about himself so far. Hearing about his life was easier this way too. The baggage felt lighter, each word less weighted, each tidbit he let slip in less painful.

"It's the only thing I ever imagined doing." His eyes were bright. His passion for his work, like so much in his life, was showcased for all to see. "You know, aside from playing wide receiver for the Patriots."

I laughed. He always had been a Patriots fan. It was the most annoying thing about him. "Must be nice doing what you love."

"Marketing's not your dream job?" he asked, and I knew the question was sincere by the discerning look he gave me.

"It's what I wanted to do. I got my master's in it to round out my English degree. But I started as an assistant at Smith & Stengel, and even though I work on other things, mostly B2B stuff, I don't know if I'll ever really be out from under that." I sat all the way back in my chair, tucking my legs under myself. "Agency life is just hard, you know? Long hours, and even when you're off, you're never really off. And then there's—"

"Harry?"

I nodded. "Sometimes, I feel like I have to work twice as hard as everyone else just to prove that I'm worthy of my job."

"That's rough." He reached out and placed a gentle hand on my arm.

That small touch felt more real than anything I'd experienced with Harry in two years. Talking about my job doubts felt good. Corey wasn't judging me or trying to fix it or talking me out of my worries like everyone else in my life would—if I could ever tell them the whole truth.

"I got a job offer to be a communications manager at this software company. It's still B2B but one client and normal hours. I'll get to do a lot of things that I only get to coordinate now—brochure design, web copy, a little PR."

His eyes shot up, and I knew he had to be wondering what this meant for my relationship with Harry. "Do you think you'll take it?"

I cocked my head. "I don't know. My life as I know it would be completely different."

"I can tell you from experience, as scary as 'completely different' sounds, sometimes it's exactly what you need. That first year with Emily was a mess, but having a daughter is not anything like I imagined, but it's everything."

I placed my hand over his where it still rested on my arm. "I bet you're a great dad."

He smiled, his cheeks flushing. "I'm not perfect, but I try every day. What do your mom and your friends have to say about the new job?"

"They don't know. You're the only person I've told." I wrung my hands. His eyes widened, but he didn't comment. "It's just that Harry gave me my start. First as an intern, then as his assistant. And I know I'm good at my job. Harry wouldn't simply promote me because of our connection, but that doubt is always there."

Talking about Harry was odd yet comforting. While I'd told Emma I was dating a married man, I hadn't said that he was also my boss. Because of that, I'd leaned into the *married* part more than I might have otherwise as a way to explain the secrecy surrounding my relationship. Emma had been the one person I could potentially talk to about my relationship with Harry, and she didn't want to hear about it.

"Then you should take the job," Corey said, glancing at his phone before returning his gaze to me. "You can be his protégé and his girlfriend."

I laughed wryly. "His wife might take issue with that."

I wanted to take it back the moment I said it. It wasn't even true anymore now that she'd signed the papers.

Corey paled, and he stared at me with a furrowed brow. He'd clearly thought he'd had my relationship with Harry figured out, but he hadn't known about the wife. He cleared his throat, pasting on a smile.

"It's not as bad as it sounds." My voice shook at the explosion of truth regarding the most secret part of my life I had just unleashed. "They've been separated for a long time and—"

Corey held up his hands. "You don't need to explain. Listen, I have to get back, but meet me at Scott and Johnson at four thirty. I can show you around, and then we can have an early dinner?"

I bit the inside of my cheek. This dinner would either give me all the answers I wanted or open a Pandora's box full of pain that I wouldn't be able to bottle back up, but I had to go. No, I wanted to go. Otherwise, there would be no point in having broken open all this angst. Corey's partnership with Ryan hurt in a way I didn't fully understand. He owed me nothing, yet I'd kept him hidden in my heart for so long, refusing to examine the feelings too closely, that his whole adult life felt like a betrayal. I had to give him the chance to explain. Even if it hurt.

"I'll see you then."

"OH, COME ON!" I NUDGED the frame straight again, but it wouldn't stay. All the others were straight, but this bottom one didn't want to cooperate. I was starting to take it personally.

With a sigh, I lifted the frame from the wall and sat down at the desk. The chair was a definite improvement from the one I'd had when I was a teenager. It spun easily and was broken in to perfection. I pulled my legs into a cross-legged position. There had to be another place for this frame. I scanned the room, and my eyes fell on the prayer card I'd taken out of my purse earlier. My mom had asked for a photo of it. The request caught me off guard, but I'd obliged. I read it, skimming the lines from Psalm 23: *The Lord is my shepherd, I shall not want.* It was fitting for a man who apparently sobered and found God.

Inspiration hit, and I slipped off the back of the frame. After removing the extra protection and padding, I lifted the coin from its central location. With a slight move to the right, the prayer card fit. I opened the desk drawer, holding the card and coin in place with my other hand. As I suspected, the contents of the drawer were completely the same—paper clips, pushpins, binder clips, tape, packing tape, rubber cement. I took a closer look. There were even several pens I recognized from trips I'd taken junior year. With the card and the coin taped onto the background paper, I held everything in place and turned it over. *Perfect.* I looked around the room again, and there, right in front of my face, was the nail where I'd once hung a collage frame. It wouldn't hide the fact that something had happened here, but it seemed a fitting spot for the final certificate. I hung the framed certificate then straightened it. Year number seven had found its home.

I sat back and let the memories of this room wash over me. So much Corey. So much Krystal. Laughter and love mixed with fear. I remembered the Christmas tree I'd put up in the corner because Ryan hadn't done anything to celebrate the holiday. I remembered afternoons sitting next to Krystal as we compared notes on Dustin and Corey and nights tangled in bed with Corey when it was too cold for our usual spots. I'd lived in Ryan's house for so short a time, but so much life had happened here.

The familiar ding of my phone brought me back to attention. I had three missed calls—two from Harry and one from my mom—and a lengthy text from Emma about an argument she'd had with Charlie the night before. I sent a quick reply to Emma as I gathered my things. Harry could wait—whatever he wanted was most definitely work related. My mom was being cagey since I'd told her about running into Corey. Her voicemail probably beckoned me home, reminding me about how we had reservations tomorrow night that had taken us weeks to get. But she had sent me up here.

I made my way downstairs and into the living room. My fit of rage the day before seemed to have banished most of the power the house held over me. I still hadn't walked into the dining room, but the sight of the grandfather clock didn't send me into a spiral. My therapist had always said I gave Fairford too much power over me. We'd tried a few things—like calling my father Ryan and accepting what had happened, feeling the panic, and then letting it go. Nothing had worked quite as well as breaking those frames, though.

I had just tossed the bag with the broken frames into the garbage when my phone buzzed with another text. I expected Emma but found Harry. He needed me to answer any email. I almost didn't do it. We got bereavement days at Smith & Stengel. But he'd said please and phrased it like a question instead of his usual demands. With a grumble, I plopped down on the couch and pulled out my iPad. My inbox had more than three hundred emails. This was going to suck. I was literally incapable of ignoring the other two hundred ninety-nine. I picked my phone back up to check the client's name just as it started ringing. *How important is this email?* But it wasn't Harry. It was Steve Alridge.

Dammit. I hadn't answered his email. There hadn't been time between sex with Harry and finding out that Ryan had died.

"Hey, Steve."

"You didn't respond to my email." His tone was sardonic, and I could picture him sitting at his desk, feet up, tossing the koosh ball he'd always kept with him up in the air.

"I know. I'm sorry. Things got a little crazy this week." I bit my bottom lip, which was already so raw. "When do you need to know by?"

"When do I—Andi, you've been asking me to make this happen for a year. I didn't think you needed consideration."

"It's just..." I didn't want to play the dead-dad card, but I was going to. Steve wanted an answer, and I couldn't make this decision off the cuff. It absolutely needed consideration. "My father died."

Steve had been in a creative writing class with me in college and had read between the lines of a story that I had positioned as a retelling of Rapunzel. I didn't often tell people about my father, but I also didn't lie if someone asked me right out, which meant Steve knew enough of the truth to know exactly what those three words meant to me. "Oh. Wow. Did you two ever reconnect?"

"No, but I'm in his hometown, and I just need a few days if possible."

"Yeah, of course. I know being there must be difficult for you." He paused. "I will need an answer either way next week."

I mumbled an agreement and let the phone drop onto the coffee table before sinking into the couch. God, it was comfortable—all plush cushions and microfiber. I wanted to burrow into its depths and never move again. Instead, I returned to my inbox and started to scroll through the three hundred three emails now waiting for me.

Chapter 22

Now

I awoke suddenly, jumping up from the couch. Too late, I remembered what I'd been doing before I dozed off. I grabbed for the tablet that should have been resting on my lap. My hands only grasped air. *Shit.* I felt around the cushions but felt nothing. *Where is it?* I looked up and swallowed a scream as my eyes focused on the slight figure sitting in the chair next to me.

"How long have you been here?" I asked, spying my tablet on the coffee table. "And why didn't you wake me up?"

"Not long."

She looked more like a teenager than she had at the funeral home. Nikki sat cross-legged on the big armchair in a pair of skinny jeans. The tips of Chucks edged out from under her knees. Her shirt had a familiar band logo on it and looked strikingly like one currently hanging in my closet.

I sat up. "You like Wilderness Weekend?"

She looked down at the shirt. "Yeah. When Corey was moving from his apartment back in with Paul and Maya, I helped by keeping Emily busy, and I swear, he just listened to them on a loop. Like nothing but Wilderness Weekend for the entire weekend. I kind of fell in love with them." She blushed at this admission, though I wasn't entirely sure why. Music was music. It transcended generations. "I'm so sad they're breaking up."

I nodded. "Yeah, I can't imagine a world without Wilderness."

The chorus of a punk pop song and the details of a shadowy weekend came back to me—Corey coming up to visit me the fall of freshman year. It was the first time we'd talked since leaving for separate colleges. He whispered sweet nothings of the punk rock persuasion in my ear, and for the first time in months, I felt whole. Everything changed in the months that followed. Everything that had seemed right was wrong, and whatever seemed wrong had turned out to be the truth.

"Corey says I'm a lot like you when you were younger, being an emo kid and all."

I laughed. I hadn't qualified as an emo kid in a long time. "Well, you definitely look like me in that outfit—at least the way I looked back then."

She eyed me skeptically. "Can I see your phone?"

After unlocking it, I placed it in her hand. There was nothing on there that she couldn't see.

Her fingers moved quickly, and I wondered what she was doing. "Exactly. Your Spotify recommendations read like a set list from Warped Tour. You can take the girl out of the emo scene, but you can't take the emo out of the girl."

I held in a laugh. "Shut up."

She handed the phone to me, a triumphant smile on her face but something else too. We were alike, at least in this small way, and it meant something to her. From the stirring in my stomach, it meant something to me too.

"What are you doing here, by the way?" I asked.

Even though she'd given me the key, based on the condition of the house, I hadn't thought anyone spent a lot of time here. But as with Corey, she seemed at ease in this place. There was a familiarity in the way she lounged on the chair, in the way they both came and went, and in the way she didn't need to examine the space around her. It might not have been her home, but it was something.

"I had to pick up some stuff," she said, her eyes on her phone. "My mom dropped me off before she went into town to take care of some things. She should be back in a few minutes."

A few minutes in Fairford time was more like a half hour. I remembered once telling my mom that Corey lived down the road—which was technically true, even though his house was a mile away.

"You have stuff here?" I asked, disbelieving.

The house seemed devoid of teenagers. Everything centered on Ryan's life. I hadn't ventured into what had been Nikki's room, equally afraid that it would be another time capsule and that it wouldn't be. But there were hardly family pictures outside the room that had once been mine. It was possible my sister was religious, too, but that wasn't her vibe.

Nikki followed my gaze and shrugged. "Dad was kind of a neat freak. The room upstairs is mine."

"Do you live here all the time?"

"No." Her gaze shifted toward the front of the house. "Do you want to see my room?"

I smiled in what I hoped was an encouraging way. "Absolutely."

As we climbed the stairs, I couldn't help but imagine how different things could have been if Ryan had pulled it together and Bethany stayed. Nikki and I would have had a relationship, and I wouldn't have minded babysitting because Corey was there. Even after graduation, we would have spent half of our breaks here—Corey sneaking in since we spent almost every night together at the college anyway. It could have been simple, happy.

Nikki stopped outside her bedroom. There was a tentativeness about her movements, and she stood in the door almost as if guarding it. After a few long seconds, she swung the door open and stepped back to let me in.

The walls were an ocean shade of blue, and the first thing visible without even entering was a framed, autographed lithograph from one of my favorite Wilderness Weekend albums. I stepped inside and found clusters of lyrics, annotated with artwork, covering the walls. Over her desk was a picture of a fishbowl with a wide-eyed goldfish, the word *life* in a sprawling script under it. Her windowsill had ledger lines and notes to a melody I couldn't read. The picture by her bed showed two theater masks connected by the word *love*. I recognized and loved all the bands and the songs.

My pain—what connected me intrinsically to the music—was not the same as hers, yet the music lived in her as well. The same words that made my life bearable made her days easier. The beauty of music was that people related to it in different ways, taking from it what they needed. That had never been clearer than it was as I stood in my younger sister's bedroom, seeing the soundtrack to my life drawn out on her walls. We were years apart, but Nikki and I were one and the same. Somehow, our roads had merged.

I sat on the edge of her bed, taking in the room from that vantage point. Artwork and band posters and lyrics and hope and pain surrounded me. "Are all of these decals?" I asked, my eyes on the artwork on the back of her door, which depicted a girl sitting under a palm tree while little lollipops danced above her head.

"I painted them," she said quietly.

"You're an artist?"

She pointed to a painting next to the door. "That's my favorite."

I walked over to get a better look. Behind me, I heard her moving around, but I was enthralled with the landscape she'd created on the small canvas: a cluster of rocks careening over the high tide of a river. It must have been farther upstate. No rivers like this were near Fairford. As I leaned in closer, the delicate nuances of each rock and the ripples in the water became clear. Nikki was talented. There was no question about that.

"Where'd you do this?"

She stopped midway through dragging a portfolio to her bed and examined her work. "Before he got really sick, Dad took me camping out by the Hudson." For the first time, there was a noticeable tremor in her voice, and her sharp breaths alerted me to the emotions she'd been trying to hide throughout everything. It was the first time I'd heard her say "Dad."

I ignored the stirring in my stomach. "You used acrylics?"

"For that one, yes," she said, her nose crinkling. She picked her portfolio back up and dropped it heavily on the bed. "I prefer oils, but they're a little messy for camping."

I sat down again, propping a pillow against the headboard, and waited. Clearly, Nikki wanted to show me more of her work. She pulled a stack of canvases out of the portfolio and laid them close to me on the bed. There were several more landscapes in oils, pastels, and charcoal, and mixed-media pieces with the calligraphy skills from her walls transferred to a much smaller surface. The detailed lettering was flawless, the shadow of the sun perfectly cast. It was a skill she'd inherited from Ryan—I remembered the drawing he'd done of the Fairford house before it had been built. But Nikki used this skill in a totally different way, and it was beautiful. As I looked through her work, a picture of her life became clear. There was more camping and more music translated into art and a drawing of Ryan that felt incomplete.

She fingered the edges of that last one. "He passed before I got to finish, but maybe it's better that way. A life unfinished."

She looked about to cry, and I couldn't handle her tears. I sifted through the art and pulled up a charcoal of a cabin. "Did you go camping a lot?"

She sniffled and nodded, the tiniest of smiles returning to her face. "We have a cabin, so we would spend a few weeks there every summer."

"And your mom was okay with that?"

Her expression shuttered, and she focused her gaze on the portrait of Ryan. "She usually came with us."

Another piece of the puzzle fell into place. Bethany and Ryan had been... friends? A couple? Nikki obviously loved her father wholeheartedly. *How did they go from sneaking away in the middle of the night to spending summers at a cabin?*

"What was he like?" I wished I could take it back as soon as I said it. Her face fell, and her shoulders shook. I was pushing her too far.

After a moment, she lay back on the bed and clutched a ratty teddy bear to her chest. Her tearstained cheeks were flushed. "He was just a normal dad. I saw him on weekends. He came to all my school events even though they were fairly far away. He loved dad jokes and singing country music at the top of his lungs whenever we drove anywhere. I think his goal in life was to embarrass me as much as humanly possible." She laughed then, covering her eyes with her hand. More tears spilled down her cheeks. "We were a family—me and Dad... and Mom. They were friends, you know, even after everything."

Her grief hit me hard. I hadn't lost anyone in the same way. I'd been sad when Sam passed away, but that wasn't close to the same. But I could imagine what it must feel like by substituting my mother for Ryan. My whole body tensed at the thought, and my heart recoiled. The actuality would be paralyzing.

She tugged on my arm until I lay down next to her. Glow-in-the-dark stars were still scattered across the ceiling. The father she spoke of was fiction to me—a joking, singing, happy man. Ryan had never seemed happy even when things were good. But he'd always been different with me. He kept me at a distance and didn't know what I was reading or who my favorite band was, and he rarely asked questions about my life. He'd listened as I babbled to Bethany about whatever drama or excitement highlighted my week, always with a beer, always just out of reach.

"How old were you when you saw him again?"

"Ten." She held up the bear. "He gave this to me that first time. I was terrified of him. I mean, sure, I'd missed him—it had been four years, but our life without him was good and full—calm. There weren't fights and broken plates and Mom crying at my door when she thought I was asleep."

Shattering glass. Chance's whine. Yelling. I squeezed my eyes shut against the same painful memories. Nikki remembered. How I wished she didn't.

We continued to lie there, sharing the silence, our arms barely touching. My *sister's* arm. I always told people I was an only child. But I had a sister.

"A few years ago, he told me about that night—what he said, the grandfather clock, how he didn't talk to you for the better part of that year, how bad his alcoholism got. Everything."

A lone tear dropped onto my nose. More were coming. And after years of holding them back and not talking about this part of my life, there would be no stopping them.

"It's awful, Andi," she said, wiping her cheek. "It had to take a lot of courage to come here." She sat up. "Why didn't you ever try to get in touch with me? I mean, you didn't know that I was in touch with Dad."

I shook my head, and a weight settled on my chest. Words were hard to come by. "I... it was..."

"Just say it quick."

"What?" I asked, sitting up.

"Mom always says if something is hard, just do it quick, you know, before you can overthink it."

"I guess that I felt that your mother should've reached out to me. She never checked on me that whole year or after. I figured if she wanted me in your life, she'd make sure I was in it." I chanced a look at my sister, but she was staring at the bedspread, breathing even, steady breaths. "It's a crappy answer. I should've—"

"No, it's fine. I get it." She started gathering her art back into the portfolio. "I looked you up on social media once. You seemed happy. It said you lived in Boston, were engaged."

That felt like another lifetime ago. Graduate school, Boston, Robert. I *had* been happy until my stepdad died, and it all came crashing apart. "But Dad said it was a bad idea since you never answered any of his letters."

Letters? I wanted to pursue that line of thought. There hadn't been letters. There'd been *a letter* too many years after the fact for me to even entertain what it said.

But Nikki stared at me imploringly, her eyes red, her cheeks splotchy. "Would you have answered me?"

I wanted the answer to be yes. A resounding, without-a-doubt yes. Had my long-lost sister resurfaced, I would have dropped everything. But if it had involved Ryan—if I'd seen one photo of her with him—it might have gone another way.

"I don't know."

"Okay," she said quietly. Her cell phone vibrated, and she typed something back quickly before shoving it in her pocket. "My mom will be here in a minute."

Silently, she packed up her art. She was meticulous and gentle, stacking the pieces before sliding it all into the portfolio. Her care for the work was something my writing had never experienced. My notebooks had always been full of bumps and bruises. I'd gone through at least five binders my senior year of high school, each one carefully collaged with photos of friends, Corey, and celebrities. The handwritten pages that I had painstakingly typed up in college were still in my bedroom at my mom's, a relic from another version of me.

Nikki dragged the portfolio back to her closet and then walked out of the room. She didn't stop to see if I followed. She didn't even look at me. *Crap.* The last thing I wanted was to hurt her. And now I'd made her cry and pissed her off all in less than an hour.

"Did you rearrange the plaques?" she asked, standing in the open doorway of my old bedroom.

I stopped in her doorway, my eyes downcast. "I did. One of them fell the other day when I was, uh, looking through my old stuff. You made them, right?"

"One a year, every Christmas."

"His anniversary is on Christmas?"

"Yeah. That's when Corey found him."

My mouth opened to comment, but nothing came out. *When Corey found him.* Every fact led to something else, another question, another suspect. The edges of the puzzle were coming together, but the picture was still unclear.

"Can I ask you something?" Nikki asked as we walked downstairs. She continued before I could respond. Just doing it quickly, as Bethany advised. "What are you doing here? It's fine. It's just…" She waited for an answer, her hands clasped in front of her.

I stopped on the second-to-last step. "I had to bring something by after I checked out of my hotel."

"You checked out of your hotel?"

I nodded. "I was staying at Cavanaugh Pond, but since I'll be here for a few more days, it's a little expensive."

"You're staying for the rest of the week?"

"Yeah, Corey asked me to."

Nikki's eyes narrowed at my mention of Corey, and I realized too late that I might have phrased that the wrong way.

"He said I had to be here for the reading of the will. Do you know what's going on?"

Nikki started to answer but stopped as the front door opened. We turned as one as Bethany stepped into the vestibule.

Her eyes skipped from her daughter to me. "Andi, hello."

"Hi, Bethany. How are you?"

"I'm well." The edge that had been in her voice at the wake was gone, but she still sounded stiff and wouldn't look right at me. She fussed with her keys, her eyes going back to her daughter. "Are you ready?"

"Can we have a minute?" Nikki asked.

Bethany nodded, turning her gaze on me again, and I thought, for a second, it softened, but then she backed away. "It was nice seeing you."

The lie sat heavily in the silence of the house. I ignored it and faced Nikki, hoping she planned on telling me why Corey had insisted I stay until Saturday.

She grasped my hand. "Don't find another hotel."

"What?" If *Nikki* didn't want me here, it was time to capitulate.

"Just stay here. It's stupid to waste money when the house is sitting here empty."

I tucked that white flag back up my shirtsleeve before anyone saw it. No foul. She released my hand, and then in a flash, she was gone. I was alone in the house. The grandfather clock chimed the hour: one, two, three.

Chapter 23

Now

S cott and Johnson Home Design occupied the three-story glass corporate building at the end of Main. Unlike a New York City building with a doorman, a visitors' log, and a buzzer system, the door to the office swung open freely, and the reception booth centered in the room was vacant. Behind the desk were two elevators with a staircase between them. Plush modern furniture filled the office—oblong chairs in front of glass tables. Through the window to the left of the reception desk, a garden was a visible distraction. The colors contrasted with the white walls and glass of the contemporary-styled building.

"Andi Scott?" a shrill voice sang from the stairs.

I would have known who it was even if Corey hadn't told me she worked here. I turned, a smile splitting my face. "Krystal!"

Krystal Rivera was the only person from Fairford, besides Corey, who'd ever met my mother and visited my actual home. We'd lost touch, as many high school friends did after freshman year of college. Our lives had gone in different directions—she'd been planning a trip down the aisle, whereas my roommate had been holding my hair back at four in the morning on a weekday.

She flew into my arms, jumping with excitement. "I thought that was you outside the church yesterday." She pulled away but kept a hold on my arms. A few stragglers in the office glanced in our direction. "Look at you, all city chic."

I rolled my eyes. "Hardly."

Her fingers curled around my wrist, and she tugged me toward the receptionist desk. When she sat down and replaced her nameplate on the counter, everything made a little more sense. Except *Krystal Berger*.

Krystal had married Dustin in the fall of sophomore year of college. I'd been invited to the wedding, but there was no way I was going—not after the disaster that had been freshmen year. But Dustin's last name was *not* Berger.

"You got remarried?" I asked, deciding to focus on the successful relationship and not the failed one.

She nodded. "Yeah, Dustin and I divorced shortly after Delia was born. But we're still friends and coparents. Nelson and I tied the knot this summer." She handed me a photo of a little girl in a flower-girl dress, who I guessed was about five. She had Krystal's thick curls and Dustin's eyes. "So, did you just wander in, or can I help you with something today?"

"Stop it." I laughed. "You know I'm meeting Corey for dinner, and I know he bought you that pastry"—I pointed to the scone on her desk—"for rearranging his schedule."

"Well, well, aren't you two just precious. Rekindling?" Her eyebrows rose suggestively.

"No, we have a bit to discuss." I rolled my eyes and waved my hand, indicating the room.

Krystal's mouth quirked on one side. "It's something, isn't it? Well, Mr. Johnson isn't here just yet, but he should be along shortly. He runs the Future Business Leaders of America club over at the high school when he's not in season."

"In season?"

The telephone rang then. Her tone changed as she answered, turning into the professional voice of a seasoned receptionist. A basket of pens sat on the ledge of her desk, with Scott and Johnson

Home Design printed on each one, along with the phone number. I put one in my purse and waited for her to get off the phone. The office was quiet. Few people walked in, and fewer wandered around.

"Sorry about that." Her eyes twinkled, and I knew she was relishing this moment with me out of the loop and her swooping in with the intel. She'd always loved gossip. She'd had no trouble keeping my secrets, though.

"Corey's the assistant football coach at the high school."

Architect. Father. Coach. His layers were peeling away like an onion. Eventually, I'd get to the core. "I see."

Corey came striding into the office, his tie loose around his neck and his jacket unbuttoned. His hair looked tousled, a sure sign he'd been stressed out. He was smiling, though.

"Hey, sorry I'm late. You look nice."

"It's fine. Krystal and I were just catching up." I was extra glad I'd changed into something that matched his attire. My black slacks and baby-blue button-down were nothing special, but blue always had been his favorite color on me.

Krystal was breathing in our every word. The gossipmongers would be happy—fresh news right from the source. *Corey Johnson and Andi Scott seen together—rekindled flames!*

"Let me show you around."

We started on the first floor, where there were offices for business support—human resources, accounting, sales, and marketing—and more than one conference room. Models of some of their projects lined the walls outside the offices. I stopped to look at one that read Library Remodel. It was beautiful, mixing contemporary styles with the homey comfort of a small-town library. On the second and third floors were offices for architects and shared meeting spaces. We passed a kitchen and a break area—complete with foosball—as we walked toward a double-doored glass office that took up an entire corner of the second floor. The sign next to it didn't say Conference Room A, like I was expecting, but Corey Johnson, CEO.

I eyed him suspiciously. Lead architect did not a CEO make.

He flushed. "Your father made me CEO a few months ago. I'm still adjusting to the title and the office."

He opened the door to his office, and I half expected another receptionist, but it opened into a lounge area. Two leather couches sat facing each other in the center of the room. A wall partitioned the back office from the front room, leaving open doorways on either side. What had to be at least a seventy-inch television hung on the wall, stock data scrolling across the screen. Music slightly better than Muzak played softly in the background, giving the space an ambience of relaxation. Sunlight came in through a big window to the right of a desk that was bigger than my bed, casting shadows on the floor this time of day. The blinds were pulled all the way up, giving us a perfect view of the bustle of Main Street. It was hard to imagine Corey here, but it was even harder to imagine Ryan behind the desk or staring out the window at the town below or in this building at all.

I sat down in one of the chairs opposite the desk. Corey took the adjacent one and turned to me. Our knees were close but not touching, and when he leaned forward, the scent of his cologne washed over me. I sat back in my seat.

"So, you've learned plenty about me," he said. "What about you? How's your mom? Sam?"

I looked up at him and clasped my hands together. "My mom's good. Busy with work, per usual. Sam passed away a few years ago."

"I'm sorry to hear that." His voice deepened, and he averted his gaze.

I looked down at my phone. A text from Emma lit the screen. "Emma and Charlie got married last year."

Corey smiled. "I wondered if they stayed together."

I nodded. "Yup, they continue to make everyone around them jealous."

Corey leaned back in the chair, getting comfortable. "Including you?"

"Especially me."

"Right—you can't marry a married man," he said, his eyes on mine. I winced. He held up a hand in apology. "Sorry, that came out wrong."

"It's okay. It's true."

I debated my next words. Corey's history was right there for all to see in the form of Emily. He couldn't hide it, though I couldn't imagine he ever wanted to. Not with the way he looked at that little girl. It seemed fair that I share mine with him, and the more time I spent with him, the more I wanted him to know the real me. "I was engaged once, but it obviously didn't work out."

If my admission had any effect on him, Corey didn't let it show. He held my gaze. "I'm sorry."

"Thanks. It was a few years ago." I stood and walked toward the window.

In the time we'd toured the building, Fairford had come alive. Cars drove by. High school kids crossed the streets carelessly, baseball bags slung casually over their shoulders. One of the restaurants down the street was setting up outdoor tables, and S&R had a crowd of teens in green and white outside it.

"What was here before?" I asked, unable to pull anything up in my memory. As much as Fairford had stayed the same, so much had changed.

"Nothing really. A small parking lot with a basketball court."

He came up behind me, though I didn't notice until he gently placed his hand on the small of my back. An uncontrollable ripple went through my body at his touch, but Corey didn't notice, or if he did, his hand didn't move.

"And a swing set," I said, remembering the park.

We'd gone there fairly often when we first started dating. It had been October, and nights were still mild. There wasn't a town curfew, but the parks closed at dusk. The diner was good for late-night brain food but not so much for privacy. It would have been easy to creep into my house—Ryan would most likely have been passed out—but this had been early days, and we weren't at that stage yet. We would sit for a while, swinging low to the ground, our feet dragging in the grass, and eventually end up in the back seat of his car before slinking home with the sunrise.

"It's really sad," he said, his hand still on my back. "The park fell to ruins. The grass ran rampant. The swing set rusted. We bought the land for almost nothing."

"And how did it turn into this?" I turned away from the window and sat down in one of the chairs again.

"We were already well on our way when we bought it," he said, not moving from his spot at the window. "We rented an office a few blocks from here at first. Back when it was just something small."

"And then?"

He turned finally, his eyes finding mine. "Let's get dinner, and I'll tell you everything."

THE RESTAURANT WAS lit by candlelight and sconces mounted low on the walls. It took a few seconds for my eyes to adjust to the dim lighting after walking to the restaurant in the bright early-evening sun. Ten tables were spread out across the small space, none big enough to fit more than four people. Each table was covered with a red tablecloth, high quality and thick, adding to the ambience of the room. No families were eating at the establishment, only a few couples and a solo businessman.

We were seated at a table along the wall. I scanned the menu, every selection sounding fabulous and expensive and far too upscale for this town. "When did this place open?"

"A few years back." Corey offered me the bread basket, and I took a warm roll. "It was featured on one of those Food Network shows about hidden treasures or whatever."

Interesting. "Fancy business brings fancy restaurant?"

He rolled his eyes. "Would you just eat your bread?" He was smiling, evidently pleased by my curiosity.

I tore a piece of bread off as the waiter approached to take our order. As soon as he turned from the table, I focused my attention back on Corey. "We're at dinner. Tell me everything."

The blood drained from his cheeks, and his eyes dimmed. He picked at his bread. But then he spoke. "It was Christmas morning, sophomore year of college. My mom had sent me to pick up breakfast from S&R. I hadn't seen Ryan in over two years. He didn't venture out much—at least, that's what my mom told me. But there he was, loitering outside S&R, drunk off his ass. The owner was outside, staring him down. By the time I came back out with the food, he was leaning against his car, playing with his keys. I wanted to leave him there, to just forget I ever saw him. I even got in my car and started it."

The waiter dropped off our wine, and Corey took a sip before continuing. "Then this image of you came back to me. It had been a year since we'd... last seen each other. But I remembered you leaving dinner in the fridge for him and cleaning up his messes. You loved him, even as you hated him. So I brought him to the detox tank at the hospital and forgot all about him. I don't know all of what he went through after that, only what he told me. But he went to rehab and got clean. That first year was hard for him. He never relapsed, but he said he came close. He went to meetings every day and started therapy. He tried to make amends where he could. After Christmas, I didn't see him for six months. Even then, he was sober but shaky. But then Sharon got pregnant, and things were such a mess. Ryan helped me renovate the basement into a studio. We had our own bathroom, a bedroom, even a nursery for Emily."

I looked up at him. "Is that why you forgave him?"

"For a long time, I hated him for everything he did to you. When he first showed up at my house sober, I accepted his thanks and sent him away." He took a breath and looked up at the ceiling before settling his gaze on me. He clasped his hands, kneading his palm with his thumb. "Sharon got pregnant right before junior year. We kept it quiet for as long as we could, but you know how Fairford is. News that I'd knocked someone up spread fast. Over Christmas break, Ryan approached me again. He offered to cover all the expenses of the basement remodel. To repay me for giving him his life back. I wanted to say no. I knew the horrid things this man was capable of. But I also wanted to finish my junior year. Sharon and I had talked to all our professors, and somehow, we worked it out, even though Emily would come before the end of the spring semester. My parents said it was my decision whether or not to accept Ryan's help."

My throat went dry. Pressure built in my chest and behind my eyes. *How does a life go so off course?* Easily, I knew. One wrong decision, one moment of fear, one careless night.

"So, you accepted his help."

"We couldn't afford to redo the basement ourselves. And I couldn't do it alone. I was a kid. Sharon and I, we needed that space for our daughter. By the time Emily was born that April, Ryan had finished it. That fall, he took me on as a paid intern at Riverwalk when no one else would even consider accommodating the schedule I needed with a newborn. Sharon and I had transferred to a closer school. We were doing online classes where we could. But that first year with Emily was the hardest of my life."

He'd been speaking matter-of-factly until that last part. His words broke my heart. I could see him as he'd been back then, disheartened from a failed football career, dedicated, and trying to find happiness in the broken pieces—and finally moving on and starting over, only to have it all crash down again. The similarities to my own journey with my ex were striking. I wanted to pull him to me and hold him through the end. I settled for placing my hand over his.

"Then Sharon left, and Ryan offered me a job when I graduated. He hired Krystal, who'd just had Delia and who had no experience, as his secretary and let us bring our kids to work. A year later, he went out on his own, and he took us with him. He put my name on the wall." Corey stopped and held my gaze. "I always understood why you didn't want him in your life. It's why I never gave him your new address or cell phone number." He squeezed my hand. "But Ryan was good to me. Raising Emily would've been near impossible without his help."

The pounding in my chest had to be audible. The last five minutes had been a marathon—slow curiosity building to a sprint through anger and uphill to compassion.

"He asked you about me?"

The thought that I mattered to Ryan had rarely occurred to me in the last ten years. As I forced myself to forget about him, I'd assumed he'd already forgotten about me. My presence in his house had been a nuisance at best.

"He knew you were the person that he'd hurt the most," Corey said with no hint of question or emotion—it was simply fact.

I cleared my throat, trying to settle the emotions swirling through my mind. "Why didn't he ever contact me?"

"He did. He wrote you letters, and even after you didn't respond, he kept writing, until recently."

My chest tightened. I pinched the bridge of my nose. I thought of my mom holding onto that letter so tightly. Of me refusing it, going so far as to toss it in the trash. Even if there *had* been multiple letters, why hadn't Ryan tried to find me? It would have been easy, especially with social media. All he had to do was look me up to find my work email. It was right on the Smith & Stengel website.

I swallowed the last of my wine in one gulp. "I only ever received one letter from him, five years after I left Fairford."

Corey's eyes narrowed. Clearly, he believed that I was as cold-hearted as I'd made myself seem. And why wouldn't he? I had years of practice pretending not to care—company events spent smiling at Harry's wife, weddings where I watched friends share special dances with their fathers, Charlie and Emma's perfect love story that I chased but never caught.

"Would it have mattered if you got the rest?" he asked, leaning forward on his elbows.

An image of Ryan and me sitting in the living room of the Fairford house when it had been new flashed into my mind. The wind shook the trees outside. Kids shouted as they rode past on their bikes. Our neighbors sat on their porch, having a last-hurrah BBQ. He sat with a beer in his hand and a smile on his face, with me next to him, sipping apple cider. The Jets were having a good season and were primed to make the playoffs. It was a relief after the dismal performance of the previous season. Ryan and I had watched every game together that season. It was the first time I'd ever spent full weekends with his family. And for those two days, we seemed like a family. We'd have lunches and birthday parties together. Bethany and I would go shopping or to the movies on Saturdays. Ryan and I spent Sundays camped out in front of the television, hoping for a win for the Gang Green.

The memory faded. It was hard to fathom how things had gone from that to disaster in a few years. Those early weekends had made me think it might be okay to live with Ryan for a year. They'd filled a hole that I hadn't even realized I had in my life, one that had been there since before I could remember.

I locked eyes with Corey. "Yes. It would've mattered."

Chapter 24

Now

"Are you sure we're not going to get arrested?" I asked, even as I pushed off the ground.

We sat on the swings at the elementary school. Each time I swung, my feet dragged in the dirt, but I kept going. Maybe it was the buzz from the wine or Corey's natural calming effect, but shoes were replaceable, and the opportunity to sit here with Corey was not.

He laughed. "We will definitely not get arrested."

I stared at the school in the distance. It looked different. I could have sworn it had been more modular before. After two more swings, it occurred to me that Scott and Johnson had probably had a hand in designing this new, trendy building. It would have been one of the projects Ryan took on to redeem himself in a town that had finally learned the truth about him.

"Did you guys remodel the school?"

Corey stopped swinging and turned to look at the building. "We did, right before your dad got sick. For way under the projected cost." He lifted his feet and started pumping slowly, gaining some momentum.

I kicked off the ground and kept pace with him, though when he was forward, I was back. It was nice, all that they'd done for the town. But a part of me wondered if both Ryan and Corey had been compensating and if it would ever be enough—if Corey would ever truly feel above their scrutiny. *Will I ever feel above my relationship with Harry?*

I stopped pumping and let myself swing back and forth. "Did you get a key to the town?"

"I did, actually. My parents keep it framed in the living room. You must've missed it." His tone was serious, but the laughter in his eyes betrayed him. I slapped at him playfully until he doubled over in laughter, his swing coming to a near stop. "No key to the town. We did get plaques, though."

I tried to imagine Ryan and Corey accepting plaques from the mayor for their service to Fairford. Even having been in Corey's office, I couldn't picture him standing beside my father. I couldn't picture them talking and confiding and building an empire together. But they had.

I started pumping again and surpassed Corey's previous height quickly. I kicked my shoes off and kept pumping. The swing went higher and higher. Corey stopped next to me, waiting. I jumped and landed a good distance away, fortunately on grass. Sticking the landing had never been my specialty, and I toppled over, getting grass stains on my good pants.

A laugh broke free, and I sat up, leaning my elbows on my knees. *This town.*

Corey trotted over and inspected me for injuries. "Are you okay?"

"I'm fine." I laughed again and waved him away. "God, I haven't done that in a decade." Finding my footing, I stood and walked back to my shoes.

"What just happened?" Corey asked from behind me. "Did I upset you somehow?"

The ground gave way underfoot, and my ankle turned. I shook it out with a grimace. Swinging and alcohol were maybe not the best combination. Corey caught my arm, balancing me. His eyes were thoughtful as he tried to figure out what had prompted my leap. I didn't even know how to explain that him getting a plaque had sent me down a spiral of questions that I didn't like the answers to. Changing the subject seemed like a great idea, but more secrets and lies were not going to make this any easier.

I sat down on one of the benches lining the playground. "No, you didn't upset me."

Corey perched on the back of the bench a friendly enough distance away. His brow furrowed, but he didn't say anything. He didn't believe me. The bench was cool against my back, the wood coarse under me. I closed my eyes and, for one uninterrupted minute, focused on my breathing. When I opened my eyes, Corey was still watching me. Our eyes met, and something passed between us. Something powerful and strong and too much.

I pushed to my feet. "We should get back."

Always the gentleman, Corey offered me his elbow. My car was still at the office, and we'd walked in the opposite direction to get to the elementary school. As casually as possible, I looped my arm around his.

"You didn't upset me." I squeezed his arm for good measure, wanting him to believe me.

He didn't turn his head, but I could feel his eyes on me. "But you are upset."

"Nothing is how I imagined. When you talk about the company, my brain just can't comprehend it. I see it, and I know it's real, but this is all just a little stressful."

Honest and to the point. It seemed the only way to deal with him. He still knew my nature. There was no use fighting it. We rounded the corner and were back on Main. I glanced at the glass structure at the end of the street. Without the sunlight, the Scott and Johnson building wasn't as intimidating. It faded into the night sky, a natural part of the Fairford landscape.

It was still early, but the town was quiet. The house would be quieter. Daytime trips were one thing, but spending a night within those walls with their ghosts, I could only imagine where my brain would go.

Back at the restaurant, I sat down on the bench in front of the building, pulling Corey down next to me. I scanned the empty street. Even with its new additions, it still read the same. The used bookstore, the local pharmacy, the library at the corner—all these things had been here ten years ago. Even the bench we were sitting on wasn't new, though the upscale restaurant used to be a stationery store. Corey and I had spent many days on this bench, drinking hot chocolate, holding hands, and going in for the occasional public display of affection.

I fiddled with my shoes and rubbed at my knee, and gradually, Corey's posture relaxed.

"What did you imagine?" he asked after I'd slid my heels back on and straightened. The noise that I emitted must have sounded worse than I'd intended because Corey's shoulders slumped. "You don't have to tell me if you don't want."

I glanced at my watch. "You should probably be getting back to Emily."

He scooted closer to me and closed his hand around mine. "Emily's sleeping at Krystal's tonight."

I stared at our hands entwined on his lap, an ache building in my heart. How easy it would be to lean in and put an end to all this pain and wonder and lost time. But I couldn't. For so many reasons. "But sleepovers are for weekends."

He smiled. "I had to make an exception after she found a girl in my bed this morning."

"Sure, blame it on me." I pointed a finger at him in mock accusation. "You're the one who didn't lock the door."

He slung his arm around the back of the bench, his fingers grazing my hair. "You know, on a clear night like this, the view at the Peak is spectacular."

I froze. The warmth that his arm had brought was doused by his words. Whether they were meant to hurt me or spark a memory or were an invitation, I had no idea, but either way, it wasn't fair. "Do you really think I don't remember anything about us?"

The idea that he thought I could just forget our story hurt more than anything had this whole trip. I wished I could forget. I'd spent nine years burying each memory. And still, I remembered every single second of my life in Fairford, from the unmentionable to the indescribable.

"I'm sorry," he said, straightening. "I shouldn't have said that."

"I know this is where we said 'I love you' for the first time after the homecoming game." I set the memory free, allowing the incredible power of first love to wash over me. "We were sitting on this bench, deciding if we were ready for the Peak. You took hold of my hand, and then you just said it like it was the easiest thing in the world."

He smiled and tucked a loose strand of hair behind my ear. "That's because it was."

Chapter 25

Now

My mind spun on a time loop of Corey and Ryan and nights under the stars and this house. In the foyer, I looked left, checking the door to my father's room as I always had. I listened for his snoring. But nothing came. Because Ryan was gone, and the house was empty. I dropped my purse on the stairs and slipped out of my shoes, wondering where I was meant to sleep. *My room?* This had been a stupid idea. A hotel would have been fine. I glanced upstairs and then to the dining room. Without stopping to think about it, I crossed the hall and walked in.

No panic. No phantom pains. No shattering glass. Just the seconds ticking by on the grandfather clock in the corner.

Corey's story had provided answers. About Ryan. About him. About Krystal. But standing in this room where my life had forever changed, it didn't really matter *how* my father had become a pillar of society. It only mattered that he had. He'd turned his life around and made the lives of so many in this town better. His amends had been grand. *Would mine have been?*

For the first time, I allowed myself to wonder what might have been in that letter all those years ago and if there really were others. It was hard to imagine my mom simply throwing away a letter addressed to me, but the alternative—that she had *read* them and kept them from me—was worse. Though the likelihood that I would have accepted any of the letters was slim.

But if I'd I known he wrote to me more than once, that he cared enough to try? I shook my head. I might never know what those letters said.

Ryan, Corey, and Nikki jumbled together in my mind, a mess of regrets and confusion. My mother was there too. Underneath all of that, Harry floated to the surface and then Robert, of all people. I thought about him often enough when I questioned my life choices—Harry, New York, all of it. I'd been happy in Boston. I could have been happy in Boston always. But life had had other plans.

Robert and I had met by chance at the public library. It was my second week of graduate school and only my third in Boston. Our romance was quick and easy and quiet. We moved in together within a year, and a few months after that, he proposed. It might have been the happiest moment of my adult life. But before we had the chance to tell our families, my stepfather fell ill. We'd seen him only two weeks earlier at Christmas. We'd all been in Minnesota with his family. But he'd felt sick after the plane ride home, and two days later, he collapsed at the gym. His battle with pancreatic cancer was short and brutal. They caught it too late. He made it to my graduation in May and celebrated his seven-year anniversary with my mom after that. A week later, he passed away, with my mom and me and his children at his side.

We stayed for a week, helping her get everything settled. Once I was back in Boston, she called me every day, more than once. Before that, I'd heard from her maybe once a week by text. She tried to cover her pain and bring a smile into her tone, but her loss traveled through the airwaves. It settled in my own heart. The same itching doubt that had kept me in bed when Corey walked out of my life started to grow in the smallest of increments. It gnawed at the back of my mind, egging me on. Robert talked of the wedding, thinking it would help my mother feel better if she had a wedding to plan. It wouldn't. She wasn't that woman. Finding Sam had been a fluke chance for her, and her happiness had been taken away too soon.

"I have to go back to New York," I said after a month of nonstop phone calls from my mother and several weekends traveling back and forth.

"This weekend?" Robert didn't look up from the vegetables he was cutting up for dinner.

"No. I have to move back to New York." My voice shook. I knew there was a good chance he wouldn't come with me.

He shook his head, disbelieving. His life was in Boston. Robert was two years older than me. He worked as a lawyer for a small Boston firm. Finding work in New York would be easy, but he'd grown up in Foxboro, spent his college years in Boston, and then moved to the city permanently during law school. It was where he wanted to be.

"Let's not rush into anything just yet. It's only been a month." He came around the island and pulled me into a hug, kissing the top of my head. "She'll be okay."

The notion was dropped for a few weeks, but by September, we were fighting daily. It was a Friday night when I left him, leaving the engagement ring on the table with a short note explaining that I had to go. I was at Emma's before he called me. He knocked on her door at three in the morning, begging me to reconsider. But we were at an impasse, and we both knew it. We spent one last night together, and then he left without a fight. He didn't even look back.

I shook off thoughts of Robert. Dwelling on the past was useless—I was already drowning in it. With a last look at the clock, I made my way upstairs. I stopped at the landing. *Left or right?*

Right. I pushed open the door to Nikki's room and flipped on the light. Her art welcomed me like an old friend. I lay down on the bed, popping in my earbuds. The music that had saved me as it had saved Nikki crashed down on me, drowning out the chiming of the hour.

Chapter 26

Then

I squealed to a stop behind Corey's car and stepped into the frigid air. The cold concrete stung my bare feet, and the wind battered my jacketless body. My cheeks burned where they were wet with tears. My body shook violently but not from the cold March night. I stepped forward, praying that his parents weren't home.

"Andi?" Corey ran down the porch steps. Concern and confusion shook his voice as he reached me. "Oh my god." He unzipped his coat and draped it over my shoulders, ushering me up the front steps. Inside, he examined me, his confusion replaced by a stone-cold anger. "What happened?"

"I didn't have my phone," I cried, my voice unrecognizable. My body continued to shake despite Corey running his hands up and down my arms. A guttural sound escaped from somewhere deep within me. "I didn't have my phone."

"It's okay. Andi, you're okay." He pulled me tight against him. He breathed deeply until my breathing matched his, and my heart calmed to a somewhat normal rate. He held me until the worst of the shaking stopped.

My hands trembled in his. When I looked into his eyes, fresh tears fell. I opened my mouth to speak, but all that came out was another sob.

His eyes scanned me from head to foot. He grimaced at my bare feet. "Please tell me what happened."

I hiccupped and tried to find my voice. "My dad kicked me out."

"What?" He palmed my face, wiping away the latest tears. "I need to know exactly what happened. You promised."

"I know," I said, my voice stronger this time. "I know."

I steeled myself against the memory so fresh in my mind that I shuddered. Terror seized me as if I was back in the kitchen, my dad standing behind me. I gripped Corey's hand so hard he winced.

"Did he hurt you?" Corey prompted.

I shook my head. "No. I... I was eating dinner at the counter. I'd made spaghetti and fried up some sausage, nothing major. He came in—it was early for him. I wasn't expecting... I left a plate for him like usual. Something was off about him from the moment he walked in. I heard something break in the hallway, but I couldn't go anywhere without going through him. So, I thought if I just ate..." My voice broke.

Corey stroked my hair and pressed his forehead against mine. "You're safe."

I sucked in a shaky breath. "He came into the kitchen, and god, he reeked. He picked up the plate I had left wrapped for him, and he... he shattered it against the counter." I closed my eyes against the sound of the plate breaking into pieces. "Then he just stood there, right behind me, breathing so hard. I didn't dare turn around, but I knew his fists were clenched. I'd heard that anger from him before. And then he screamed at me to get the fuck out of his house."

Corey held me impossibly closer.

"I had no shoes. All my coats were in my room. I didn't have my phone." My voice grew louder, and I started to panic again. "How stupid am I? I mean, I didn't have my phone! What if something had happened? I wouldn't have been able to call you or anyone. What if it had been more than my wrist this time? And I didn't have my phone."

"It's okay."

I shook my head, tears blurring my vision. "I got complacent because he's been somewhat normal. You've seen him. But it's his wedding anniversary. I should've remembered. It's on a freaking framed plaque at the entrance to the house. I see the date every single day."

And so did he until he smashed it tonight.

"It's not your fault. None of this is your fault."

"Yes, it is. I should've known what day it was. I should've made sure I wasn't in the house."

He held me by the arms, his eyes boring into me. "It is not your fault, Andi. Now, come on."

This wasn't the first time I'd come over to avoid my dad's moods, though those had been fewer and farther between in the last few months. It was, however, the first time any of his anger had been directed at *me* since the summer. Usually, I heard his bad mood from the safety of my bedroom.

Upstairs, Corey handed me a pair of sweats and his Fairford Baseball hoodie. Silence closed around us as I changed and Corey paced.

"What about your parents?" I asked once I was tucked into his bed. Though I'd stayed well past curfew before, I'd never slept over. And we usually made a show of me leaving before he'd sneak me in again through the back.

"I'll deal with my parents," he said, pulling me into him, my back against his chest. We fit perfectly as if we were designed only for each other. "You just sleep and know you are safe."

He didn't say "for the night," but I knew we both still heard it.

I WOKE TO SUNSHINE and the smell of bacon. Corey was passed out on a sleeping bag on the floor. When I'd fallen asleep, Corey's arms had been around me, though it made sense that he'd moved to the floor. His parents finding us in bed together would not go over well. They had to know I was there—my car was parked in the driveway. But if they'd come in at any point, they hadn't woken us up. Or at least, hadn't woken *me* up.

A knock sounded at the door. "Breakfast, you two."

Corey groaned and rolled over. He gave me a sleepy smile before climbing into bed, pulling the covers up over us. His lips skimmed mine.

His dad knocked a second time. "Now."

"Two minutes," Corey called back, his voice heavy with laughter.

"Thirty seconds." The door swung open. "And door open." Mr. Johnson's eyes found mine. "Morning, Andi."

"Morning, Mr. J. We'll be right down."

He pointed at his watch, pushed the door all the way open, and walked downstairs. Once we were downstairs, our plates filled with pancakes and bacon and the fluffiest scrambled eggs I'd ever eaten, Mr. Johnson turned his attention back to me in his son's bed this morning.

"Explain," he said evenly.

"Dad..."

Mr. Johnson narrowed his eyes at his son and pointed a finger at him. "The only reason you aren't grounded for the rest of your life right now is that I found you on the floor." His expression lightened but barely. "And you look far too unhappy for anything uncouth to have happened. Now, explain."

"It's my fault," I said, even though he'd directed his request at his son. Corey would have come up with a cover—because he loved me—but part of him would die doing it. I wasn't sure we could ever be the same after that. "My dad, he, umm, sometimes, he drinks too much, you know, since my stepmom left. And last night was one of those nights, and I was scared, and I didn't know where else to go."

Mr. Johnson pulled a face. "How often is *sometimes*?"

"It's not usually enough to send me out of the house." It wasn't technically a lie. "Yesterday would've been his wedding anniversary, so I guess he was just upset."

Mr. Johnson's gaze bored into me. I prayed my answer both satisfied and placated him, because if not, he was definitely going to call someone.

"Did he hurt you?"

I shook my head, hoping he wouldn't follow up with "Has he ever hurt you?" I pushed the hair back from my face and could feel the tears coming. Corey must have sensed the shift because he placed a protective arm around me.

Mr. Johnson watched us, his gaze flitting between Corey and me. I knew what he saw—his son calm, too calm, shielding me like he always did. *We wouldn't be this calm if something like this hadn't happened before.* I tried to shift away from Corey, but he only tugged me closer. Mr. Johnson gave his son an assessing look, his mouth flattening into a thin line. Any hope that he might believe Corey hadn't known what was happening in my house until the night before vanished.

"He broke a plate," Corey said when I couldn't find the words. "And told her to get out. So she did."

Mr. Johnson's jaw clenched, and he didn't say anything for a full minute. "Well, next time..." He paused, his eyes saying he knew without a doubt there had been a last time and there would be a next time. "You can stay in the guest room, no questions asked. And you're staying here for the rest of the weekend."

Relief overwhelmed me, and some of the tension I'd held since last night dissipated. I was not ready to go back and sleep in that house. Not yet. I leaned into Corey, not caring that his dad was watching us. "I'll have to go home and get a few things. Shoes, for starters, and my jacket," I said.

Mr. Johnson arched an eyebrow at the word *shoes*.

"And my dress for the dance."

"Don't worry—I'll drive you over," Corey said, kissing my cheek.

"You'll do no such thing," Mr. Johnson said, his coffee mug rattling as it hit the table.

Corey met his gaze. "We're not missing junior prom, Dad."

"Of course not, but I'll take the two of you over." He drummed his fingers on the table. "I think I'd like to have a word with Mr. Scott."

COREY LEANED AGAINST the car door, his arm wrapped around me. Even though I wore his winter coat and a too-big pair of his sneakers, cold seeped in. I burrowed deeper into him, watching Mr. Johnson start toward my house. He'd driven us here as soon as we were all dressed. For me, his expression had been warm and comforting. But when he thought I wasn't looking, it turned to stone. His words for his son had been clipped, and I wondered what awaited Corey after I went back home.

"Dad, is this really necessary?" Corey called across the lawn.

Mr. Johnson stopped halfway to the house and walked back to us. "Your girlfriend showed up at our house with no shoes and no jacket, terrified of her own father last night." Corey opened his mouth to respond, but his dad went on, his voice dropping to a hiss as he got closer to us. "Don't think for a second that I believe you knew nothing about this before last night. Because you damn well would've told me what was going on if you weren't trying to hide something worse."

"We thought we had it under control." Corey's voice was quiet, his execution weak.

Mr. Johnson turned to me, the anger in his face softening but not as much as it had at his house. "I can either have a conversation with your father, or I can call child protective services."

"Dad!"

Mr. Johnson held up a hand. "It's her choice."

"I don't know if he'll talk to you," I said through tears.

"Then let's find out."

We followed him to the house. Corey gripped my hand, the pressure saying more than words could. I pulled us to a stop at the bottom of the stairs, forcing him to meet my eyes. "This isn't on you."

He nodded but looked past me, his eyes clouded.

I touched his cheek with my cold hand, bringing him back to me. "None of this is your fault."

He kissed me, tugging me close. His fingers slid along my spine until they tangled in my hair. I knew I should stop him—I could feel his dad's impatient glare on my back—but the desperation in his kiss kept me in place. What had happened to me had happened to him as well.

"Kids," his dad said in a voice tinged with annoyance and worry.

Corey broke away from me, trailing his fingers down my arm until they entwined with mine. I led him up the porch and let him and his father into the house. There hadn't been another adult in the house in six months. I surveyed the foyer, but per usual, any sign of what had happened the night before was gone.

"Dad?" I called after the front door clicked shut behind Mr. Johnson.

Unconsciously, I had directed my question to the bedroom, but he wasn't sleeping. No, he was sitting at the dining room table. I shuddered as he approached, and Corey pulled me against him.

"Paul?" My dad sounded strange. I stared at him as he stepped into the foyer. He was sluggish, his eyes dry, his words crisper than usual, and instead of his normal can of beer, he held a bottle of water.

Is he sober?

"Dad—"

"Ryan," Mr. Johnson said at the same time as me. "We need to talk."

My dad's gaze lingered on me. He didn't appear angry, as I thought he'd be, or even worried—he simply looked resigned.

"Kids, why don't you go get Andi's things?" Mr. Johnson said.

I couldn't move. I wanted so badly to run up the stairs and be away from my dad, but I couldn't look away. Not only sober. Hungover. He'd stopped drinking long enough to be hungover.

"Now," Mr. Johnson said, nudging Corey—and, by extension, me—toward the stairs.

We went, and I could feel both fathers' eyes on us until we crossed into my room. Corey closed the door, his eyes scanning the space. "What do you need?"

I grabbed my phone off my bedside table, where it had been charging, and then pulled my basketball bag out from under my bed. "Clothes, my backpack, bathroom things. My dress."

We packed in silence, never too far from each other's side, our hands brushing constantly. I dropped my bathroom bag on top of the pile of clothes. "That should be it."

Once downstairs, we could just hear Mr. Johnson and my dad in the kitchen. We both stopped before the last step, holding our breath as the words floated over to us. "I really don't care if you want to drink yourself to death. But when your daughter gets back here on Monday, you'd better have figured something out." I couldn't make out my dad's reply, only Mr. Johnson's rebuttal. "Because I swear, Ryan, if I see one scratch on her that looks out of the ordinary, I will call the police. One scratch."

They rounded the corner, and Corey and I scurried to the front door, my bags at our feet. My dad looked at me—directly at me. His brow furrowed, and something like regret flashed across his features. A sadness so deep it hurt to witness peered back at me from his eyes. "I'll see you Monday."

KRYSTAL TUGGED AT MY hair, twisting it until it was tight against my head. I winced as bobby pins pushed against my skull.

"Suck it up, buttercup," Krystal said with a sardonic grin. "Beauty is pain."

"How many have you put in there?" I whined as she found a spot for yet another one. My phone chirped in my hand—another text from Emma. She'd been begging for pictures for the last hour, even though I'd told her I wasn't ready yet. Fortunately, it was too late in Paris to expect to hear from my mom. Her requests would come in the morning.

Krystal's eyes met mine in the mirror, her expression serious. "Listen, I know you and Corey are all forever and always, but my door is always open too. No questions. I'll even cuddle with you, you know, if you need."

I hadn't told her everything but enough to account for the weird vibe surrounding me and what I suspected would be a highly overprotective Corey. I squeezed her hand. "Thanks, Krys."

"I still can't believe Mr. Johnson laid into your dad," she said, pinning another pin into place. "He's so mellow."

"Yeah."

"Knock, knock." Dustin's voice cut through the conversation, followed by Corey's laughter. "Everybody decent?"

Krystal thrust a lip gloss at me before opening the door and jumping into Dustin's arms, despite the fact that she was wearing a floor-length dress. Corey slipped past them, shaking his head. He pulled me into his arms and held me for a second longer than normal. His hands skimmed across my bare shoulder, and his lips met mine. Every kiss from Corey felt like coming home and like my body would combust if we didn't kiss again. This kiss was no different. My body lit up, and sparks radiated through my extremities. But there was also a weight to it, a chain connecting us in a new way, as if we were irrevocably bound by last night's events.

He pulled away first, his hand caressing the soft skin at the back of my neck. "You look amazing."

"Corey, Andi, come here. I need a picture of you two," Krystal called from the doorway.

He turned us so we faced her, his arms around me, our hands clasped. I leaned against him, resting my head against his shoulder.

"Say cheese!" she said, holding up a camera.

As she said it, the upbeat pop song faded into the opening chords of a ballad. Our song. The lyrics had felt so personal when I'd heard it over Christmas break. And hearing them now, wrapped in Corey's arms, I felt safer than I had in my whole life.

As soon as Krystal dropped the camera, turning it to try to snap a picture of her and Dustin, Corey spun me out of his arms and into a dance position. His hands fastened around my waist. I linked my arms around his neck, and we swayed to the music, our heads close together.

"How was your conversation with your dad?"

"Not great. He's going to be pretty pissed at me for a while, I think."

"I'm sorry," I said, my eyes on his. "I never meant to bring all this drama to your life."

He shook his head. "Your drama is my drama. Nothing is too much. Nothing."

"I love you," I said as my lips found his, bringing me home.

"I love you too."

He hummed along with the song, slightly off-key but perfect to my ears. We spun, in our own world, oblivious to the pictures being snapped or the rest of our friends arriving. We danced until the song changed, and Krystal pulled me and Bella onto her bed for more pictures, and I knew without a doubt that Corey and I would face whatever happened next together. Always.

Chapter 27

Then

"Do you think he'll come home today?" Corey pulled another photo off the wall, tucking the tape around the corners.

I turned from the stack of clothes I was folding and shrugged. "I honestly don't even know if he knows I'm leaving."

After Mr. Johnson's conversation with my dad, things in the house had changed. He disappeared for days at a time. When he was home, he stayed in his room. One afternoon, he brought home a minifridge. After that, he didn't even have to go to the kitchen. We'd moved around each other in silence for months, but now we were tenants in separate apartments. He was still drinking—I knew by the trash bag full of cans he put out at least once a week and the smell that emanated from his bedroom door.

He must have ventured into the rest of the house on occasion—though never when I was there. There'd be milk in the fridge in the afternoon when I had finished the last of it that morning, or I'd find my laundry basket at the top of the basement stairs even though I'd left my clothes in the dryer, or a mug that had been missing would appear in the dish drain. On my birthday, there'd just been a stack of cash on the kitchen island. The imminent danger might have been gone, but the new arrangement was cruel, and every day that he avoided me turned the knife a little deeper.

"Anything else you need me to pack?"

The room that had been so full of life looked like a shell of itself. Tape stained the walls, and dust outlined where my belongings had been. The bed was still made, the furniture in place. I was taking only what was mine. The rest didn't matter.

I dropped the clothes into a suitcase. "I don't think so."

"What about this?" He held out a green hoodie with his last name and jersey number on the back and the Fairford mascot on the front. "I know you won't take my letterman jacket, so this is the next best thing. I slept with it for the last few weeks, so it's nice and smelly."

I hugged it to me. "Thank you. It's perfect."

"I'll wear it for you whenever we're together so it always smells like me."

I pulled him down onto the bed, our lips colliding. This was what it had been like between us for days. Denial and acceptance and crying and laughing and a blistering heat as we kissed our way through the pain. Our hands explored and our kisses grew deeper. Corey's shirt came off and then mine. He skimmed a hand down my chest and over my stomach, making me tremble. I fumbled with the button on his jeans, and our eyes met, wide and feverous and wanting. We'd agreed not to have sex for the first time with our emotions running so high from my departure. We had sound reasons—I was sure of it. But in the face of goodbye, I didn't care what those reasons were, and from the way he looked at me, Corey didn't either. I pressed my hand over his heart. We stared at each other, not moving, until Corey slanted his lips over mine. The world narrowed to the two of us and that moment. And then the front door slammed.

We jumped apart but then went still, listening. No second door closing. Corey pulled his shirt on and passed me mine. He fixed his jeans and stopped in front of my closed bedroom door. He flipped the lock, effectively trapping us inside.

"Let's just go," I said, zipping up my suitcase. Most of my stuff was already in Corey's car. I wasn't taking the car my dad had bought me, which was registered in his name. That would be too much of a connection. "He never wanted me here. It's not like he's going to stop me."

Corey crossed the room and picked up the suitcase by the handle. I slipped on my backpack and lifted the box with the last of my belongings. Together, we walked down the stairs. My dad sat at the dining room table. He didn't look over at our approach. He just sat there, staring out the front window. I watched him, but he didn't turn. I wondered what his eyes looked like—cloudy from a buzz, heavy-lidded from too many beers, or clear like the morning Mr. Johnson had come over. *How does he feel, knowing his last family member is walking out the door?* Probably, he was just happy to have his house back.

I nudged Corey forward and walked out of the house for the last time. He'd parked on the street as a precaution. The last thing we needed was to force a conversation with my dad if he blocked Corey in. We walked down the lawn to the car. I didn't want to look back, but as Corey rearranged the trunk, I turned and stared up at the house that had become a monster.

It stood as it had when I'd arrived—a perfectly manicured lawn, blooming flowerbeds, and two cars in the driveway. The house was unchanged, but I never would be the same again. I shifted my gaze to the dining room, where everything had changed. My father stood at the window, staring in our direction. I didn't meet his gaze.

"Ready?" Corey's shoulder grazed mine.

I mentally went through the list of my things. The only clothes I'd still had to pack had been those in the laundry. *Dammit.* I'd left a load in the dryer. Well, I wasn't going to get it now.

I shook my head. "I'll never be ready to leave you."

Our hearts were bound—of that there was no doubt—but the moment we pulled away from the house, the miles would stretch our bond to its limits. One hundred miles. One year. Separate lives. My chest constricted.

He grasped my hand. "We survived this whole year, Andi. We can handle a few hours between us."

He was right. Our love was strong enough to withstand the distance. But these weren't normal circumstances. And when the truth about my time in Fairford came out, I wasn't sure my mom would ever let me come back. Even if she did, how could I drive the now-familiar roads without remembering the anguish of this year?

He opened the passenger-side door, and I climbed in. His car had never felt so much like a prison. I glanced up at the house, but the curtain to the dining room window was drawn.

I took a deep breath. "Are your parents home?"

"Yeah, why?"

Because I wasn't ready to say goodbye to the love of my life. Not without cementing our connection. Not after we'd agreed to forget reason less than ten minutes ago. "Let's go to the Peak, then."

The tips of his ears reddened as the intention behind my words became clear. "It's daylight."

"Then that motel on the way to Robinson."

He eyed me skeptically. "You want our first time to be in a roadside motel?"

The first of what would be many tears spilled onto my cheeks. My wrist ached as it did lately whenever my emotions were high—a psychosomatic pain, Dr. Greenwald had told me. I buried my face in Corey's shoulder. He held me close, and his scent—deodorant and shampoo mixed with sweat—washed over me, bringing more tears.

"I just need more time with you."

"I'm staying with you for a week. We have more time."

"My mom is going to freak out when I tell her the truth." I had considered not telling her, but there was no way to explain no more weekend visits, never talking to my dad, or the lack of child-support checks without revealing the whole story.

"And I'll be there by your side when she does. And every day after that for the rest of our lives."

"Not every day."

He wiped the tears from my cheeks. "It's one year. We can get through one year. Then we'll leave on our graduation road trip and head right to whatever campus we chose. We'll be together, and none of this will matter."

I pressed my forehead to his. "I love you, Corey Johnson."

He kissed me, and it was desperate and messy and flavored by our tears. It was extraordinary and simple and perfect. It was everything. "I love you, Andi Scott."

Chapter 28

Now

I padded into the kitchen, a battered copy of *Wuthering Heights* I'd found on Nikki's bookcase tucked under my arm. It had always been my favorite. My stomach growled. After picking up a late breakfast at the coffee shop and clearing my inbox as best I could, I'd wasted the day away with Catherine and Heathcliff. Corey was due to pick me up in an hour for some surprise event, but my stomach wasn't going to wait that long. I turned toward the cabinets that used to house cereal, snacks, and assorted other food. My stomach growled again.

An unorganized collection of boxes waited behind the privacy of the cabinet door—Triscuits next to Golden Grahams next to Cheez-Its and Special K bars. The bowls were where they'd always been, in the wall cabinet to the left of the sink, near where I had found a party of tasty treats. I took out the Golden Grahams and poured them into a bowl until it was brimming. From one of the drawers in the breakfast nook, I pulled out a spoon.

Dinner of champions. I shoveled a handful of grahams into my mouth and then pulled open the fridge door in search of milk. Nothing on the main shelves, but yes, on the bottom shelf of the door was a quart of milk. Fingers crossed, I glanced at the expiration date—good until next week. The first spoonful of golden honey deliciousness awaited, and my stomach groaned in anticipation. I hopped up on the counter, bowl in hand.

Before I could scoop a spoonful, there was a knock at the door, and I heard it open.

"Andi?" Corey called from the foyer.

"In here!" I said, putting my cereal down on the counter.

A moment later, he appeared, an easy smile on his face. It was the most relaxed I'd seen him all week. My stomach fluttered and not from hunger. Each time I'd seen him, he'd been dressed for work or bed, but today, he looked like the boy I knew in jeans and a powder-blue Henley that complemented his eyes. Both items of clothing were way more fitted than anything he would have worn back then. And man, it worked for him.

I forced my eyes up to his. "Hi."

"You got my text, right?" He leaned casually against the wall across from me, his arms crossed. His eyes rolled over me, taking in my leggings and skimming over the lacy edge of my cami and the loose cardigan that hung off my shoulders. He bit at his bottom lip.

Somewhere between the bedhead and the honesty and his brazen invitation to go to the Peak, something had changed between us. We hadn't gone to the Peak—we hadn't been that tipsy. But the walls between us were falling, the awkwardness fading. When I'd gotten his text earlier, still in bed, I'd smiled like an idiot. And now I was ogling him. I hopped down from the counter, hoping he couldn't see the blush his once-over had caused and hadn't noticed that I'd given him one too—a twice-over, actually. That was how good he looked in those damned slim-cut jeans.

"Are you saying that whatever we're doing isn't leggings appropriate?"

He laughed. "I guess it could be if you want."

Damn. I'd thought for sure he'd let something slip about where we were going. I dumped my uneaten cereal into the trash. "Are we leaving now? I thought you said seven."

"If that's okay with you," he said, shoving his hands in his pockets, "I thought we'd make a pit stop."

A savory thought popped into my mind, one that sent a surprising ripple of desire through me. I pulled my cardigan tighter around me, realizing just how much skin this outfit showed. *Pit stop* had been code for "Let's go park and make out" when we were in high school. We'd made *a lot* of pit stops. The blush that crept up his cheek proved he'd realized his mistake too late.

"I just want to show you something," he amended, his eyes downcast.

"Sure." I reached out and touched his arm, hoping to stave off any further awkwardness. His bicep was solid beneath my hand. *Double damn.* "That sounds great."

I sized up his outfit. I had no idea what we were doing now or later, and my options were limited. But there was that blouse I'd packed in case Harry decided to whisk me away to Des Moines, and if I paired it with skinny jeans and my ballet flats, the colors would complement his outfit well. Not that color coordination was necessary.

"Give me ten minutes," I said, squeezing his arm before I turned toward the stairs. I stopped halfway there. "Hair up or down?"

His smiled. "Down. Always down."

COREY'S HANDS FUMBLED with the padlock on the stairway gates. I glanced around us nervously. We'd just broken into the high school. Well, technically, Corey—Coach Johnson—had used a key. The lock clicked free, and he shoved the ancient gate to the side, letting me slip past him. The unused stairwell led to the roof. Back in high school, the combination lock had been broken and hung so it looked secure. Many a skipped class had been spent up here. He pushed open the door to the roof. The sun had already started its descent, blanketing Fairford in pink and orange.

"Remember the night we got locked up here?" He stood at the edge of the roof, his hands folded behind his back.

I stepped up next to him, taking in the view of Fairford from three stories up. "You mean the night Dustin and Krystal trapped us up here?"

"What?" His whole face softened with laughter. "That was planned?"

I stared at him in shock. "You seriously didn't know? They wanted us to 'do it already,'" I said, affecting Dustin's deep voice.

"And they thought we'd do *that* on the roof of the high school?"

I half laughed, half coughed at the memory of that night—the Power Rangers comforter we'd hidden in a bin, the warm May breeze, Corey's hand on the zipper of my dress. "We almost did."

Redness seeped into his cheeks, and his eyes glistened. It was a good memory. And honestly, by the time they'd locked us up here, even I was surprised we hadn't done it already.

"Yes," he said, trying and failing to smother a grin. "Yes, we did."

I slapped at him playfully. "Stop remembering what we *did* do up here!"

His grin went wider, if that was even possible. "That poor Power Rangers comforter."

"Shut up!" I laughed, loud and long. It had been a long time since I'd laughed like that.

"That poor janitor."

"Oh my god." My cheeks went bright red. "Janitor Bob found us."

I'd forgotten how we'd been discovered a few hours later, missing key pieces of clothing and any dignity. Not that we cared about dignity in that moment. Corey had been far too pleased with himself.

"I promise that reliving that moment is not why I brought you up here," Corey said, sitting down on the edge of one of the heater units.

I sat down next to him, close enough that our knees banged together and I could rest my head on his shoulder if I wanted. Too big a part of me wanted to do just that. And something about his relaxed posture made me believe he'd allow it.

"Then why did you bring me here?"

"It's one of my favorite spots in town," he said, his lips quirking into a smile. "I come up here whenever I can use a time-out from everything. And I thought if anyone could use a time-out, it's you."

"Thank you," I said, inclining my head toward his.

He tucked a piece of hair behind my ear, his fingers lingering on my cheek. My breath caught until he dropped his hand. Even then, the memory of his touch lingered on my skin.

"You never told me yesterday," he said, clearing his throat and inching back, "what you imagined."

I shrugged. "I guess I didn't imagine it—not really. Thinking about you wasn't something—" *Crap.* There was honest, and then there was saying too much to the extremely hot former love of my life. "Well, I figured you were some big-shot architect in someplace like Chicago or San Francisco."

"Never in New York?"

I shook my head. "No, you always hated the city. Remember when we went there after prom?" I sat down next to him. "If I thought about it, I guess, Ryan was still a drunk, and maybe ten people would be at his funeral. Possibly, I'd get to see my sister, who would be there for the same reason I was—closure—but nothing else. I never thought he'd be the town hero."

Corey worried the hem of his shirt. "He's not, Andi. I know what it must look like—all those people at the funeral, the company, me and Krystal, but a lot of those people were employees. We closed for two days so everyone could come. Trust me, Ryan was not universally loved. He's been banned from S&R for eight years. They won't even deliver to Scott and Johnson. I mean, the rest of us still go there but not Ryan. Not once since I've known him." He cleared his throat. "Not once in the time that I knew him. There's a doctor in town who refused to see him."

Memories popped up—seeing Ryan arguing with the owner of S&R, Dr. Greenwald imploring me to call my mother—and I let them through. I was tired of hiding from that part of my life—of banishing anything Fairford because I'd pushed away the good with the bad. I'd lost people I loved and friendships that mattered. The memories hurt. They would always hurt. But this time, they were bearable.

"Fairford has a long memory," Corey continued. "You of all people know that."

"Yeah. The Cavanaugh Pond lady recognized me." I nudged him with my shoulder. "Felt the need to comment on my lack of a wedding ring and remind me of how you and I had spent an uncouth weekend there senior year."

He laughed halfheartedly. "That's Dolores. I learned the hard way not to take dates there."

My chest constricted. *Dates.* "Oh? Do tell."

I saw the tug-of-war behind his features and realized this might not be a story he wanted to share. "Well, basically, I was seeing someone I probably shouldn't have been seeing, and we went to Cavanaugh Pond one night. Dolores knew the both of us, and clearly, I wasn't Lauren's fiancé. I don't know what she said to Lauren, but she told her fiancé everything the next day. And I got a really nice black eye for Christmas. Not my best moment."

Corey didn't seem the affair type, but then again, neither had I. Sometimes these things happened, and the choices we made weren't always sound or honorable. Sometimes those mistakes needed to be made.

"So, where do you take your ladies now?" I asked with a grin.

"The rooftop of the high school, of course." He stood up and pulled me to my feet by both hands. "It's the best view in Fairford aside from the Peak."

I rolled my eyes, but he was right. Depending on where you stood, you could take in the bustle of Main Street, the woodlands to the west, or farmland for miles. It painted the whole picture, capturing all the intricate details of what made Fairford *Fairford*.

We stood side by side. Our shoulders touched, and our hands hung near each other. I wondered what would happen if I slipped my fingers between his. His finger twitched, and then his fingers slid between mine. Every inch of my body ignited. Every nerve focused on the way his fingers fit with mine. Corey and I had been bound together so young, and the tether between us was still there. It pulsed between our palms. I looked from our hands to his face and found him staring back at me. There was a question in his eyes that I desperately wanted to answer.

But then he stepped back, letting our hands fall. "Seriously, though, I don't really date much. It's difficult, between Emily and the company. I learned the hard way that it wasn't fun having to explain a black eye to a five-year-old."

I knew the feeling. Though Emma wasn't five, explaining to her why I couldn't bring my plus-one to her wedding had been the opposite of fun.

"Come on," I said, nudging him. "I bet you work that single-dad mojo."

He glanced down at his watch, and when he looked back up, his lips were pursed, his nose scrunched in chagrin. He sighed exaggeratedly. "We should probably go. Emily will be upset if we're late."

I rolled my eyes. "Please tell me that wasn't your mojo."

Chapter 29
Now

We drove through the upscale areas of Fairford. It was fancy, contemporary, and filled with mansions, many based on sketches I'd seen at Scott and Johnson. We'd rarely ventured to this side of town, and driving through it now, I couldn't quite believe it was still Fairford.

"Where are we going?" I asked after a few minutes of comfortable silence.

He'd been humming along with the radio—some pop song that hadn't been popular in years—but stopped and fixed me with a smile. "My house."

"Come again?"

"I said we're going to my house."

I stared at him incredulously, but his eyes remained on the road. "I wasn't aware you had a house."

We turned down another copycat street. The houses were nice, each one similar to the last but with one unique piece—a showcase window, a widow's walk, a wraparound porch.

"It's a new construction. Emily and I lived in those condos off Honeysuckle for a few years. We moved in with my parents when my mom was sick."

"Your mom was sick?" I pictured Maya from the day before. She'd lost weight, and her hair was shorter than before, but the change wasn't enough that I'd thought anything of it.

"Yeah, she had breast cancer."

"I'm sorry," I said, putting my hand over his on the gear shift. I waited for him to say something. My eyes focused on the air conditioning vents and the smudge near the handle of the glove compartment.

"Thanks. She's been in remission for a few months now, but at first, my dad needed the help, and our house was still under construction, so we moved back in. I thought we'd just stay in the basement again, but my parents had already refashioned it as part fitness center, part office, part crafting space. And Emily was used to having her own room, so we ended up upstairs."

We stopped in front of a large two-story house. It was stone-faced, with several windows at the front of the house. A chandelier was framed in a window on the second floor, highlighting the vaulted ceilings. And I just knew there was a grand staircase inside. It reminded me a little of Harry's house on Long Island.

"Wow. Corey, it's beautiful."

"Thanks. It was the last thing Ryan and I designed together."

He pulled in behind a few other cars in the driveway and then came around and opened my door, a gesture so foreign I stared at him for a second before getting out.

"When are you moving in?"

He pocketed his keys and guided me toward the house, his hand against my back. "This summer, after Emily's done with school."

The inside was just as spectacular as I'd imagined—grand staircase, office tucked into the front window with empty built-in bookcases lining the walls. Before I could investigate further, Corey motioned toward the back of the house.

Feet pounded down the stairs, and then Emily slammed into Corey. "Daddy! I missed you!" Before he could say anything, she'd released him and wrapped her arms around my waist. "Hi, Andi."

Shock coursed through me, but I hugged her back. She let go and grinned at the two of us before taking off again. A moment later, another set of footsteps sounded, and a girl with thick brown curls ran by. I recognized her as Krystal's daughter, Delia, from the picture at Krystal's desk.

"Slow it down, girls."

That voice. I hadn't heard that voice in a decade.

"Well, well, look at you two. Late as usual," Dustin said, crossing the room and pulling me into a hug. "Welcome back to town, Scott."

Dustin looked the same as always in jeans and a long-sleeved polo shirt. Only this time, the word Coach was stitched over the pocket. Nothing had made more sense than those five letters on Dustin's shirt.

"Hey, Dustin," I said, stepping out of his embrace. "Looking good."

"You know it."

I laughed. He was still too much. Corey and Dustin did that handshake, half-hug thing they'd always done, and we could have been right back in high school.

"Thanks for coming, man," Corey said.

"Of course. Anyway, Delia left Mr. Snuggles at my place, and you know how she is if she doesn't have that damn dragon. Be back in a few."

The front door closed behind him, and I turned to Corey, a smile on my face. "Dustin and Krystal really had a kid."

"They did."

I shook my head, disbelieving, even though I'd seen the photos. "So, you and Dustin coach the football team *together*?"

"We do. He's actually a teacher at the elementary school."

Dustin shaped young minds. In some crazy way, it made sense.

"So, who else is here?"

As if I'd summoned the other guests, a round of laughter sounded from the back of the house.

"Come on," Corey said.

In the living room, Krystal sat on a couch with a man who had to be her husband, Nelson, and Corey's parents. They waved a greeting. Opposite them, Nikki played a board game with Emily and Delia on the hardwood floor. Krystal's face twisted with laughter as she continued her story.

"And I walked into Ryan's office that first day. He was such a mess. His tie knotted, almost unrecoverable, his button-down shirt wrinkled, the ironing board just sitting in the middle of his office. You couldn't help but wonder how he'd ever gotten this far alone."

Corey grasped Krystal's shoulder in welcome. "He was nervous. We'd just launched our own firm with one and a half architects and a sassy assistant."

Moving us farther into the room, he motioned to two chairs next to the couch. I took the one closest to Krystal. He sat down next to me, his body turned toward mine, our knees bumping.

"Oh, I know." Krystal's eyes twinkled as she glanced over at us. "He had me go pick up that damn apple cider drink at Dorthea's three times that day."

Nikki groaned. "Oh god, don't mention the apple cider."

"Wait, wait." I looked between Krystal, Nikki, and Corey. "Explain."

"Ryan loved the stuff. I don't even know why he picked that, of all things," Corey said, his nose crinkling. "But whenever he was nervous or stressed or happy, he'd drink it. And then it became this thing. Dorthea's started carrying it year-round for him."

"He learned how to make his own at home." Nikki groaned again. "We'd go apple picking every fall, sometimes three or four times. The house reeked of apples half the time. I literally cannot eat apples anymore."

"That makes two of us," Krystal said with a laugh. "I knew it was going to be a bitch of a day if I smelled that stuff before noon."

And on they went. So many stories. Ryan trying to coach the youth baseball team that Scott and Johnson sponsored and handing over the reins to Dustin in the bottom of the first. Ryan's superstition about which tie he wore for certain clients and how Corey had bought out the store's supply so that his boss was never without it. Ryan embarrassing Nikki the first time she brought a boy over by making him fill out a questionnaire.

Each anecdote chipped away at the walls of my fortress. I'd spent a year locked inside my own head in a silent house, and the confident girl who'd walked through the door in June never came home. She'd put on a brave face and forced herself to concentrate on the things she could control, but the Ryan-shaped hole grew bigger. The edges had cauterized but never healed. But surrounded by the people my father had loved best—and some of the people I had loved best—I could feel those scars starting to fade.

Corey handed me a glass of wine and retook his seat. He slung his arm across the back of my chair. Between that and his knee, there had barely been a moment he hadn't been touching me in some way. Even passing the wine, our fingers brushed when they hadn't needed to. I glanced around the guests, but only Krystal seemed to notice, her eyebrow arching as her gaze met my mine.

"Andi?" Emily tugged on my arm. "Do you want to know my favorite Uncle Ryan story?"

"Yes!" My voice went high and excitable. I found I really wanted to know. This little girl had superpowers that seemed to work on anyone she came in contact with.

"Uncle Ryan and Daddy... they designed our new house."

"I know. Your daddy told me. It's beautiful."

She smiled, her eyes flitting to Corey and then back to me. Maybe Krystal wasn't the only one to notice Corey's attention. "Uncle Ryan let me design my new room. We spent the whole day together, went to Home Depot, picked out the colors, and then we looked through catalogues for furniture. He wrote it all down and gave it to my daddy. Uncle Ryan drew it and colored it and gave it to me. It's not ready yet, but it's going to be the *perfect* room."

She passed over a sheet of paper. It was the drawing, full of purple and blue and all things Emily. Ryan hadn't just drawn a room and colored it in. There was a whole reading nook, complete with a beanbag. Each book had a title on the spine. Lacrosse sticks were stuck in one corner of the room, and the exact shoes she was wearing were by the door.

"It really is perfect, Emily."

She took the paper back and hugged it to her chest. "Maybe you can come back and see it when it's done."

Corey and I exchanged a glance, and so many things he'd said to me over the last few days flashed through my mind. How he'd told me he couldn't just drop everything for me anymore. His confession about how hard it was to date. He hadn't just been talking about himself.

"Maybe I will."

She smiled. "One day, I'm going to take over the company."

"I'm sure you will." And I meant it. She might have had an absentee mother, but Emily had family—a big, messy, loving family. And Scott and Johnson was at its heart.

"All right, you," Paul said, coming up to us and placing his hands on Emily's shoulders. "Time to go home."

"You too, Delia," Krystal said from her position on the couch.

Paul and Nelson packed up the kids. Hugs were given all around. I took the opportunity to stretch my legs and give myself some space. I'd barely gotten across the room before Krystal pulled me down onto the couch with her.

She hugged me close, her head on my shoulder. "In case I haven't said it yet, welcome home."

Chapter 30

Then

My hand shook as I crossed another day off the calendar on my wall. The date had a giant red heart around it with the initials AS + JC inside it. Tears streamed down my cheeks as the black marker covered the heart. It had been one year since Corey had kissed me at the Robinson Diner and changed my whole life. It had also been twenty-two days since he'd spoken to me.

I didn't blame him. I was the one who'd skipped the kickoff dinner and then the first game of the season without warning or explanation. Senior dinner was another football tradition, held the night before the first game of every season. All the alums came, speeches were given, a team photo was taken, and a football was signed by all the seniors. Later that night, the freshmen would be tasked with stealing Mr. Langen's tractor. My mom, in a rare show of deference to my relationship, had told me I could skip my afternoon classes to go even though it was only the third day of school. She'd taken me dress shopping and talked to Corey's parents about me staying with them for the weekend. It was the first time she'd even considered letting me go to Fairford. All summer, Corey and Krystal had trekked to visit me without complaint.

But the pressure of going back there, to that life, had felt like a burden, not a gift. I'd spent my lunch hour huddled behind the back row of lockers in the girl's locker room, crying through a panic attack. So when the bell rang for seventh period, I'd gone to physics class and then calculus and then practice. I'd ignored all the calls from all my Fairford friends until finally sending a text to Corey saying that I wasn't coming when I realized he was about to leave the dinner and drive to my house.

The next night, after the team lost their first game of the season, Corey had called and ended things. Maybe he was happy I hadn't come. Maybe it had given him the out he'd been waiting for. There were so many uncomplicated girls in Fairford he could easily love.

My chest constricted, and I felt the beginnings of a now-familiar panic attack. My wrist ached, and my head throbbed. *No. Stop.* I breathed deeply and counted to ten. I pushed all thoughts of Corey away. I blasted music from my computer, the sound filling the heavy silence. Another big breath. *Okay. I'm okay.*

My bedroom door swung open, and Emma and half the volleyball team stumbled in. I wiped at my cheeks, but it was no use. Emma eyed me and the calendar behind my head and then pulled me into a hug. Three of my teammates sat down on my bed, and two more stayed stationed at the door.

"What's this?" I asked my assorted group of friends. It was weird seeing Emma and my teammates together. They normally didn't mix.

Emma's eyes drifted to the calendar again. "This is an intervention."

"Get up," Lila, team captain, said, pulling me to my feet. "We're going to Joe's party."

Joe. Great. Joe Kell was popular, and he'd had his eye on me since sophomore year. My year away had done little to squelch his interest. If anything, he'd been trying harder, even though I had the boyfriend of all boyfriends. Seeing Joe sounded like an awful idea. A wonderful, awful idea. My therapist had just told me that maybe I should look at my breakup with Corey as a way to rid myself of any remaining connections to Fairford—that without Corey tying me to the place, I might feel free.

Emma held up a Forever 21 bag. "We brought presents."

An hour later, dressed in the slinky tank top my friends had bought, with my hair straightened courtesy of Lila and shimmer lip gloss in place, I walked with them into the party. It was already in full swing, but it took less than twenty minutes for Joe to find me and hook an arm around my waist. I hadn't seen my friends since. Emma might have already left—this totally wasn't her scene.

Now, Joe and I were smushed together on a love seat in his basement with four other people. In front of us, a group played pool, and behind us, a beer-pong tournament raged. His arm rested along the back of the couch, his hand on my shoulder. I tried not to flinch at the touch. I didn't particularly like Joe. But I didn't need to like him.

"Do you want to go somewhere more private?" His face was so close to mine I felt his breath on my cheek. If I turned my head, we'd be kissing.

"Sure." I stood and pulled him to his feet.

His hand was warm in mine, but our fingers didn't fit. We walked up the stairs and out of the clatter of the party. His parents were out for the night, but most of the guests were in the basement—less evidence should his parents come home unexpectedly.

When we reached the quiet of the hallway, he leaned me back against the wall. His lips found mine, and there was no hesitation. His tongue invaded my mouth. His hands went to my hips, his fingers gliding along the bare skin at the hem of my shirt. I slid my hands under his shirt, splaying my fingers across his back. He moaned against my mouth and pushed himself closer to me. His leg slid between mine. My body lit up, missing being touched. I leaned into him, attempting to let the feeling consume me. But my heart recoiled, and images of Corey smiling, his eyes half-lidded—happy, serious, in love—flooded my memory.

My body went frigid under Joe's touch. I pulled back, letting my head smack against the wall. The pain washed away my idiocy. Joe was not Corey. No one was ever going to be Corey.

Joe stared at me, wild-eyed and confused. "Why are you crying?"

Crap. I could not be crying in front of Joe and half the kids at school. I pushed past him, my heart hammering in my chest, breaking again into a million little pieces. I'd been right—this awful idea *had* put things into perspective. I didn't want to be free.

COREY'S HOUSE WAS DARK by the time I reached Fairford. This was my second awful idea of the night, but at least I'd had two hours to sit with it. Two hours to go over the conversation in my mind endlessly. *He loves me. He loves me not.* I had to believe he loved me still. There was no way I could still love him this much, hurt this much, and he didn't feel it too. But if he didn't, how would I survive? My heart raced in my chest as I sent him another text he was bound to ignore. I picked up a handful of rocks from the garden below his window. The first one hit siding, the second one barely grazed the balcony, but the rest rattled against his window. My phone buzzed at the same time the light in his bedroom turned on: *Go to the front door.*

A few minutes later, the porch light turned on, and then the door opened. Corey stood there—the boy I loved and also not that boy. His sweatpants hung low on his hips, and he wore a zip-up hoodie over an old tee. It was the one he'd set aside for me to wear when I used to stay over. The shirt used to be too small on him. I stepped closer, examining his face. His eyes were heavy and shadowed, his jaw tense. This month had been as unkind to him as it had been to me.

I moved slowly up the porch steps. His eyes tracked my movement, but neither of us spoke. My very presence on his porch in Fairford in the middle of the night on our anniversary said everything that I could possibly say. In one more step, I'd be in front of him. I steadied myself and then took the final step.

Corey wrapped me in his arms, pulling me against him. His breathing hitched as we held the embrace. Tears streamed down my face, soaking his hoodie.

"You're really here," he said, stroking my hair and then caressing my cheek and trailing his hand down to my neck and collarbone as if he couldn't not touch me.

"Yes," I said, my eyes blurry with tears. "I'm so sorry."

He shook his head. "No, I'm sorry. I never should've—"

I kissed him then. I didn't need apologies—I needed him. Always.

He pulled away and tugged me toward his house, his eyes never leaving mine as we walked through the front door and the living room.

"Your parents?" I whispered as we walked up the stairs.

"Away, remember?"

Right. I'd known that—relished that fact—twenty-two days ago. A night alone with Corey in his house on our anniversary. There had certainly been plans. Plans I'd banished from my mind. A shiver ran through my body as he pushed open his bedroom door. It had been one hundred two days since I'd seen this room. It still felt like the safest place I'd ever known. And I still loved the boy who lived in it.

"You got a new comforter," I said, running my hand over the plush navy blanket.

My pulse pounded in my ears. We were alone in his house. We were together after nearly a month of silence and tears. There was so much to figure out, but none of it mattered. Not with Corey sitting next to me, staring into my eyes, drinking me in as if it had been a lifetime.

His lips pressed against my neck and worked the opposite trail that his hand had traveled minutes before on the porch. When his lips finally found mine, I fell into him. There was no breakup or complications or things to figure out. There was just me and Corey, as perfect as we'd always been. After a long while, Corey laid me back on the bed, our hands roaming and our kisses deepening until nothing remained between us.

And as our bodies connected in a new way, our hearts pounding parallel melodies, we found our way back to each other. We became more than we'd been. We became better. We became who we were always meant to be.

Chapter 31

Then

"**D**ude, this room." Krystal sank back into my bed, her eyes still scanning the space. "Oh my god, this mattress."

I laughed and shoved her over so there was room for me on the bed. "It's the same mattress from my old room, dork."

My mom, Sam, and I had moved into a three-bedroom house on the ritzy side of town a few weeks before. The move made sense when they explained it to me—Sam's house was old, and our house was small—but still, it seemed like overkill. Until you put it through the Ryan filter. My mom had already changed my phone number and our landline and had forced me to get a new email, as if my father had any interest in contacting me. But I'd gotten a bigger bedroom, and there was a guest room, which meant Krystal and Corey could come visit without having to sleep on the pull-out couch. Not that Krystal ever made it to the guest room. Each visit with her was an all-weekend slumber party. I would roll into school on Monday, barely conscious, still finishing my homework. But the exhaustion was always worth it.

"Really?" she asked, bouncing her butt up and down on the bed. "It feels softer. I mean, I can just melt into it."

"That's the comforter," I said, smoothing out the bedding set I'd picked out the weekend before. It was fluffy and warm, and you could get lost in it for days.

"Your stuff looks different in here," she said, sitting up and inspecting each piece of furniture as if it would suddenly become recognizable.

"Yeah, I was able to space stuff out more, and the built-ins really helped keep it open in here."

"Look at you, HGTV."

Sometimes I missed Krystal so much it hurt. I pulled her into a hug, a smile spreading across my face. "I'm so glad you're here."

The door swung open, and Corey walked in, his eyes zeroing in on us. Before we could pull apart, he jumped onto the bed and wrapped his arms around the two of us.

"What are you doing?" Krystal asked, untangling herself.

"I was feeling the love," he said.

"Well, keep your love over there." She pointed to the other side of the bed where I sat.

Corey scooted over until he was sitting so close to me the outlines of our bodies touched. I giggled and climbed onto his lap.

"So, what did your mom have to say about the ring?" Krystal asked, her eyes averted from our public display. She and Dustin had broken up around the same time Corey and I had gotten back together, and it was obvious she was still feeling the aftereffects. She barely looked at me and Corey half the time we were together now.

I glanced down at the silver infinity ring on my left ring finger. Corey had given it to me last weekend, when I'd been in town for the annual Fairford Classic that signaled the start of basketball season. My mom had noticed it immediately. She'd stopped midsentence and pulled my hand up to her face. After staring at it for too long, she must have accepted that it wasn't an engagement ring because she just smiled and told me it was beautiful before returning to our original conversation—which had been totally unlike her. But then, my mom had been totally unlike my mom since I'd come home from Fairford. It was as if she was afraid to say anything lest she break me—especially where Corey was concerned.

"Nothing really," I said with a shrug. "She had much more to say about my college application list."

The door opened again, this time unveiling Emma and Charlie with the pizzas. They sat on the floor opposite the bed. Corey, Krystal, and I relocated to the floor. Charlie threw open the first pizza box.

"You shouldn't have told your mom the plan." Krystal rolled her eyes. "No mom is going to just shrug and say, 'Yes, follow your high school boyfriend to college.' You know, because that always works so well. No offense."

"That list includes Brown and Dartmouth," I countered. I still didn't understand how any parent could be upset with a list of colleges that included two Ivy Leagues.

Corey and I had made the list together. Some were reaches, and some were safeties. Brown was my top choice. Corey was keeping his top choice close to his vest, but I knew that if I wasn't in the picture, it would easily be University of New Hampshire. He talked about their football program often and the allure of a big school where it was easy to get lost in the crowd. In between those schools was a carefully selected group of colleges that would give Corey and me everything we needed individually so that we could be together.

"And Corey and sex and no parental supervision," Emma added in her best parent voice.

I refrained from throwing a pillow at her only because I didn't want it stained with marinara sauce. The finger would have to do.

"What? You know that's all she heard."

"We literally had no parental supervision almost the entire first year of our relationship," I said brazenly.

I never talked about Fairford in that way, but my doctor had thought that perhaps it would help if I didn't give it more power than it already had. I didn't put much trust in most of the things Dr. Singh recommended, but I had to admit that the nightmares had gotten less frequent, and when they did come, they weren't as intense. Plates clattering could still send me into a panic attack if it was unexpected, and my mom had promptly sold the grandfather clock that Sam had brought from his house, but it was still progress.

"I don't think that'll help your argument," Charlie said, picking up a second slice. *Boys.* Corey was going on three. It was a good thing we'd gotten two pies.

"There's no argument," I said, giving Corey a kiss on the cheek. "We're going to college together."

He pulled me into him. "Hell yeah, we are, baby."

Slowly, the conversations turned toward other things. I watched my friends—all of them, from the various parts of my life—coming together. Corey and Charlie talked sports. Emma and Krystal debated whether the new *Twilight* movie we were all going to see that night would be better than the first and whether they were Team Edward or Team Jacob. Team Edward was the only right answer, though Krystal would never agree. The four of them had made it so easy. They'd embraced each other so that when the two sides of my life collided on weekends like this, I felt whole. There was no conflict or competition, no awkwardness over who was the best friend. There was just me and the four most important people in my life. I'd take the teasing from all sides if it could stay like this forever.

Chapter 32

Then

We are pleased to inform you that your application to Brown University has been accepted.

The words had been haunting me since they'd arrived six weeks ago—when they'd been paired with Corey's rejection letter. I'd held true to our plan—we were going to the University of New Hampshire together. There wouldn't be hundreds of miles between us or our parents' prying eyes. In a few short months, I'd be cheering on the Wildcats. Corey had a recruited walk-on spot—there was interest from the coach, and he had to try out for the team over the summer, but at least the coach knew his name. There were no guarantees, but Corey was good, and not just Fairford good. So, while we'd both gotten into other schools, I couldn't let him turn down the chance to see his dream through. But I couldn't bring myself to send in my admissions deposit either.

I stared at the acceptance form from Brown, which was due in a week. It was now or never. I could delete this email, shred the form, and forget all about Brown and its peaceful campus. I could embrace the idea of being a football player's girlfriend with the travel and the parties and the commitments. It wasn't the quiet life we'd planned for Brown. It wasn't a life I wanted, not really. But I'd promised him.

"Everything okay?" My mom stood in my doorway, her arms crossed. From the look on her face, she'd been watching me for a while.

"I'm just filling out my acceptance forms," I said, tucking the one for Brown under the one for UNH.

She stepped into the room and pulled the paper back out. Her mouth pinched in, and she squeezed my shoulder. When she spoke, her voice was soft. "No one would blame you for going to Brown."

A bitter laugh escaped my lips, one I wasn't sure I'd ever made before. "I'm pretty sure Corey would."

"He's asking a lot of you to give up Brown for him." She shifted her weight so that she sat on the edge of my desk, the form she'd picked up tucked under her hand.

This again. She hadn't said these exact words before, but we'd had variations of this conversation for the past few months.

"He isn't asking anything of me." Which was true. Corey hadn't asked me not to go to Brown—he just hadn't told me to go without him. He'd assumed I'd go with him. Because I'd promised him.

"Andi, you know—"

"I wouldn't have survived Fairford without him, Mom."

She blinked several times and then looked away from me. Every time I said "Fairford" or "Ryan," it was like a visible current ripped through her. This time, she composed herself quickly.

"I understand that. I do. And I like Corey. I will be forever grateful for what he did for you when I was away."

That, I knew, was only half the truth. My mom had accepted Corey as part of my life, but that didn't mean she wasn't pissed off at every single person who hadn't forced me to call her or found her on social media or done anything besides give me safe haven.

"But I don't want that year of your life to define you or mold your decisions." Her words were gaining traction, and I was terrified of what she was going to say. Because all I needed was permission, for one person to tell me it was more than okay to do what I'd been sitting here thinking about doing, and I might just do it. I hadn't even let Krystal or Emma get far enough into conversations to broach the topic. Case closed. UNH was my only option.

My mom sighed. "You can love Corey and still have your own dreams. Brown and UNH are only two hours apart. You both have cars. Would it really be so different from your relationship now?"

"I *promised* him."

She ran a hand over my hair, the motion comforting and familiar. I leaned into her, willing some of her strength and resolve into me. Whatever I decided, she'd support me—that much I knew, and part of me knew she was right even while the rest of me screamed that she was completely wrong. Loving Corey was not a byproduct of what had happened with Ryan—it was what had set me free.

Her finger brushed against the ring he'd given me. "I know, honey. But Corey loves you. If he can't forgive you this—did he offer to give up his team spot so you could go to Lehigh together instead?"

Lehigh was one of the other schools we'd both gotten into. It had been third on both our lists. I shook my head. We hadn't even talked about Lehigh.

"Did you ask him to?"

"No. Playing football at UNH is his dream."

"And Brown is yours."

I wanted to say it wasn't the same, but it was. The shape of the dream was different but not its heart. My face crumpled and tears threatened behind my eyelids. My whole body shook with the weight of this decision. But it wasn't even a decision. The moments I'd spent at Brown when we'd visited over the summer had been peaceful. I'd felt more at home there than I had in almost two years.

But what does it matter if Corey isn't with me? I looked down at the ring on my finger. Our relationship flashed by—moments big and small, quiet and loud. Forever and always. *Forever* could survive four years of college. *Always* would figure out a way for us both to live our dreams together. Corey would forgive me.

I picked up a pen and quickly filled out the form. I stuffed it an envelope and finished writing out the blank check my mom had given me for the deposit. My hands trembled as I handed it to her. "Mail this, please. *Now.*"

"You're sure?"

I nodded, afraid that if I spoke, only sobs would come out. Once she was out of the room, I picked up my phone and sent the text that would shatter everything: *I decided to go to Brown.*

"HI!" I JUMPED INTO Corey's arms before he'd even stepped into my house. It had been more than three weeks since I'd seen him in person, thanks to summer training at UNH. "Come on." I pulled him through the house and into my bedroom then shut and locked the door behind him.

"What are you doing?" he asked as I unbuckled his belt.

"Mom and Sam are gone for the whole day." I grinned.

My mom *never* left us alone in the house. Like ever. And now she was in the city for dinner and a play, and Corey was here after so long. I kissed him and let my hands caress the taut skin of his stomach. He groaned as my fingered dipped under the waistband of his boxers, and he brought his lips back to mine hungrily.

Corey hadn't been thrilled with my decision to go to Brown, but after a few tense days, he'd come around. We'd finished out the school year strong. We'd gone to two proms. Graduated. Spent a week in Wildwood with my mom and Sam. And then he'd gone to training camp. He'd spent the first few days texting me about all the ways he could sneak me into his dorm. And then practices picked up, and half the time we talked, he would fall asleep in the middle of our conversation. But as hard as it was being apart, it hadn't felt like the war we'd waged all year to be in each other's lives. Instead, it felt like the natural evolution of our relationship. We could make this work.

"Do you think you have a spot on the team?" I asked as I pulled his shirt over his head.

He shook his head. "I'll probably be on the scout team."

I knew what that meant—the practice squad. The guys who made the starting line better, who got the roster spot and the jersey but no playing time and no traveling.

"And you're okay with that?" I genuinely wasn't sure. Corey had been a starter in Fairford as a sophomore. It seemed a big step down, but he'd still have the chance to move up if he stood out.

"It's not like I have a choice in the matter," he said tersely.

I paused in my strategic removal of his clothing and really looked at him. He was the same Corey I'd said goodbye to three weeks earlier, but he was also bulky and muscular in places he'd once been soft. And how had I not noticed the desperate look in his eyes?

"What's going on?"

"Come with me, Andi," he said, his eyes pleading. "I don't want to be at school without you. I don't want two hours between us and distractions and temptations and one week turning into one month, and then it's Thanksgiving before I see you."

My heart skittered. *Temptations?* I could only imagine the doubts his teammates had planted in his mind and all the ways they'd tried to prove their point. I'd thought we could make it, but Corey had been questioning our ability to survive another separation.

"I'm literally leaving for Brown in the morning." I stepped back from him. Annoyance dripped from my words, but I couldn't rein it back in. He'd had two months to have this conversation. Two months during which I could have rescinded my acceptance and paid my mom back the deposit money. But I wasn't backing out now.

He tugged his shirt back on and buckled his belt. "So? *Fuck* Brown. I need you with me."

"What happened at camp?"

"Nothing happened except I missed you. I barely had the energy to talk to you, and that's going to be my whole semester. But if you're with me, I can bear it."

In another situation, his Hail Mary might have been romantic. But at this moment, it was cruel. "I can't, Corey."

His eyes bored into me, dark and desperate and resolute. "Then I can't be with you anymore."

Before I could even muster a response, he walked out of my bedroom, slamming the door behind him. The right thing to do was run after him. He couldn't mean it. He didn't drive four hours to break up with me in person. *Or did he?*

Bile rose in my throat. The room closed in. All the anger I'd felt at his request drained out of me, replaced by a hollow feeling I remembered from the last time he'd walked away. My hands shook as I stared around my empty bedroom, my eyes landing on the Brown pennant I'd left over my bed—further proof of my impending departure and awful betrayal.

I swiped at my eyes with a tissue and walked to the window. His car still sat in the driveway. I could fix this. I just had to walk down those stairs and come up with a Plan B. We could work this out. We could trudge through the semester until we found a better solution. Maybe I'd consider transferring in the spring. But I couldn't make more promises I might not be able to keep. That wouldn't fix what I had broken. I didn't move. This was it—the last thread tying me to Fairford. If I let it break, if Corey really walked away, I would shatter, and the pieces of me would never fit together again, not in the same way. But there'd be nothing tying me to Ryan. There'd be no chance encounters in Fairford. Maybe the panic attacks and nightmares would stop completely. I'd be broken but free.

I heard the front door slam, and then he was there, shoulders slumped as he walked to his car. He didn't look back. He just got in and drove away. Pain like I'd never known before rippled through my chest as my heart splintered. A sob broke free, guttural and raw, and I crumpled to the floor, drowning in my own tears. Corey was gone. And this time, he wasn't coming back.

Chapter 33
Now

Corey, Krystal, Dustin, and I lounged on the couches long after everyone else left, picking on leftovers and reminiscing about the year we'd been a unit. It was so *easy* with them, even with all that had happened and all that had kept us apart.

"So, settle a bet," Dustin said through a yawn.

"Dust!" Krystal chucked a pillow at him. "Don't you dare."

"Oh, come on. It was ages ago."

I looked from Corey to Dustin to Krystal—she had definitely been on the other end of the bet. "Go on."

"At prom, when you two disappeared, you were totally who the teachers caught f—"

"And we're done," Corey said, standing up.

I giggled. It had been ages since I thought about prom, particularly the Fairford prom. We *had* gotten caught making out in the girls' locker room, but we'd been clothed if a little disheveled.

"I should get going anyway. Delia has soccer at the butt crack of dawn tomorrow." Krystal turned to me. "Do you need a ride?"

"I've got it," Corey said too quickly.

Her gaze swung between the two of us, and I expected a smirk but instead found something like concern. "All right. Come on, Dust."

He nodded at the two of us. "Always a pleasure, Scott."

After they left, I helped Corey clean up. Downstairs, some of the rooms were furnished and others not. The living room, for instance, had couches and a coffee table but not much else. The dining room was empty. The kitchen was full of appliances but had mostly empty cabinets.

"Come on," he said, pulling me off the couch, which I'd returned to while he took out the trash. "Time to go home."

The idea didn't sound appealing. The evening had been perfect, and I didn't want it to end, especially considering that I had no idea what was going to happen the next day when the will was read. "Can't we just sleep here? There are beds, right?"

His eyes met mine, and I felt the crackle between us. "There's *a* bed."

"Fine," I said with a pout. "Take me back."

The drive across town was too fast, and when we pulled into the drive, I still wasn't ready for the night to end. All night, with Corey's hand on my back or his knee bumping mine, I'd felt like we were on the cusp of something. And then came my stupid request to sleep at his house. I needed to get out of the car before we couldn't go back.

I stared up at the dark house, my hands in my lap, willing myself to go inside. "Do you want to come in for a bit?"

He glanced at his phone and then turned off the car. "Sure."

We settled in the living room with glasses of water. Because, of course, there weren't nightcaps in this house. Surrounded by our friends, conversation had been easy, but alone in Ryan's house, words failed us. We sat both too close and too far away.

I sipped my water. "It's 11:11."

Though I'd stopped making wishes years before, there was still something enchanting about 11:11—a magic, a hope that maybe it was okay to believe in dreams.

Corey's eyes trailed over me, the corner of his mouth quirking up. "Make a wish." I shook my head. "Suit yourself." He closed his eyes, his face relaxing.

I watched him until he opened his eyes with a contented sigh. "What did you wish for?"

"If I tell you, then it won't come true." He snaked his arm along the back of the couch, like he had earlier. His fingers tangled my hair and drew a line across my shoulder—an answer in and of itself.

I inched closer. His fingers continued their path along my shoulder and neck. I shivered at the touch, desire rocketing through me. It would be so, so easy to tilt my head up and bring his lips to mine. My lower abdomen twisted with want.

I linked our fingers. "I had a great time tonight."

His expression softened, and he shifted so that we faced each other. "I'm glad."

He was so close I could smell his aftershave and the wine on his breath. "Can I ask you something?"

"Anything." His hand worked its way around my collarbone and up my neck and caressed my cheek.

I shuddered and leaned into his touch, craving more. I ran my hands up his chest, feeling the solid body beneath his shirt. I tilted my head, moving even closer. And then his lips crashed into mine. I let him in, taking everything he offered. And there was so much—want and desire and hurt and forgiveness and giving in and letting go. I pulled him closer, and the years separating us didn't matter. We were together now, and in his arms, I knew exactly who I was meant to be.

A loud buzzing sounded in the quiet of the house, and all at once, the world crashed back into focus. We pulled apart, our eyes meeting for barely a moment.

Holy shit.

On the table, my phone continued to buzz. A picture of Harry flashed on the screen. Corey snorted and then moved an entire cushion away from me. *Fuck my life.* I silenced the call and turned my phone off. I took a deep breath, but it did nothing to calm the pounding in my chest or the adrenaline coursing through my veins.

Corey had kissed me. And I had kissed him back.

Holy shit.

Next to me, Corey's breaths came fast, and he sat with his head in his hands, his fingers shaking. This would be fine. Totally fine.

I reached out and tentatively touched his arm. "Corey?"

He shook me off and stood, lacing his hands behind his neck. "This is such a disaster."

I moved toward him, but he stepped back. "It's okay, Corey."

"This is not okay!" He backed up a few more steps. "I have a daughter, and you have a boyfriend, and—fuck, I knew this was a bad idea."

His words rooted me in place, and my pulse quickened for a completely different reason than before. "That what was a bad idea?"

"All of it?" His expression was guarded, and something like panic flashed in his eyes. "But he was so confident you'd come. 'Corey, be nice to her. She's going to need you.'"

What? "So, you kissed me because my father asked you to?"

Corey's face, usually so gentle and calm, turned hard. "All these years, I understood why you cut him out, even after he wrote you letter after letter. I understood that what he did to you in that year was unforgivable. I mean, I lived it with you." His hands clenched into fists. "But you cut me out of your life like everyone else in this town. Like I was just some fucking guy who meant nothing to you. And I stood by you through everything. *Everything.*"

"Everything except Brown." I crossed the room until we stood face-to-face. His eyes bored into me, but he didn't get to put this on me. "You're the one who slept with me in October and then brought a girl home with you over Christmas break. You moved on long before I had even dried my tears."

Corey grasped the counter so hard his knuckles whitened. "Are you kidding me? You willingly went to a school two hours away from me when we agreed to be together." He gritted his teeth. "You left me on your porch with no explanation. You did this, Andi, not me."

Memories of that lost Christmas assailed me, and I forced them back. "I was going to transfer for you!"

"What?" He straightened and met my gaze head-on for the first time since the truth had come tumbling out of our mouths.

"I applied to UNH to be with you. I drove all the way to Fairford to surprise you with the news." I forced down the bile rising in my throat. "I pulled up near your house, and there you were with some big-breasted brunette wearing your letterman jacket." I sucked in a breath. "*My* letterman jacket."

His eyes widened, and recognition dawned on his face. "Big-breasted brunette? You mean Sharon?"

I gasped. I hadn't considered that the girl I'd seen that day in Fairford could be Emily's mother or even that they had known each other while Corey and I were still figuring out the status of our relationship. The decibel level and desperation in my voice rose with every word that passed through me. "The mother of your child? You dated her freshmen year?"

"No. We met freshmen year. We were *friends*. If I remember correctly, I gave her a ride home because she lived a few towns over, but when we got there, she didn't have her keys, and no one was home. And she wasn't wearing *my* letterman jacket. She was dating Joel at the time."

"Oh."

Something more eloquent would have quelled his anger better, but I had no words. The truth I'd held to so tightly was a fallacy. Seeing that girl had made my impossible choice easier. It was what had gotten me through the months that followed. And now not only was my belief shattered, but the girl had ended up giving him Emily.

"When Sharon left after Emily was born, I thought it was me," he said, his voice cracking. "I was the reason why you gave up on us and why Sharon didn't love me enough to stay."

I stopped pacing. We hadn't talked much about him and Sharon. We'd talked around her, but this was his truth. I gripped the television for support, not sure that my legs would hold me. "You were in love with her?"

Again, his stare, cold and unyielding, met mine. The synapses between thought and speech were failing. Things had spilled out of my mouth that I'd never had any intention of saying out loud to anyone, especially Corey.

"Why does that surprise you? You were engaged to another guy!" He gave me a cruel, wretched smile. "Did you really think I sat around for nine years, waiting for you to come back into my life?"

His words forced their way between the scar tissue surrounding my heart and split it open. The dull ache that always resided there burst into overwhelming heartbreak. This was the breakup we'd been waiting nine years to have. And there'd be no going back. Tears flooded my eyes. I wrapped my arms around myself, but it was useless. I was bleeding out.

"Get out."

Chapter 34
Now

Sunlight streamed in through the windows in Nikki's room. I rolled over with a groan. My whole body hurt, and my head pounded. *Damn this day.* The last thing I needed was a hangover—emotional or otherwise.

I sat up, rubbing my eyes. Across the room, the goldfish taunted me, and the dancing lollipops grinned in derision. I wanted to be anywhere but here. But I couldn't bring myself to leave. After kicking Corey out, I had cried myself senseless while packing my meager belongings. I'd gotten in the car. And then I'd carried it all back inside. Nikki didn't deserve me disappearing in the middle of the night. And I needed to see this through.

I flipped off the lollipops and headed to the bathroom. Downstairs, the coffeepot beeped its completion, and Emily's voice reached me. *Great, company.* I glanced at my watch. It was already after nine. *Stupid emotional hangover.* I padded downstairs.

Corey and Bethany sat in the dining room, speaking in hushed tones, their heads close together. Nikki was perched on the kitchen counter, eating a bowl of cereal, looking like a memory of me. The smell of coffee, rich and nutty, drew me fully into the kitchen. As I rounded the bend, I saw Emily in the living room watching cartoons. She waved and offered me a toothy smile.

"The lawyer will be here soon," Nikki said between spoonfuls of Golden Grahams. She picked up a cup of coffee and took a sip before handing me a mug. "You look like hell."

I took the cup. "Thanks."

I doctored my coffee and took a big sip, the caffeine calming my frazzled nerves. Whatever was about to happen, I had a feeling it was going to change my life. Across the way, Bethany and Corey had stopped talking. She stood at the front window, and he sat at the table, staring at his phone. The muscles in his jaw twitched, and too large a piece of me wanted to go to him, to wash away the harsh truths of the previous day. It didn't need to be like this between us—always so rife with angst. His eyes met mine for the quickest of moments, sadness flashing in them, before he turned back to his phone.

"Scoot over," I said, hopping up on the counter next to my sister.

She rolled her eyes and handed me the Golden Grahams. "Eat up, sis. You're gonna need it."

An hour later, the four of us were gathered around the dining room table. Bethany shuffled through papers, and Nikki stared at her phone. Corey had taken the seat next to me, but gone were the casual touches. Except for a terse "good morning" when he'd come to scoop up Emily from the living room, he'd hadn't acknowledged my presence. Which was perfectly fine. My stomach roiled every time I thought about everything we'd said and that stupid kiss and his hands warm on my skin and his lips—I inwardly groaned and forced my thoughts back to the present. I was mad at him. Furious. I had a boyfriend. *And yet you kissed him back.*

The lawyer cleared his throat. I had never been so happy to be pulled away from my own traitorous thoughts.

"Now, this is more a formality than anything else, but as the will had certain suppositions in it, I thought it important for us all to gather today and execute Ryan's will as he wanted it done." The lawyer flipped a few pages and then trailed his finger down one and stopped about halfway. "If you will all open to page four, paragraph three, we can discuss the division of assets."

I hadn't taken much time to look at the document, though it had been sitting in front of me for ten minutes. Emily had caught my attention since she'd ambled into the dining room from the backyard. She was sitting in the corner, nudged up against the grandfather clock, reading a book, a doll tucked under her arm. Even with the confusion of the adults around her, Emily seemed at peace, lost in her own world, unaware of the troubles that were unfolding in front of her.

"Since Andrea is here"—he motioned toward me, and I felt my hand start to rise and willed it back onto the table—"the total property of 19 Washington Road will be transferred from Ryan Scott to Andrea Scott. The ownership of the cabin in Hudson, New York, will be transferred to Bethany Scott. The rest of the estate shall be split equally between Bethany Scott, Andrea Scott, and Nicole Scott."

The lawyer was still talking, but his words passed over me. *The house?* I stood up abruptly. Four heads turned, and even Emily looked up from her book.

"Excuse me." I walked out of the room at as normal a pace as I could muster and then leaned against the door for support. Ryan had bequeathed me the house. A tirade of obscenities ricocheted around my mind, and I doubled over as a wave of nausea hit me. This couldn't be real.

"What are you doing?" Corey hissed.

I breathed in a few times and then straightened. His eyes were harsh. All the compassion and understanding of the last few days was gone. Corey wasn't acting anymore. Not for my benefit.

Anger bubbled in my chest. "The fucking house?"

Corey's eyes flickered to the dining room, and then he motioned to the door. I stepped outside, and he pushed past me down the stairs. In the front yard, he whirled on me. "What is wrong with you?"

"*Me?*"

I glanced back at the house, but the windows in the dining room were sealed. They wouldn't be able to hear us. A breeze shook the trees on the far end of the yard, and I tucked my hands into the pocket of my favorite hoodie. Brown University was embroidered across the chest in big letters—a silent *screw you* to Corey. A shiver struck me in the cool morning.

"Yes, you." He looked skyward before settling his gaze back on me. "Do you think this is easy on any of us? On Nikki?"

Nikki's words from that morning came back to me: "You're going to need it."

Corey wasn't the only one who knew *why* I had to be here for the will. He was just the one tasked with making sure I did so. "You all knew this was in the will."

Corey took a step toward me, and his voice softened a fraction. "Ryan discussed it with us, yes."

I looked away from him, trying to get my emotions under control. Anger was mixing with betrayal and despair, and god, I felt like such an idiot. For staying, for caring, for thinking this trip could be more than it was. I pressed my palms to my eyes, stopping the tears. Question after question tumbled through my mind, but all of them ended in the same place: *Why?*

"Why would I want this house?" I asked, turning back to Corey. "Why would I want anything from him ever? In ten years, I have not asked for one thing." My voice rose with each sentence. I took a breath. *Stop.* It had to stop.

Corey grimaced. "It was his way of—"

"And you! What the fuck, Corey? You trick me into staying here, make me think you still—" The words got stuck in my throat. "You *kissed* me."

"I wasn't the only one on that couch last night."

"No, you weren't." I shook my head. "But I was there because I wanted to be there. Because I thought..." The anger from yesterday slammed back into me. "How could you spend three days with me, acting like that, and not mean it? And don't tell me it's what Ryan wanted. No one is that dedicated to a person. No one."

Hurt flashed across his features, and he ran a hand through his hair. I took in his appearance for the first time all morning. There were bags under his eyes, and their normal blue looked stormy. Small creases crossed his forehead, and his hair was a mess.

"Do you really hate me that much?" I asked, my voice cracking.

"You think I hate you? God, you haven't changed. Not one bit. Everything is always about you. You had to stay in Fairford even though we *easily* could've called your mom. You *had* to go to Brown. You had to cut everything Fairford from your life." His chest heaved, and his hands were white-knuckled at his sides. "Did you ever stop to think about what any of that did to *me*? Or Krystal? Or my mom and dad? Did you even consider what not answering his letters would do to him or Nikki?"

His words stirred an already kindled fire. I hadn't done anything wrong. All I had done was protect myself from pain, hurt, and heart-break—from this horrible feeling of inadequacy.

"There weren't *letters*!" I screeched. "He lied to you. I got one stupid letter. Real effort on his part."

He shook his head. "Do you even hear yourself? Who do you think *mailed* the letters to your mom's house? Me. Every fucking year. I watched him die, carrying the weight of your silence."

Doubt sliced through me, but I shoved it away. "Fuck you, Corey. You can all keep living in your little bubble of Ryan Scott lies, but I'm done."

I turned, ran up the porch steps, and slammed the door behind me. Inside, Emily stood in the dining room door, biting her thumbnail, her eyes focused on her shoes. My heart lurched at the sight, but I couldn't stop. I ran up the stairs two at a time, something that had once been as natural to me in this house as breathing. I grabbed my bag from the end of the bed and my purse from its perch on Nikki's desk chair and then ran back down the steps.

I was halfway to the door when Corey grabbed my arm. "Andi, wait."

I pulled my arm free and shot out the door, not stopping until I reached my car. Footsteps sounded behind me, and I froze with my hand on the door.

"Please don't leave," Nikki pleaded. "*I* want you here."

A sob clawed its way up my throat, but I swallowed it down. How many different ways could my heart shatter? I turned to face my sister. Her face was a picture of sadness and desperation. I wanted to cast it away, but instead, I memorized it. *My sister.*

"I can't stay. But you have all my information if you want to see me again." I placed a hand on each of her shoulders and stared into her eyes until I knew she would hear me. "I will answer you, Nikki. I promise."

Chapter 35

Then

"Heading to the caf. You want in?" my roommate Kelsey asked, leaning against the doorjamb, her hair still wet from the shower.

I glanced at the clock—it was nearly eleven. I'd woken up from a nightmare at five. The nightmares had returned full force after Corey broke up with me. I had a few recurring nightmares, but this one was always the worst: I sat on a pile of glass shards, blood dripping down my arms and over my fingers as I silently cried. Figures I couldn't make out but who I knew were there watched from the darkness. The silence weighed down the dream, the pressure so great I couldn't even move from the shards or stop the bleeding. Usually, this was when my father would step from the darkness, a sneer on his face, and watch until the me in the dream fell to the ground, waking real me up. But in the latest variation, Corey had stood there. Since there was no way to go back to sleep after *that*, I'd been working on a paper for several hours. All I'd had to eat was a granola bar and some boxed iced coffee. Real coffee and a waffle sounded amazing. My stomach grumbled in agreement.

"I think your stomach just said yes for you." Kelsey tied her hair back into a ponytail.

"Can I meet you there?" I asked, realizing I was still in my pajamas and unshowered, and five-hour-old bedhead wasn't a good look on anyone.

"Sure"—she pulled a winter hat down over her wet hair—"but hurry, or you'll miss Steve."

Steve was the hot junior who worked the early shift at the cafeteria every weekend. We'd been ogling him for weeks, and he ogled us right back, though he mostly had eyes for Kelsey.

I'd just returned from the showers when my cell phone rang, rattling against my desk noisily. It hadn't even been ten minutes—Kelsey could be so impatient. I picked up the phone, ready to make a sassy retort, and froze. The number flashing across my screen was one I knew well. I couldn't forget that number if I tried. *Corey*.

"Hello?" I asked, full of trepidation.

"Hi," Corey said, his voice both familiar and foreign. "It's Corey."

Something about the tone let me know that this wasn't a friendly call. I refrained from mentioning that I recognized both his voice and his number and instead focused on the reasons he could be calling me. It wasn't an anniversary, nothing had seemed abnormal on any of my Fairford friends' social media, his football team wasn't going to be in the area. Corey had unfriended me and blocked me online. But in a moment of weakness, I had googled the UNH football schedule, even though I didn't know if he'd earned a spot on the team. After only two months, Corey might as well have been a stranger.

"Is everything okay?" I asked for lack of anything else to say.

"Dustin was in a car accident."

I sat down, worry flooding me but also dread. I could feel Corey working his way back into my system like a drug I'd missed, and he'd only said nine words. "Is he okay?"

"He will be, but he shattered his arm."

"His throwing arm?" I asked, my voice rising.

"Yes."

Dustin wasn't at a Division 1 school like Corey, but unlike Corey, he was a starter at a smaller school. This was career ending and life altering. "Holy shit."

My thoughts swung to Krystal. She and Dustin had been teetering on the edge of reconciliation since they'd gone to prom together. When we'd talked two weeks earlier, it had seemed they were almost there. But she hadn't told me about the accident.

"Does Krystal know?"

"Yeah, she's with him. And I came home to see him as soon as I heard," he said. I wondered what his coaches had thought of that. "Do you think I could stop and see you on my way back?"

I almost said no. It was a bad idea. I felt it in every part of my body. But like an addict, I couldn't pass up a fix. "Okay."

He coughed, and I wondered if he was covering his surprise. Maybe he'd expected me to say no. Maybe I should have. He hadn't exactly been a glowing example of a boyfriend the last time we'd spoken. Not that I'd been the best girlfriend those last few months either. We made so many mistakes and too many promises that had been impossible to keep.

"When will you be here?" I asked, angling my phone between my shoulder and my ear.

"Now."

"Now?" I stared down at my clothes. Perfect clothes for a late-morning breakfast—leggings, Brown T-shirt—but completely imperfect for seeing my ex-boyfriend for the first time in months. Not to mention that my hair was currently dripping cold water down my back.

"Jameson-Mead, right?"

I stood and looked out my window as if I'd be able to see him standing in the quad. *What is he doing here? What does this even mean?* My heart sped up. *What do I want it to mean?* I pulled my hair back into a clip and slipped into my sneakers. What did it matter what it meant—Corey was outside my dorm.

I took the stairs two at a time and skidded to a halt as soon as I was outside the main doors. My eyes landed on him immediately. He stood out in his blue-and-white hoodie among a sea of brown and red and white—it was a game day after all.

"Hi," I said, stopping in front of him.

His eyes met mine, and the smallest of smiles formed on his face. "Hi."

Chapter 36

Then

I sped past the car on my right as Route 17 opened in front of me. The sky looked ominous, and snow was in the air, but the news had promised that more wouldn't fall. I reached across the car, my fingers finding the printout I'd put there.

Congratulation, your transfer application to the University of New Hampshire has been accepted.

I would make it to Fairford. I had to.

An image of Corey's face popped into my mind. His hair mussed, his eyes bright, his lips skimming across my shoulder. It had been two months since he'd shown up at my dorm. Two months since our hearts had collided again. Two weeks after that, I'd applied for a transfer. And today, I'd been accepted. My mom hadn't known I applied. She didn't even know Corey and I were talking again. But when I squealed in excited and then sprinted out of the house, calling out that I was going to Fairford, she caught on pretty quickly. She'd rolled her eyes and handed me the keys to her car—which had better traction control—telling me to drive safely.

Corey and I were not back together, a fact that Emma reminded me of daily. But we'd talked nearly every day since that weekend, and though he hadn't come home for Thanksgiving because of football, he'd asked to come see me over Christmas break. And last night, he'd texted, *Good night, babe.* With a kiss emoticon. That had to count for something.

The track turned to my favorite Jimmy Eat World song. I swiveled the volume to blasting. The door panels shook. I laughed, giddy with excitement, drumming my fingers against the steering wheel. Fifteen miles to Fairford—fifteen miles to forever.

Not surprisingly, Liberty Road was crowded. Several of our classmates lived there, and everyone seemed to be home from school. Brian was unpacking boxes from his truck. Ann carried only a duffle bag as she climbed the front steps to her house. I parked just short of Corey's driveway. He was on his way home from New Hampshire, but I hadn't thought to see where he was in his trip when I left. But his car was in the drive. I breathed a sigh of relief and hugged the printout to my chest. Then he was there, backing away from someone, his hands held up in surrender. His face was crinkled in laughter. He wore his University of New Hampshire football jacket, a matching hat pulled down over his ears. He threw a snowball and then turned to run. It had to be Dustin, who was well on his way to recovery, according to both Krystal and Corey. Whether he would ever play again was still up in the air.

I checked my appearance in the visor mirror and applied a fresh coat of lip gloss and was ready to leave the car when a high-pitched laugh stilled my hand on the door handle. I whipped my head back to Corey, spying a pretty brunette wearing a Fairford letterman jacket. My eyes flittered to the WR on the sleeve. *Corey's* letterman jacket. She clung to Corey's back, smashing a snowball into his hair. He swung her off him and pummeled her with snowballs. She ran back toward his house. He followed, only stopping to pick up more snow.

This wasn't happening. There had to be a logical explanation. Steve often gave me piggyback rides across campus—it didn't *mean* anything. Yet I couldn't get out of the car.

Krystal would know. She always knew everything. And I owed her a visit. I hadn't seen her since before I left for Brown.

U in town? I texted her. Corey hadn't reemerged from the yard, but I could still hear that girl's squeals. His name in her mouth made me want to throw up.

R U!?

Meet u at library in 5, I typed back before finally pulling away from Corey's house. I didn't look back or check my mirror or anything. If I didn't see anything, there was still a chance that it was all completely innocent.

Krystal was already sitting on the library steps by the time I pulled up. She had two S&R hot chocolates with her. As she handed me one, the sun glinted off her hand. *No way.*

"You and Dustin got engaged!"

She blushed. "Two days ago."

"Oh my god!" I squealed, enveloping her in a hug. "Congratulations!"

"Thanks," she said, adjusting the small solitaire diamond. "I know it's fast, but when you know, you know, right?"

I tried to nod encouragingly. I was happy for them. Really. But Dustin had just gone through a huge trauma. As long as they'd been together, Krystal and Dustin had never seemed like they were on the marriage track. They loved each other, they had fun together, but Krystal hadn't once mentioned getting married. Even Corey and I, at our best, had never talked about that, and we'd been all in on forever from the start.

I studied Krystal. *She can't be...*

Krystal's eyes narrowed as she took my expression. "I'm not pregnant. Quit looking at my stomach."

I half laughed. "When's the big day?" I asked, sitting down next to her.

She started to rattle off dates in the fall—at least they were waiting a little while. I tried to listen, but all I could picture was that girl, her long hair falling across Corey's chest, her lips on his, his hand coming up to cup her face. *Shit.* I looked away from Krystal, into the sun, hoping to blind my mind of these fallacies. I choked on my hot chocolate at the sight in front of me. Ryan stood outside S&R Deli. He was arguing with the owner over something. He stumbled back onto the street.

The town dropped away from me. I hadn't seen him in eighteen months. When I did go to Fairford, it was to Corey's or Krystal's or the high school hangouts. We avoided spending time in town. And being away from him—from all of it—at Brown had helped. But I'd come to his territory. Willingly. Stale beer filled my nostrils. It wasn't possible. He was three stores away. The familiar ache that had vanished in the past year set up residence in my wrist. Fingers tightened on my forearm. I startled, pulling my arm free, forgetting that it was Krystal next to me and that I wasn't standing in his living room.

"Andi?" she said loudly, most likely not for the first time. She placed her hand back on my arm tentatively.

I watched Ryan's head turn toward us at my name. Our eyes met. This wasn't happening. "I'm sorry." I hurried down the steps. "Krystal, I have to go."

She watched me, looking from me to my father. Her face twisted in a frown. I saw her reach for her phone and knew she was going to text Corey. I was going to tell her to stop, but then Ryan started toward us. Then he was at the stationery store, only feet away from me, clearly drunk. Maybe drunker than I'd ever seen him. From where I sat, I could smell him and see his bloodshot eyes. Coldness leached onto me, an all too familiar foe.

He gave me a crooked smile. "Hello, my darling daughter."

Without a word to either of them, I sprinted to the safety of my car and locked the door. Krystal stood there, her mouth agape. I watched her type frantically into her phone. I pulled into traffic, keeping an eye on Ryan as much as possible. But he'd already returned to his argument at S&R.

By the time I got back, my mom and Sam were home from work. Through the front window, I watched Sam chop vegetables at the island. Sam, who had walked into a family rife with baggage without a second thought. Who only ever argued with my mother over me and what they referred to as my "condition." I knew what I had to do. That couldn't happen again. I'd successfully escaped Fairford and Ryan. I couldn't go back. With a last look at the acceptance letter, I dumped it into the recycling bin.

My mom stood in the doorway. "I didn't expect you home tonight."

"Mom, please, okay?" I said, walking up our porch steps, keeping my head down so she wouldn't see my splotchy cheeks. "I'm not going to transfer. It was a stupid idea."

"He doesn't want you to transfer?" she asked, sounding surprised.

"I didn't tell him." I walked past her into the house, but she stopped me with a hand on my shoulder.

"What happened?" she asked, her eyes clouded with concern.

"Nothing happened," I said, attempting to hold her gaze and failing. "Dr. Singh is right. It's better to look forward than to dwell on the past."

"Andi?"

We both looked up at Corey's voice. It sounded raspy, as if he had a cold, and more than apprehensive. *Does he know I saw him and his girlfriend?* I'd convinced myself on the two-hour drive that that was who she was. It was easier than facing what I had to do.

"I'm going to go help Sam with dinner," my mom said, backing out of the doorway.

"Why were you in Fairford? I thought I was going to meet you here next week." His eyes traveled over me. "Are you okay?"

I stepped back outside, closing the front door. He looked scared, his blue eyes paler than normal despite the rosiness of his cheeks. I longed to go to him, but where had his lips and his hands been before Krystal's text? *Except he must have dropped everything to get here so quickly.* I pushed that thought away. "It doesn't matter."

"Andi, what happened?" He reached for me, but I backed away from him.

"Let's not do this."

He pulled a face. "Do what?"

I motioned between the two of us. "This. Us. That weekend was..." *Everything. Perfect.* "A mistake."

"Don't say that. You don't mean it."

I *had* to mean it. "I'm at Brown. You're at UNH. And that's not going to change anytime soon, and you made it perfectly clear in August that you didn't want a long-distance girlfriend. That you couldn't handle the temptations that came along with it. And you're an athlete. I'm sure there are plenty of girls trying to get in your bed."

He wrapped his hand around mine, and I'd never been so glad to be wearing gloves. His touch would have undone me. "I don't want plenty of girls. I want you. I love you."

No, no, no. I forced myself to recall images of Ryan, both from reality and from my nightmares. Bloodshot eyes flashed into my mind. The smell of stale beer, only a memory, crippled my stomach.

"I can't go back. I thought I could, but I can't." Maneuvering my hand from his, I stepped away and opened the door to my house. My heart raced, and my head pounded. I shoved my hands into my pockets so he wouldn't see them shake. In another moment, I would break. "You should go."

I turned on my heel, closing the door behind me. I took the stairs two at a time until I was safely in my room. He didn't follow. This time, I wouldn't watch him leave. I sat on my bed, still in my coat and gloves, my back to the window, until I heard his car start and his tires squeal on the slick pavement. Only when the last sounds of his car faded away did I let myself cry.

Chapter 37

Now

"**M**om?"

When I'd left Fairford, I had intended to go straight to my apartment and drown my sorrows in cheesy teen soap operas and ice cream, even though it meant finding street parking on a Saturday in Williamsburg. But with Corey's words still rattling around my mind when I reached the exit that would take me to my mom's, I'd changed my mind. I needed to find out why my mom would have given me one letter and kept the others from me.

"Mom?" I called again even though I knew she'd taken to going into the office on Saturdays.

I flipped on the hall light and basked in the comforting smells of this house—Downy and sugar cookies and vanilla coffee. These four walls had only been ours for one year before I went to college, but still, the place smelled like a lifetime of Mom. I walked up the stairs, not sure what my plan was. I couldn't tear apart her house, looking for letters that might no longer exist. At least not inconspicuously.

On the landing, I glanced at the door to what had been my room and still held a good many relics from my younger life. Then I turned toward her office. She loved that office and spent more time there then anywhere in the house. I crossed the short distance and entered the room, its familiar decor covering me like a warm blanket.

At her desk, I wriggled the mouse to wake up her computer and typed in her totally hackable password—Sam0711. You could tell my mom's mindset by what picture she had on her backdrop. The last few times I'd been in here, it had been Sam. But today, a little girl with dirty-blond pigtails and bangs running into her hazel eyes greeted me. My left arm was in a sling, but I was dressed in a soccer uniform. I was eight. I'd broken my arm that summer on a Sunday with Ryan. My mom had forbidden him to see me for weeks after that. It was a strange picture for her to have up on her computer. *What is she trying to remember?*

My fingers hovered over the keyboard, itching to let out my racing thoughts. I let the picture rest and opened Word. The morning's events—the will, the company, Corey, the letters—were all tangled in my mind. I stared at the blinking cursor, willing the knots to come apart. My muse had deserted me long ago, but now words spilled from me and sprinkled the page. When I looked up again, three pages had been filled, and the room seemed out of focus.

I pushed back from the desk, letting my gaze wander across the space. There were more words in me—I could feel them under the surface, itching to get out. I blinked, trying to get my eyes to readjust, and my gaze fell on the mail tucked into the letter holder. I knew that handwriting. Where did you hide letters you wanted to keep secret? In plain sight, apparently. I picked up the envelope with shaking hands.

Andi Scott was written in a cursive I remembered from child-support checks. But the address was in Corey's familiar scrawl. Just like he'd said. *Fuck.* I ran my thumb over the return address, one I wouldn't have recognized until this week. The postmark was just over two weeks old—only days before Ryan had died. I could picture Corey sitting at that giant desk, writing my last known address on a final letter he knew would go unanswered. Like all the ones before it.

I flipped the envelope over, my hands shaking. It was open. The steady, measured tock of the seconds from my watch was the only proof that time was still moving. I pulled out the folded sheet of legal-pad paper. It felt cruelly short, but after seven years of unanswered attempts, maybe there wasn't much left to say. I unfolded it, flattening the paper against the desk. My father's handwriting littered the page in front of me.

Dearest Andi,

I have hoped for your response for many years, but none ever came. Did you get any of my letters? Did you know I wanted to see you? That I love you? That I'm a changed man? When I last saw your mother, she said you were better off without me in your life. Maybe she was right.

My vision blurred. *Saw.*

The last time he *saw* my mother.

She'd more than known all this time.

An out-of-place creaking floorboard drew my eyes away from the letter to my mother standing in the door. Her eyes were wide with a mix of shock, sadness, and regret. Without a flinch or a hesitation, I met her gaze. "When's the last time you saw Dad?"

Her expression hardened. "You spend five days in Fairford, and he's *Dad* again?"

I held the letter out in front of me and read, "When I last saw your mother, she said you were better off without me in your life."

"He came to my office just after you went back to Brown for the spring semester your freshman year," she said, her voice resigned.

Before he'd been clean. Because he'd seen me with Krystal that day. "Was he sober?"

"No, he wasn't." Her gaze, as it swept over me, felt heavy. "Sam almost got arrested that night, and you were already such a mess after breaking up with Corey. It just wasn't something you needed to know."

That sounded like the truth. I'd barely gotten out of bed that whole break. My mom and Sam almost hadn't let me go back to school. Knowing that my father was trying to reach me outside the confines of Fairford would have been catastrophic for my mental health.

"And the letters?"

She crossed her arms. "The first one came about a year later to my office, and I just couldn't, Andi. You were finally smiling again. And then another one came to my office a year after that. The third one came to the house."

"The one you told me about."

She nodded. "Yes."

"Did you read any of them?"

"I read the first two that were sent to *me*. But I didn't read the others." She crossed the room, took the letter out of my hand, and folded it back along its crease. "Until this one. And I read this one too late to do anything about it."

My whole world felt like it was shifting. I had told Corey it would have mattered if I'd received more than one letter. But I hadn't really believed they existed or that my mom would actively keep me in the dark. "When you gave me that third letter, you didn't think to tell me he was sober?"

She tucked the letter back into its envelope but kept her hold on it. "It wasn't the first time he'd tried to get sober, honey. Remember when you didn't see him after he dislocated your elbow? He'd gone to rehab before. He always relapsed eventually."

I thought of all the times throughout my life I'd gone weeks and months without seeing him, thinking my mom was angry with him or he didn't love me or some combination of the two. I'd never suspected his absences had nothing to do with me.

"Then why did you ever let me move up there in the first place?" I asked incredulously.

"He had been doing so well, at least I thought. He married Bethany. They had Nikki. And then when they built that house, you *loved* weekends there. Before your first overnight at the house,

I made him come see me, and he was so clearheaded, going on and on about 'his girls' and the house. I'd never seen him so excited. I thought he'd finally found a reason to stay sober.'"

I couldn't picture my parents in the same room. I'd always thought it only ever happened on other sides of doorways or in tense situations. But they'd been talking to each other my whole life. Otherwise, after that first dislocated elbow, I never would have seen him again. He must have done *something* to convince her to let me back into his life every time.

"After you told me Bethany left, I almost forced you to come to Paris. But you never said anything. You didn't even hint at anything. Our phone calls were filled with laughter and stories about your friends and Corey." She looked heavenward. "That should've been my first clue, but I chalked the intensity of your relationship up to first love."

Everything tracked. I could see how this new truth fit into the outline of my life as I knew it. It seeped into the holes, explaining the absences and the silence and so much more. But broken or not, I hadn't been a child when those later letters had come.

I stood up, bracing myself against the desk. "But by the third letter, you must have seen that he was still doing well."

"I told you, I didn't read it." Her features sharpened, and she fixed me with a glare. "And don't act like it would've made a difference. You didn't even look at that letter. I left it on the counter for a week, waiting for you to see that boy's handwriting. Because god knows, you didn't want to talk about Ryan, but you would've read every word of that letter to know how Corey was involved."

I shook off the weird feeling brought on by the fact that she would have recognized Corey's handwriting and that she'd known early on that Corey and Ryan were connected.

"Why didn't you force me to read the third letter? Didn't you think I deserved to know what he said? I mean, he apologized in the first two, right? You didn't think that was something I needed to hear?"

"Maybe it was," she said, defeated. "But I couldn't risk it."

I threw my hands up. "Risk what exactly? It's not like I was going to start giving him World's Best Dad mugs because he apologized in a letter."

She met my disbelieving gaze with one so sad that it made me recoil. "Ryan wasn't the only one who wrote to you."

"What?"

"Corey wrote to you junior year."

My eyes went wide, and a tremor shook my body. I clenched my hands, but it did nothing to stop the shaking. *The only reason for Corey to have written to me that year...* "You knew about Emily."

"Yes, and Ryan's letters mentioned him quite a bit, and I know you—you would've gone running back to that boy in an instant. You would've thrown it all away to take care of someone else's mistake."

Anger swept through me. Emily was not a mistake. "You had no right."

"I had every right. You almost gave up Brown for him—twice. But you got away somehow. You had dreams, and he was the one thing you would've given everything up for."

Fury swallowed me, and all my walls caved in. "How could you?"

"I had to protect your future." Her tone was sharp. "And look at you now. You graduated with honors and earned a master's degree. You're a successful marketing professional at a renowned firm."

I balked at how completely wrong her image of me was. "A successful marketing professional whose been sleeping with her *married boss* for two years!"

Her face contorted. "You... what?"

"You heard me. That meeting you interrupted the other day, not really a meeting. *That's* who I am. So please, tell me what, exactly, you were saving me from." I ripped the envelope from her hands, tearing one of the edges. "Where are my letters?"

She walked to the bookcase lining the back wall and trailed her fingers across the titles until she came to a copy of *Wuthering Heights*. She slid it out of its spot, revealing the manila envelope hidden behind the row of books. "This is all of them."

"Corey's too?"

She nodded. "Corey's too."

I snatched it from her hand, grabbed my purse off the edge of the desk, and stalked toward the door.

She trailed me, and when she spoke, her voice was thick with desperation. "Andi, please wait."

I stopped at the top of the stairs, afraid that if I turned around, I would break. And so would she. "You should've told me."

"I know. I'm sorry. I was wrong, but it was an impossible situation. Do you remember what you were like after that year? You couldn't drink things out of a can, and if we accidentally dropped a plate, you'd have a panic attack. Sam and I had a fight once, and we found you huddled in the closet, crying. And the years went by, and you were finally happy, and you were so adamant that you didn't want to hear about him ever again."

Betrayal urged me forward, but love rooted me in place. "Fine. I get it. You couldn't tell me back then. But why wouldn't you tell me before you sent me up there for the funeral? Did you think no one would say anything?"

"I just didn't know how. When the letter first came, I didn't think it was out of the ordinary. It was only a few weeks after they usually arrived. People get busy. But then Bethany called, and it was too late."

I gripped the banister as pain lanced through me. "Did you know about Scott and Johnson?"

"Only since last year." She sniffled. "And only because that letter came in a branded envelope."

I shook my head. How different this week could have been. How different my *life* could have been. I faced her, matching her tears with my own. Regret and fear were etched into her features. I wanted to absolve her of this—she'd been my only parent for my whole life—but she'd sent me up there blind. She'd let me get hurt again. Her silence had made me cruel.

"You should've told me, Mom."

The rest of the house passed in a blur as I ran to my car, the letters clutched to my chest. Twilight had fallen, and a cool night breeze rustled the trees. I queued up a Wilderness Weekend album, and the opening piano soothed my broken edges as I debated where to go. There was no way I could go to Emma like this. But Harry was a free man. Darlene had even handed over her keys with the signed papers. I shifted into drive.

Chapter 38
Now

I drove into the cul-de-sac a few blocks down from Harry's and parked in front of a house having a confirmation party. Balloons were tied to the mailbox, and cars filled the driveway and lined the street. It was the perfect cover for my car. Not that I needed to sneak in anymore. I glanced in my visor mirror and groaned. My hair was a mess, my face splotchy. Grabbing eyeliner from my purse, I focused on what I could fix. I brushed my hair back into a ponytail and wriggled out of my shirt, pulling it out through the arm of my Brown hoodie. Skinny jeans, ballet flats, and a tattered sweatshirt. I looked like a college student—Harry would love it. With a last glance in the mirror, I headed toward his house.

I knew he was spending the weekend ridding the house of the last of Darlene. Even though I hadn't returned his call or answered any of his texts, he'd been sending me messages all day—mostly about all the things he wanted to do to me when I got back. And a few pictures of him sweaty and shirtless. I'd finally answered the last one with a dirty idea of my own as I pulled off the highway, though I hadn't told him I was on my way.

After confirming that his was the only car in the driveway, I rang the doorbell. He opened the door in loose-fitting jeans and a quarter-zip pullover that was unzipped enough to show off just a smidge of his hairy chest. His hair, usually slicked to perfection, sat in loose curls, and his glasses hung too far off his nose. My Harry. The one I only saw in his most unguarded moments.

"Surprise," I said.

His eyes trailed over me like a caress, and then he ushered me inside. He shut and locked the door. "What are you doing here?"

I wrapped my arms around his neck. "I thought we should rechristen the house. Now that you're a single man."

His eyes darkened, and his fingers tightened against my waist. "You don't know how much I wish we could."

"Why can't we? The house is yours." I pressed against him and brought his lips to mine. "I'm yours."

"Babe."

"Come on." I smiled at him mischievously. "Which room should we start in?"

"We can't. Stephanie's here."

I jerked back, releasing him. Stephanie was his daughter. She was a few years younger than me and still flailing about, spending her father's money until she decided her next move. I glanced behind me as if she was going to materialize with a disgusted look on her face.

"Here as in, in the house?"

"Well, no." His eyes trailed over me. "She's out with some friends, but she could come back."

I rolled my eyes and pulled him back to me by the collar of his sweater, letting my fingers dip under the soft material. "It's barely eight o'clock. She won't be home for hours."

He dropped his hands from my waist. "Let's go to your place. I'll text her that I got called away on business."

"It's Saturday night."

He smirked. "And it wouldn't be the first time *business* has called me away over the weekend."

"What does it matter if she finds me here?" I asked with a pout. "She has to know you have a girlfriend. She isn't stupid. You and Darlene have been apart for ages."

"Where did you park?" he asked, unlocking the door and picking up his keys.

"Come on." I grabbed his hand and pulled him back toward his study. "We'll make it quick."

"Babe, no. What do you think is going to happen if she finds out my girlfriend is practically the same age as her—and is my assistant."

I was *not* his assistant. Yet I always would be, as far as he was concerned. I stalked from the house, not waiting to see if he followed. By the time I reached the mailbox, he was at my side. He didn't take my hand. The night had turned brisk in those few minutes inside, and I hugged myself against the breeze.

After we were both in the car, he linked our fingers. "You okay? You have your bad-day sweatshirt on."

Of course, he knew that. The shock of emotions that had fueled my drive to his house and subsequent attempts to screw away the pain were ebbing. His words about his daughter hurt. I didn't usually need much from Harry. But I needed him to let me stay. And I needed him to know that without me having to explain it. I turned the car on but didn't move to go anywhere. Music filled the space, the melancholy soundtrack to an already disastrous day.

"We're never going to be normal, are we?" It was a whisper, an escaped thought that should never have made it to the surface.

"Don't be dramatic." He sighed. "You need to give me some time to adjust. To figure out how to explain *you.*"

I sighed. "You're never going to introduce me to your daughter."

"I wasn't aware that was something you would even want."

It *hadn't* been something I wanted. I'd been content to hide out with him, keeping myself safe from the possibility of heartbreak. Until I saw my old friends and their full lives. Until Corey kissed me, and I realized everything I was missing. There'd been vacations when Harry and I were a normal couple. Holding hands, walking down the street, checking in as Mr. and Mrs. Scott. Stolen moments in an otherwise torrid romance. I could easily love him all the way. But he would never let me.

"I want a lot of things, Harry. Being allowed in your house for starters. To fall in love. To get married, have kids. Do you want any of those things again?"

Our eyes locked in a silent showdown, and then he set my hand back in my lap. "No, I don't."

"I'll clean out my desk next week."

"This doesn't mean you have to leave the firm."

I leaned across him and pushed open his door. "Yes, it does."

He stared at me, his eyes fixed on mine. He opened his mouth and then closed it again, apparently unable to muster up an argument. With a shake of his head, Harry stepped out of my car for the last time.

I locked the doors and leaned my head against the steering wheel. The music, with its heartache and longing and sorrow, flowed through me. I'd just quit my job. And lost Harry. *On top of everything else I lost today.* I reached into the back and pulled out the manila envelope with the letters onto my lap. Flipping through them, I finally found Corey's tucked in the middle. I needed to know what all of them said, but Ryan was already gone, and nothing I read would change that. But Corey was real and solid, and I *had* to know what he'd written to me. I scanned the envelope. He'd mailed it on October 3. Tears pricked at my eyes. I knew what I'd been doing on every October 3 since I'd met him. That one, I'd spent dancing with my roommate and making out with some guy whose face I couldn't even remember and puking all the grief away. I pulled out the sheet of paper, my hands shaking, and finally read his words.

I promised myself I wouldn't do this. You made your decision, and I need to accept it, but I need to see you. My girlfriend's pregnant. And we're keeping it. I haven't even told my parents yet, but it's been almost four months. We won't be able to hide it much longer. God, Andi, I'm 20. How am I supposed to raise a child?

At first, I was terrified, but I thought Sharon and I could do this. We've been together for a while. Maybe it would force me to finally get over you, for real. But every day I think about you more. I want you here with me. Which is crazy because I'm having a baby with someone else. She doesn't want to get married. I've asked three times. She says she loves me but that a baby is no reason to get married. But you know how Fairford is. This is going to be my legacy forever. Unwed high school football star knocks up Liberty alum at 20.

How did this happen? No, I know how this happened. I saw your dad. I sent him to the drunk tank last Christmas. And he showed up at my house in June. Sober. It got me thinking about you. Which is why I went to the party at the Peak. Which is where Sharon and I did something stupid.

You know, today would've been our four-year anniversary. Was it really four years ago that I kissed you in our booth at Robinson? When I inextricably tied my fate to yours? It feels like another lifetime and yesterday all at once. Even with everything that happened, I'd kiss you again. Hell, I'd kiss you sooner. I'd fight harder. If you give me the chance, I'll fight now, somehow. It's a lot to ask, Andi. But I'm asking. Because I love you.

I'm in Bremerton 314. It's on the south side of campus. I'll be home for Christmas. I'll come to you.

The song reached its climax. Images of Corey—the man, not the boy—flooded my mind. The kiss followed by shattering revelations, harsh words, truths. And now the letter. It all fit together. Ryan wasn't the only one who'd carried the weight of my silence all these years. A sob racked my body as I thought back to each moment with

Corey that week, the push and pull until we finally gave in, and it had felt like coming home.

The song faded, quiet piano keys breaking what was left of my heart.

Chapter 39
Now

It was warm under my comforter, too warm, but it had been a full day since I'd crawled into bed, and I didn't have plans to emerge anytime soon. My Spotify was on a perpetual loop of the same twenty songs. My phone blinked with dozens of notifications, but it didn't matter. Tomorrow was Monday, and I didn't have a job to go to, so bedhead with a side of Cheez-Its seemed the perfect solution. With a groan, I sat up, reached for the letters on my bedside table, and spread them out in front of me. They'd been my only reading material since I arrived back at my apartment, tear soaked and weary.

Seven letters, eight if you counted Corey's—and I did because his story was intrinsic to Ryan's. The letters explained so much about the years we'd lost. They changed everything and nothing at all. I pulled Corey's out of the mix and tucked it under my pillow. He hadn't just told me about getting Sharon pregnant. He'd asked me to be with him. And my mom was right. If that letter had been an email or text, if he'd unblocked me long enough to write me a message on social media, I would have been in New Hampshire before I finished reading. That was what we did for each other even now. But email and texts and social media were all traceable, as I well knew after years with Harry. And how would he have explained to his girlfriend that the only thing he needed in that moment was his ex?

I stacked the five letters from the middle years. Those were a storybook. Each letter was pages long, detailing Ryan's year, his journey,

Nikki and Corey and Emily and Bethany and Krystal. He'd loved them all with a fierceness that matched theirs for him. Those letters had little to do with me. He didn't apologize, and he didn't justify. He simply told me about his life and signed each one the same way: *You know where to find me.* In those pages, Nikki had grown up, and Corey had become a man, and Ryan and Bethany had fallen back in love. It hurt but in a good way. One day, if my sister ever spoke to me again, and if I found the courage to reach back out to Corey, I would ask them about the memories in those pages. But after how I'd left, who knew if that would happen. Nikki hadn't tested my promise, and Corey hadn't called.

I stared at the two remaining envelopes. A beginning and an ending. I'd read each enough times to have them memorized, but I still wanted to see those words again. The words that had been for me and me alone. I picked up the first letter he'd ever written me, five months after his encounter with Corey that Christmas morning.

Dear Andi,

I've written more of these letters than I care to admit. This step has been the hardest so far. Apologizing. Atoning for all the wrongs I've done. This is the last one I will write. It's taken me a long time to come close to being able to write your name. And now to ask for your forgiveness.

Maybe I should explain. I'm in rehab. You'll never believe who dropped me off—that boy of yours, on Christmas on top of everything. I heard (yes, there's a grapevine even in rehab) that you two went your separate ways a few years back. So much of that time is a blur, but I do remember him and you, the laughter that filled the house when he was there. But these things happen, I guess. My bet would be that he still loves you. Why else would he help a drunk like me?

I'm getting sidetracked. I hear you're at Brown now. I hope you know I'm proud of you. I hope you even care. I probably shouldn't even send this, not like this. But this is who I am now—now that the liquor's gone. My brain wanders. They tell me it'll pass once I'm out of here and back to my life.

The point, Andi, my beautiful daughter, is that I am more sorry than words can express for what I did to you. The things I said that night, shunning you, making you live in fear and neglect. I was in pain, but there's no excuse. You'll probably never see this—if the tables were turned, I don't think I'd give it to you, but your mother always was the better of the two of us. I hope you can find it in your heart to someday forgive me. And when you do, find me. I'll be in Fairford. I'm not going anywhere you can't find me.

With hope and love,

Dad

I tried to imagine a version of my life where I'd gotten this letter, but nothing materialized. It could have changed everything. Most likely, it would have changed nothing. At twenty, I was angry and lost. My father's words would have sent me down a spiral I might not have come out of because I'd given up what felt like everything to be rid of him. And he would have been back but not any of the other people I'd pushed away. And that was if I'd even read it. Which I probably wouldn't have unless my mother had forced me, and with the glib comment about Corey's love for me still existing, she never would have forced me.

I folded it back up and turned to the ending, which really was just his hope that in his absence, we'd all find a new beginning.

Dearest Andi,

I have hoped for your response for many years, but none ever came. Did you get any of my letters? Did you know I wanted to see you? That I love you? That I'm a changed man? When I last saw your mother, she said you were better off without me in your life. Maybe she was right.

For the past seven years I've written you a showcase of my life, of my change. I've wished for you to reconsider your silence with me and with your sister and with Corey. They need you. They always have. And now they will need you more than ever.

The doctors say I don't have much longer—maybe a few weeks. So I thought I'd try one last time. If you've been reading these all these years, know that I understand your silence, and I've accepted it.

There's not much left to say. I've written you the story of my new life. A wonderful second chance at love and family. I only wish you were a part of it.

When I'm gone, please find Nikki. Go to Corey. They'll be in Fairford. Learn about them, love them. Take the house and make it your own. Fill it with happy memories. Erase the pain and sadness from its walls. Know that I am eternally sorry for my actions and that I have always loved you, my daughter.

With hope and love,

Dad

I skimmed my fingers over Nikki's and Corey's names and my father's assertion that they needed me. The words were almost exactly what Corey had told me Ryan said to him—"Be nice to her. She's going to need you." Ryan had been right. I would never have stayed in Fairford if Corey hadn't come to the house that day. I wasn't sure Nikki or Corey needed me. They'd lived full lives without me. The more important question was whether they wanted me. I glanced at my phone, where too many missed calls and texts waited. But none were from either of them. From the front of the apartment, I heard the front door open. *Emma.* She was the only one who had a key and the only one who would walk in unannounced.

She stuck her head through the door to my bedroom and pulled a face. "Boyz II Men—really?"

I laughed. She couldn't have timed her entrance better if she'd tried.

Her gaze paused on the letters on my lap before coming back to my face. "Please don't go all Seth Cohen on me. I literally cannot handle it today."

"What are you doing here?" I asked, stuffing the letters under my pillow.

Emma sat down at my desk and scrolled through my playlist. "Did you seriously make this?" She paused the song but kept scrolling. "This is just depressing." She turned to me with a frown. "Your mom called me. She was worried about you."

I sighed. "We had a fight."

"Yeah, I gathered that." She sat down on the edge of my bed. "What's going on?"

"With my mom?"

"That mixtape isn't about your mom."

I pulled the pillow from under my head and covered my face. There was too much to rehash. Emma nudged me and pulled the pillow away. She stared at me until I spoke.

"I pretty much screwed up everything with Corey and my sister." Emma had only been given the bare minimum of information—Corey was in town, my sister was back in Ryan's life, I was staying in Fairford for the week—and I could see the wheels in her mind spinning as she tried to glean anything from the meager details I'd given her.

"I'm going to need more than that." She motioned for me to continue.

I really didn't want to talk, but Emma wasn't going anywhere. "Corey helped my father get sober eight years ago. They started an architecture firm together called Scott and Johnson Home Design, of which Corey is now CEO. And Krystal works there too."

"Wow."

I nodded. "Yeah, so the whole time I was up there, everyone kept talking about these letters Ryan wrote me and how I never responded." I took a breath, steeling myself. "But you know that I only ever got the one, which is exactly what I said until Corey told me *he* was the one who mailed the letters."

"Oh no." She palmed her face, already seeing where this was going.

"Oh *yes*. My mom hid them from me."

"Why would she do that?"

"Well, she gave me a lot of reasons. Some of them pretty sound. But mainly, she didn't want me to find out that Corey had a daughter."

"He has a what?" Emma's eyes narrowed as she realized just how much I'd been keeping from her all week.

The sound of my laughter surprised me, but it was also a comfort that despite the situation, I could still laugh and find the good in some of it. If anything was good about this week, it was Emily.

I reached for my phone and scrolled through a few pictures I'd taken while up there. "That's Emily."

"Oh my god. I thought you meant, like, a baby, not—wow." She placed the phone on the bed between us and turned to me, her eyes still narrowed, her nose scrunched.

"And did I mention that Ryan left me the house in his will and a third of his estate?"

"Holy shit. You made it seem like a boring visit."

There it was again—laughter. Either I was losing my mind, or we really had entered a parallel universe. It had felt like the latter ever since Corey had stood in the vestibule of my father's house. From then on, it had gotten more tangled. Yet telling the story now, I missed Emily's hugs and Nikki's voice, Corey's smile, and Krystal's laugh—the sense that my world was changing despite my protests.

The small room I'd occupied for two years in my own apartment now seemed foreign. The beige walls, bareness, and strategically placed framed photographs didn't represent who I was but who I thought I should be at twenty-eight. Nikki's room had held my heart, but it was illogical to paint lyrics on every inch of my walls to drown out the demons. From my bed, I could just reach my desk and hit Play on the laptop. The crooning sadness returned. Emma didn't say anything, but she didn't look pleased.

Crawling back under the covers, I pulled them over my head and burrowed into the mattress. "Hiding."

I could feel my best friend's eye roll through the comforter. She pulled it back down and fixed me with a pointed stare. "That's all a lot, but it doesn't add up."

She wasn't looking at me. Her eyes were trained on the laptop screen that was too far away for her to read. The song had changed to a Wilderness Weekend track that Emma knew well. In the days after I'd left my fiancé, she'd sat with me while I cried to this song repeatedly.

"What doesn't add up?" I purposely avoided her gaze when she turned back to me.

"The last time you listened to music this sad was when you and Corey broke up the first time. But now, with all these secrets and lies, shouldn't you be *angry*?"

I was angry. So beyond angry that I'd skipped right into despair. Everything I'd thought I knew was wrong. My life had been defined by half truths. And I'd made it that way. But Emma hadn't been in Fairford. She hadn't kissed Corey or found a sister only to push her away. She hadn't seen the Ryan renaissance. She hadn't just ended a two-year affair and quit her job. And I hadn't told her about any of it, not really.

I sighed. "This week just made me see that I needed to make some changes."

"Like...?" Her tone implied that she already had an idea, and it was probably a correct one.

"I ended things." I knew she would understand without any further explanation.

"Thank God. I'm sorry, but I hated that you were seeing a married man. And I know his marriage was a technicality, but still..." She reached out and took hold of my hand.

"I know. I also quit my job." I said it calmly, hoping she didn't put together that ending the affair and quitting my job were connected.

"What?" There was a look of alarm in her eyes.

I held up my hands placatingly. "I have another one."

"Lead with that next time," she said, rolling her eyes.

I bit my lip, hesitating on the last part, but she was my best friend. If I couldn't tell her, there was no hope for me. "Oh, and Corey might have maybe kissed me before everything went to hell."

She groaned. "I should've known this was a Corey-induced playlist." Without warning, she tossed the comforter onto the floor. A draft blew through my thin clothes, sending a shiver through my body. The room went silent as she reached for my computer. Based on the look on her face, there was no way I was going to be able to refuse whatever plan she'd just decided on.

She crossed her arms. "Get out of bed."

I sat up and let my feet touch the ground for the first time in too many hours. "Turn the music back on, and I'll get out of bed."

The weariness of the mix blanketed the room again, turning everything a shade blander. Her finger was poised above the pause button.

I stood. "I'm up. Why am I up?"

Emma began digging through my dresser. She threw a pair of jeans, a shirt, socks, and even underwear onto my mattress. Then she picked up my duffle bag and emptied the dirty clothes I hadn't bothered to unpack into the hamper. "You're going back to Fairford."

"What?" My body ached to sit back down. I straightened my shoulders, stretching out the kinks that had settled in my back.

"You've spent your entire life running away." She stuffed the clean clothes into the bag. "You said going up there made you realize you needed to change things in your life—it made you end a two-year affair and kiss a guy whose name you haven't even been able to say in forever—all of which you will tell me about later in excruciating detail. So, obviously, when things got tough up there, you left everything unresolved and came back here to hide under the bed."

A spark of resistance ignited in me, and my lazy limbs perked back up. "I spend one week up there, and I'm supposed to just have things be normal and be in all of their lives?"

My heart recoiled from the thought of returning, thinking of the last words I'd said to Corey and his admission that he didn't want to be nice to me, but he had to be. And I'd left Nikki asking—begging—me to stay. To face them would mean complete denial of everything I'd trained myself to be.

"You went up for a funeral and came back with photos. Those people *are* a part of you. They always have been. You're the only one who never seemed to know that." She stared me down. "Now, get dressed. You have a long ride ahead of you."

Protesting wouldn't help. If I refused to make the trip, she would drive me herself, even missing work if she had to. She was still packing but also glaring at me and then the bathroom door and then back at me. It was a warning that if I didn't move my feet, she was going to start throwing soapy water on me.

I held my hands up in surrender. "You'd better start some coffee."

Chapter 40
Now

There was no logical explanation as to why it almost always rained on my drives to Fairford. It must have been a sign that life was about to get cloudy and full of doubt because that seemed to be what every trip turned into—one catastrophe or another. That needed to change. The pattern needed to be adjusted. There was only so long someone could spend avoiding a town or a memory. Another ten years couldn't pass.

The rain worsened as the miles between my car and Fairford got fewer. The storm was moving north. Fairford would be underwater by the time I got there. The speedometer slowly inched closer to seventy, despite the blurred vision and the rain. Monticello passed by—only a few more exits.

Corey's house was mostly dark, but in the pale light of the porch lamp, I could just make him out, sitting in the far corner, facing the storm. So many rainy nights, I'd sat up with him. He loved the pitter-patter against the windows, the splash against the ground, the rolling thunder—it put him at ease. There would be no waiting for a break in the rain. It had no intention of stopping anytime soon. Parked across the street from his house, I doubted he recognized me or my car. He didn't move from the chair, though he did turn his head for just a moment when my engine sputtered off.

I'd thrown on a raincoat on my way out the door, but it wasn't going to help much. The string was pulled as tight as it would go against my head, yet pieces of hair snuck out. It was time to reconcile myself to the fact that I was going to get wet.

As I ran across the street toward his house, Corey must have finally recognized me because he stood up and walked to the edge of the porch, still protected from the rain but close enough that he would be able to hear what I was saying. He was dressed in what was apparently his nighttime attire—gray sweats and a tank top. A loose-fitting zip-up hoodie hung off his shoulders.

"Andi, what are you doing here?"

I stood at the base of the stairs as rain pelted my head. "I'm so sorry." The words came out in a cry, a plea. "I was wrong about everything."

I wiped a wet strand of hair out of my eyes. This whole trip was one big improvisation, and there was always the possibility that he wouldn't let me inside. His eyes met mine, but he didn't say anything. Water seeped into my sneakers. My socks were mush on my toes. My fingers, rigid with cold, were tucked into the pockets of my jacket. It was pointless to worry about my hair—it was a rat's nest under my hood.

"Come up here out of the rain," he said finally.

In a few short steps, I was at his side. The hood of my jacket hung heavily off my neck. I tucked my matted hair behind my ears as much as possible.

"I'm sorry," I said again. I would say it until he heard me.

"You drove up here in this? Are you crazy?" He pulled his hoodie off and held it out to me. "Give me your jacket."

I peeled the soaked vinyl off my arms, handed it to him, and slipped quickly into the hoodie. "You needed to know, what I said—I was wrong. I didn't—"

He held up a hand to stop me. "You were upset. I shouldn't have said what I said about being nice to you. Or any of it really."

"But it was the truth." My eyes fell to my feet, tears welling up. This was going to hurt. He was inside my heart and my head, and an apology might not be enough.

"It wasn't." His voice was quiet. He didn't look at me. A rumble of thunder followed quickly by a flash of lightning grabbed our attention for just a moment, and then our eyes met. "I mean, Ryan did tell me you were going to need me. But he followed it with 'and you need her.'" He took hold of my hand. "It was just hard feeling us again. And then I kissed you, and you're in a relationship—"

"I'm not."

His eyes met mine. "What?"

"I'm not in a relationship." I gently touched his cheek, leading his lips to mine.

Corey pulled me into him—wet hair and all. Our bodies melded into each other. We breathed each other in, and still, it wasn't enough. I clung to him, my body finding new ways to touch him, to connect. My poor, fragile heart started to knit itself back together.

We crashed into the house, still wrapped around each other. Each time we broke apart, we came back together, hard and desperate and wanting. He tugged at the zipper on my hoodie. "You're all wet."

"I don't care." I pulled him back.

"Wait." He paused, his lips still on mine. At first, I didn't hear anything, but then the toilet flushed, and I could hear slow, light footsteps overhead.

"How did you even hear that?"

He gave me a lopsided grin. "Let me go make sure she goes back to sleep."

I followed him through the downstairs until he deposited me outside the laundry room. He came back a minute later and held out a pair of sweats and a blanket. "Drop your stuff in the dryer and meet me in the living room." He kissed me thoroughly. "I'll be right back."

I'd barely had time to change into the sweats he'd given me and get situated on the couch before he sat down next to me. I offered him the throw. "Are you sure we won't bother your parents?"

He shook his head. "They're not here. My mom has a doctor's appointment in the city tomorrow."

"Is everything okay?"

"Just routine follow-up." He smiled and mussed my damp hair. "You warm enough?"

I nodded, bringing my knees up to my chest. There was an ease between us, the same one I'd sensed at the dinner party. Except it had ignited into a flame I could still see in Corey's eyes and feel in my abdomen. Yet I couldn't ignore the chasm between us. Nine years of life. There was so much to learn, and we couldn't do that in one night. But we could start. I wedged my toes under his leg and pulled my purse onto the couch.

"Your toes are cold," he said, rubbing a hand over my foot.

They were always cold. I felt him lean into me, his eyes half-lidded.

"I found the letters," I said too fast, turning my head just so. He straightened. "My mother kept them from me."

"It's okay. He knew that was always a possibility."

I played with the hem of the blanket, keeping my eyes on the pattern along the edge. "If only I'd read that one letter. If only I'd known that it would be the only choice I got to make."

He squeezed my foot. "Look at me."

"I found the one you sent me," I said, untangling the letter from the mess of my purse and offering it to him. "About Sharon being pregnant."

His body tensed as he took it. "I couldn't not tell you." He walked to the window. The rain had worsened. Branches battered the windows and the siding. "We hadn't talked in almost two years, but to have a baby and not tell you." He shook his head and looked down at the page, reading out loud. "'Even with everything that happened, I'd kiss you again. Hell, I'd kiss you sooner. I'd fight harder. If you give me the chance, I'll fight now somehow. It's a lot to ask, Andi. But I'm asking. Because I love you.' God, I was such an asshole."

True. In that moment, he'd been a complete asshole to Sharon. But that didn't change the fact that he'd written these horrible, amazing things to me.

"I wish I'd gotten it. It was really beautiful." I walked over and hugged him from behind. "I would've come in a second."

He sucked in a breath and placed his hand over mine. "No, it's better that you never saw this. I can't believe I sent it. I started an email to you, but I kept deleting it. I knew how ridiculous my request was. I mean, I had asked Sharon to marry for the third time less than a week before I wrote this. But I just... I knew if I didn't try, I'd end up driving to Brown and figuring out how to find you. So I wrote it in a letter and mailed it to your mom's house." He sighed. "Could you imagine if you'd gotten this, Andi? I loved you entirely. I would've left my pregnant girlfriend without a second thought if you'd shown up. And if somehow I stayed with her, it would've been obvious to everyone—most of all her—that I loved you."

"But you loved Sharon too," I said, her name sticking in my throat.

"To an extent." He turned and stepped out of my embrace. "And I believe she loved me in her own way. But we weren't in love, not then at least. When I finally accepted that you weren't coming, I did fall in love with her, especially after Emily was born. But..."

His gaze met mine, his expression completely open. Fear, heartache, longing, understanding, want—it was all there.

"Yes?" I whispered, inching back toward him until we were toe to toe.

"Would you really have come?" His fingers grazed mine.

I nodded. Even with the news of his pregnant girlfriend, if Corey had tried to get me back, I wouldn't have had the strength to say no. I wouldn't even have wanted to. "There's no question. If you'd needed me, I would've been here."

He kissed me, politely almost, with his fingertips just barely touching mine. His scent washed over me—Tide and remnants of cologne mixed with a day's worth of sweat. A chill ran down my spine the same way it did every time someone with that cologne passed me by. Memories of that night on the roof of the high school—and other nights spent tucked into his arms—tumbled through my mind.

Goose bumps sprouted on my arms as his fingers brushed my shoulder, and he kissed my neck. His hand tangled in my hair. Electricity flowed between us as we kissed slowly and then more urgently. I slid my hands under his shirt, warming them against his chest. Everything touched—arms, hands, lips, legs, toes. My heart thrummed in time with his. I breathed him in, shivering as his fingers reached again for the zipper of my hoodie.

"Daddy?"

We broke apart at Emily's voice. He gave me a commiserating look and mouthed an apology. I just shrugged and kissed him lightly. This was his life, and if I wanted him, I had to accept all of him.

"We're down here, sweetie," he called and headed toward the stairs. I returned to the couch, his words reverberating through me. *We're down here.* As if it was the most natural thing in the world. And maybe, as he'd told me before, it was.

Emily rubbed sleep from her eyes and walked down a few steps. "Daddy, the storm is scary."

"It's all right," he said, tucking her into his arm as she reached the bottom.

"Andi!" She squirmed out of Corey's embrace and jumped into my lap. What this little girl saw in me, I didn't know. But for her, it was only right that I was in the living room, in her dad's clothes.

"Hi, sweetie." I stroked her hair.

Corey settled in next to us with his arm across the back of the couch and my head against his arm. Emily lay down between us, putting her head in my lap.

"What are you doing here?" she asked.

"I need to take care of some things at Uncle Ryan's tomorrow." It was incredible how easily that phrase flowed now—how normal it was beginning to sound.

She peered up at me through her bangs. "Can I come?"

Corey cleared his throat conspicuously. "Someone has school to-morrow."

"Can we watch a movie, Daddy?"

After a moment of pretend deep thought and a nod from me, he smiled. "Sure, why don't you go grab my phone from my room. Pick whatever you want."

She jumped off the couch before he'd even finished his sentence.

"She'll be out after the first ten minutes," he whispered, his lips lingering on my ear.

My heart fluttered. *Are we going to do this?* There would be no going back. Despite the years, despite the challenges, it would all come back. The spark between us was undeniable. Everywhere we touched lit up with excitement.

His lips moved past my ear to the soft spot just behind it. A tingle radiated from that spot to my whole body. I watched Emily until I couldn't see her anymore. Corey's fingers ran small circles on the bare skin between my shoulder and neck, and his lips worked their way down to meet his fingers. With effort, I kept my eyes on the stairs.

As sudden as his touch had been, so was his departure. Somehow, he'd heard her again before I'd even registered the opening and closing of his bedroom door. Dad tricks.

In and out. Inhale and exhale. With each breath, my overstimulated senses calmed down.

"What did you pick?" I asked as Emily lay back down, and the television came to life with the familiar Disney opening.

"*Beauty and the Beast*. It's my favorite."

I smiled. "Mine too."

Belle was barely singing about a provincial life before Emily's breathing settled, and her grip on my hand loosened. I leaned over and kissed Corey lightly on the lips before settling back into his arms. We watched the movie in silence for a few more minutes. The enchanted objects of the Beast's castle were coming to life when Corey flipped off the television.

He picked Emily up, and she curled into him in her sleep. "Meet me upstairs?"

My choice. My heart pounded in my ears. My body was electrified from his caresses. I could live with the consequences of whatever happened. I couldn't live without knowing. There was no other choice. It had always been Corey.

His room was messier than the last time I'd been there. More of Emily's stuff had migrated into it, though it seemed like some of his things had made their way into the box under the windowsill—a few books, a collection of picture frames, Emily's artwork.

The rain was slowing down, but a constant patter assaulted the window. I leaned in closer. The glass was cold against my palm, and a cool breeze snuck through a crack.

The door clicked shut. My pulse quickened before he even touched me, and then he was there. His arms wrapped around me, and he nuzzled into my neck. He trailed kisses across my shoulder as he finally unzipped my hoodie. We both paused as the zipper released. Then he drew slow circles on my skin, his hand traveling higher each time until he skimmed my breasts. I shuddered under his caress and the slow movement of his lips on my skin.

"Corey," I whispered as he nipped at my ear and then kissed along my jaw until his lips parted mine. I turned into him. His warm hands slid over my skin as he pushed the sweatshirt off.

"I've missed you." He kissed down my chest. "The smell of your skin. The taste of it." His tongue slid over my nipple, and I gasped. He stroked my curves and my stomach until reaching the loose waistband at my hips. His fingers flexed on my skin. "May I?"

Our eyes met, and so many years of unspoken apologies and regrets and love passed between us. The last time we'd done this had been desperate and messy and so very full of hope. We'd known everything and nothing of love.

I nodded, and he pushed the fabric down, his eyes going dark as he took in my lack of underwear. Those, too, were in the dryer. My body vibrated with anticipation as his hands trailed over my hips and he cupped my ass. I gripped the edge of his shirt and pulled it over his head, touching the taut skin of his stomach and the firm muscles of his chest—a chest that now had hair on it.

He pulled me to him, maneuvering us until we were at the bed. He laid me back, settling himself between my legs. I pushed at his pants until he was free, and the truth of his desire pulsed against me.

Our mouths smashed together, and our tongues danced the same dance they always had, yet the song had changed. We were no longer fumbling teenagers. We were no longer each other's only. We were broken and bent, but still, we fit in all the ways that mattered and in new ways that made each touch that passed between us hotter. So much hotter.

"You're beautiful," he said, his hands still roaming.

I groaned as he skimmed a finger over my most sensitive part. His eyes asked me a question as if I hadn't already told him yes in every kiss and touch. I slanted my lips over his in response, and his fingers found their mark. I moaned as pleasure spiked through me.

Corey grinned as my moans turned to whimpers and finally to a scream he swallowed with a kiss. We played for a long time, losing ourselves in the pleasure of each other, in caresses and kisses and teasing and love. And when I thought I might die if we didn't take the next step, he slid into place between my legs. His cheeks were flushed and his hair mussed, and he was so beautiful it hurt in the best way. Awe settled across his expression, and one thing became blindingly clear—Corey Johnson loved me. He always had, and he always would.

Our lips came together again. My existence, as I knew it, fell away to just the two of us.

Giving in.

Coming back.

Together.

Home.

Chapter 41
Now

The morning was hazy. Corey lay next to me, his arm slung casually across my body, his breathing shallow, his hair sticking out in every direction. I caressed his cheek, feeling the beginnings of whiskers he'd never let grow.

He opened one eye and smiled, pulling me to him. "Good morning."

I burrowed into him, trying to keep warm as a chill went through me, and I reached for the hoodie he'd given me the night before, but he tugged me back with a laugh, pulling the comforter over our heads.

"Of the two of us, you have more clothing," he said, his lips finding mine. "So you get to keep me warm."

I looked down at the boxers and tank top I'd stolen during the night and then at him, completely naked. My body stirred as the morning haze dissolved.

I yanked the tank top off and held it out to him. "This should help."

He laughed silently against me as his hands traveled the curve of my waist. "You're right—this is much better."

"I agree." I rolled on top of him and almost gasped at how hard he was. "What were *you* dreaming about?"

"I'd show you, but—"

"No buts," I said, taking him in my hand.

He moaned as I stroked him but shook his head. "What time is it?"

I glanced at the clock on his bedside table, picking up my pace. "Almost six thirty."

He sat up with a frown. "Emily's going to be up any minute."

Emily. My eyes widened, and I pulled on the sweatshirt and zipped it up to my chin. "Sorry, I forgot."

Corey kissed me lazily, his erection pressing into me. We moved together, the friction like kindling. His fingers flexed against my hips, restless. "Never apologize for what you were just doing."

"You should really get dressed," I whispered as his cold fingers crept up my abdomen.

"This is the best morning I've had in a long time." He brought his lips to that spot on my neck he knew I liked to have kissed. "Thank you."

I blushed. "You say that to all the girls."

He shook his head, his tongue running along that spot until I purred. "Only you."

A knock low on the door dragged us back to reality. We stared at each other, not moving.

"Did you lock the door?" I whispered as I moved from his lap to the bed.

Panic flashed in his features. "I don't remember."

He pulled the blanket over our laps as there was more scuffling on the other side of the door. The doorknob turned but met resistance.

Holy shit.

He let out a breath with a strangled laugh. "Holy shit."

"Daddy! Let me in!"

We scrabbled into clothes—me pulling on his sweats and him a pair of mesh shorts from the hamper. Emily's knocking persisted. He opened the door, pulling a shirt over his head. "Yes, honey?"

Emily's face brightened at the sight of me. She bounced into my lap. "Can you drive me to school, Andi?"

Corey's face didn't register an answer, so I shrugged. "Sure."

"Yay!" She squeezed me tight and then bounced back off the bed and out the door.

I turned to Corey, who was watching Emily run down the hallway. He looked different than he had the past few days—his smile more natural, his stance relaxed. He shut the door once Emily's footsteps on the stairs faded.

He wrapped me in his arms, kissing me lazily. "I guess we should get going."

"School and work—right."

He nuzzled my neck. "I have meetings this morning, but I can cancel the rest of my day."

"That works. I have some things to handle this morning anyway."

He kissed me again, harder this time. I felt his desire down to my toes. This was going to be a problem, but what a good problem to have.

"Daddy, where's my unicorn bowl?" We jumped apart at Emily's voice, but it was fortunately coming from the kitchen.

Corey linked our hands and kissed my knuckles. "Meet me at the office at lunch? I know a place with a bed and no interruptions."

"That sounds perfect."

Chapter 42

Now

I pulled the car to a stop along the edge of the hill. The sky was clear and the day already bright after yesterday's storm. A brisk wind kept the day chilly, and I zipped Corey's hoodie as far as it would go. His scent wafted over me, and all the memories of the night before returned. I basked in them for a minute before pulling a blanket from my trunk and heading up the hill. Ryan's grave was halfway up, hidden under a blossoming tree. In a few weeks, with the branches in full bloom and the tombstone in place, it would be beautiful. Now it was a muddy mess, but I spread my blanket out nevertheless and sat down cross-legged.

"Hi, Dad."

A few leaves on the tree fluttered to the ground. It seemed like a sign that he was listening. I pulled a notebook out of the pocket of my sweatshirt—a pen was strapped in, ready for use. We had never been the talking kind, and speaking to a grave seemed superfluous. Maybe I could write it out, though—answer his unanswered letters. The pen hit the paper, and before I could think of what to write, my hand started moving across the page.

Dear Dad,

Just writing that salutation is strange. The last time I referred to you as Dad was so long ago. You were a different person, and so was I.

I got your letters, all of them at once, about two days ago and finally read them. I wish I'd seen them sooner, especially the last one. Perhaps I would've come... that's probably not true.

I wish I could say I was the sort of person that would've seen your change and forgiven you, driven up to Fairford and been in your life, but I'm not. After all the years I spent lost in my own anger, I don't want to be angry anymore at anyone—not you or Corey or even Mom for keeping your letters from me. I just want to be.

Over the past decade, I've lost so many people, and I've always blamed you. You made me afraid to trust a man, afraid of my own feelings. I would cling onto a relationship so hard until it was time for the grand gesture, and then I'd run, like with Robert in graduate school. We were engaged, but then I left him in Boston, and he let me leave. It's why I left Corey. God, I loved him, and I was afraid to have that connection to you for the rest of my life, to know that every Christmas I'd have to risk seeing you. It was too much. So, I picked Brown, a great school but a better hiding place. And I missed him every day of the past nine years, and now we're together, and I've never been so happy and terrified in my life. Can it ever be the same? How do we tackle a decade of regrets? I know what you would say from reading your letters and watching you build a family from the ashes of your old self. You do it together. And I think we can. I think he thinks we can too.

All these years, I've tried to figure out why—*why it happened, why I stayed, why Bethany left—but I will never know because you're gone, and no one can answer for you. Your letters help, but they can't replace whatever truths you took with you. The way I figure it, you were really yelling at yourself. I was just in the way. But it doesn't justify what you did to me.*

Something, the hum of a car or the breeze rustling through the leaves, shook me from the letter. I rested the notebook against my knees and let my mind wander back to his letters. His letters had been informative and sometimes questioning, like he was reaching for me to give him any sort of information about my life. His main question had been about forgiveness—could I forgive him for that day, that year. The pen felt heavy in my hand, but I had to give my answer.

You asked if I could forgive you, and I've spent a lot of the last week thinking about forgiveness and that year. We all made mistakes. And while I didn't think I'd ever even think these words... I do forgive you. I'm letting go of the pain and the anger. It's going to take some time for me to reconcile who you were to me with this new version of you that I'm slowly getting to know, but as the days and years go by, and I see your empathy in Nikki, your passion in Corey, and your laughter in Emily, I'll know you better. It's only been a week after all. But if there's anything this week has shown me, it's that you didn't expect forgiveness from those you hurt—you worked to earn it. And while it may be too late for us, I do believe you earned mine.

Footsteps snapping the leaves and weeds brought me out of my thoughts. I squinted into the sunlight, making out the outlines of an SUV and a person approaching, the familiar scribble of a band logo on her shirt.

"Thanks for coming," I said.

"Anything to get out of bio." Nikki smiled, her cheeks flushing. "What did you want to talk about?"

I'd called my sister this morning to see if she could meet me here, knowing that after the way we'd left things Saturday, I needed to see her. Fortunately, Bethany had given her permission to miss her morning classes, though Nikki had to be back by fourth period if she wanted to play in her lacrosse match that afternoon. Oh, how I remembered those days.

Closing the notebook, I pushed myself to my feet and scanned the cemetery, noting a bench a few plots away. I motioned toward it, and we crossed the short distance in silence. From the outside, we probably looked like the average family, our features so similar we could only be sisters. We would get there—average, normal—when seeing the quirk of my smile reflected in hers wouldn't feel weird. One day.

"So, listen," I said after we sat down. "I have to tell you something, and I don't want you to take it the wrong way."

"You're not accepting the house." Her tone was resigned, and she visibly deflated.

"No, I'm not." I took her hand in mine.

She looked at me with a frown, the lingering grief evident in her features. "He kept it for you. He didn't even stay there most of the time, but he didn't want to—"

"I know. I found his letters."

"Then why can't you keep it?"

I sighed. "I don't have a use for it or the finances to support it. But I'd like to sign it over to you. I'm going to talk to that lawyer and see what needs to be done—if I need to keep it until you're eighteen or if I can just forfeit my rights or whatever."

"But you'll come back?"

"Yes, whenever you want me to. Or you can come see me in the city or stay with me for the summer. I'm sure we can find you an awesome internship."

"Really?"

"Yeah. I mean, I have an ancient couch and a crappy air mattress, but we can make it work. And you might have to share the bed with Emily every so often, but..."

She laughed. "I knew that fight wouldn't stick."

"At least one of us did." I pulled her into a hug. "Thank you for giving me that key."

She sniffled. "Thank you for coming back."

We sat like that a while longer and then walked back to the car. Bethany waited in the driver's seat, reading.

"Everything okay?" she asked.

Nikki nodded. "Yup, and I'm not even going to get to miss gym."

"Sorry. Next time I'll talk slower." I turned to Bethany. "Can I speak with you for a minute?"

We walked a short distance away. Nikki studiously studied her phone, but I had a feeling she'd cracked her window to eavesdrop.

"What can I do for you, Andi?"

"I got Ry—Dad's—letters. You two got back together."

She bit at her lip. "We did, about two years ago. There was a lot to work through. A lot of forgiveness all around." Her eyes met mine. "I so wanted that year to be perfect for you. Wanted so badly for you and Nikki to really feel like sisters. And it all went so wrong so fast."

I thought of everything that had happened that night and that year and all the ones that followed. My choices, hers, my mom's, Corey's. "Maybe you shouldn't have left me there. But I should've let you call my mom. I should've called you from the hospital. It was an impossible situation, and we all made mistakes."

She hugged me, her arms so tightly around me I was afraid she might break if I let go. "I'm sorry you never got to know the version of him that we all loved. But I know he's smiling up there because you're here. His girls are finally together again."

We stood in the embrace for a long moment. And she wasn't my dad's wife or the woman who'd left me or any of the other ways I'd thought about her in the last decade. She was my stepmother, and she was a woman grieving for the love of her life.

I stepped back and took her hands in mine and said what I hadn't been able to say a week ago. "I'm so sorry for your loss, Bethany."

Chapter 43
Now

S cott and Johnson was bustling when I walked through the glass doors. A group of men in suits chatted in the front lobby, another group dressed in considerably more business-casual style chatted as they walked from the back of the building, and a cluster of people stepped off the elevator, laughing. Krystal's desk was empty, an "I'll be back shortly" sign in place of her nameplate. Next to it was a list of extensions for what looked like everyone in the building. And next to that was a folded sheet of paper with my name on it in Krystal's loopy handwriting. I unfolded it, smiling at her directive—*You better tell me everything. And I mean* everything.

I glanced at my phone, which lit up with notifications. One was Corey telling me to come right up. Nikki had sent a picture of herself frowning in her gym uniform. Then there was a missive from Emma that was very similar to Krystal's note and, finally, one from my mom. She'd been texting me since I walked out of her house on Saturday. I hadn't replied yet, but if there was anything I'd learned in my life, it was that silence was a deadly weapon.

I read her latest message. *Just let me know you're okay. Please.*

I'm fine, I typed as I headed up the stairs to Corey's office. *I need some time to sort through all of this. I'll text you when I'm back in town. We'll go to yoga.*

I pocketed my phone and crossed the short distance to the corner office. Before I'd even stepped into the room, Corey had me in his arms. He embraced me and pulled me back against the wall that wasn't glass. "I thought you'd never get here."

I laughed—he'd literally texted me fifteen minutes ago. That was barely enough time to gather my things from his parents' house and get across town. "Patience is a virtue."

His lips found mine. "I think we've been patient enough."

I glanced at the doors to his office, but no one could see us. I tugged at his lapels. "What has gotten into you today?"

"You." He quirked an eyebrow. "Or the other way around."

I rolled my eyes. "Wow. That was awful."

He kissed me again. "Do you care?"

No. Really, I didn't. After so long without him in my life, I'd take any version of him, but I was particularly fond of this happy, light one. And I was going to have too much fun working him out of his suit. "You know we could've met at the place with the bed."

"True, that would've saved time." He released me but only long enough to wrap an arm around my waist and lead me farther into the office. "I have something to talk with you about actually. If you're up for it."

That was definitely code for things that were going to dampen the mood. I sighed. "More Ryan stuff?"

Corey glanced at me, his brow furrowing. "It can wait. Really, there's no rush."

I shook my head. *Better now than more surprises later.* "Lay it on me."

"Oh, I plan to," he said with a grin. I stared at him incredulously until he burst into laughter. "Sorry, I couldn't resist."

We sat on one of the couches in the front of the office. I leaned into Corey, craving his warmth, and he draped an arm around my shoulders, pulling me closer. Apparently, this Ryan news was something I could receive while cuddling. That seemed a good sign.

"So, what's going on? I'm actually kind of hungry," I asked. He opened his mouth, and I held up a finger. "Don't you dare say, 'So am I, baby.'"

He grinned again. His face was going to get stuck that way if he didn't quit it. "You know me too well."

Corey reached forward, keeping me in his grasp, and picked up a file folder. "Before Ryan passed away, he made sure I owned fifty-one percent of the firm. Then he asked me to do two things for him, the first being to split his half of the company into two trusts—one for Nikki and one for you. If you want it." He took a sheet of paper out of the folder. "All you do is sign this letter, and I can get that started."

More money. More Scotts to partner with Johnson. "Okay. And if I don't want it?"

He took out another sheet of paper. "Then you sign this paper, and the full half will go into Nikki's trust. This request does have a fairly quick turnaround as we execute his estate, but you have some time to decide."

I nodded. Time was good. I had no idea what to do with a quarter of a company, particularly one in an industry I knew little about. "And the other?"

"Ryan also had me draft a provision that would create a chief communications officer position for you. This one has no timeline. The position only exists if you want it. It will never be filled otherwise. So today, a year from now, twenty years from now, it's yours. All you have to do is sign the letter and give it to me. I'll handle the rest."

I looked at the sheet he held in front of me. It was on Scott and Johnson letterhead and had Ryan and Corey's signatures. But nothing about either of the papers he'd shown me read contract to me. And in my job, I'd seen plenty of client contracts. "These aren't legally binding."

"No. But I know what Ryan wanted. I have it in writing and notarized. His lawyer also has a copy. Look, there's no pressure here.

Sign this or don't. It's up to you." He tucked everything back into the folder and placed it on the table before turning to me. He leaned in close. "But either way, you're stuck with me."

I grinned. That sounded like a very good problem to have. "Is that so?"

"Yup. I'm not ever letting you go again." His fingers skimmed across my cheek, and *holy shit*, his touch was electric.

I groaned, catching his hand before it could reach my neck. "Why aren't we in the place with the bed?"

He laughed. "Oh, we're going to the place with the bed, but we need to make a pit stop first."

"I thought we were already making *a pit stop*," I said, eyeing him.

He shook his head, pressing a quick kiss to my lips. "That's an all-night detour, maybe going through tomorrow and the next day. In fact, if you like, we can make it our permanent destination."

His words were full of promises. So many promises for today and tomorrow. For forever. My pulse jumped, and in my chest, my heart broke free of the remains of the fortress I'd built. I kissed him there on that couch in view of anyone passing by, and nothing had ever felt more right. Because this Scott belonged next to Johnson. Always.

"I love you, Corey Johnson."

He smiled, slow and real and true. "Good. Because I love you, Andi Scott."

TWENTY MINUTES LATER, we stood in front of the Robinson Diner. Corey linked his hand with mine and rang the bell. A familiar, though now older, waitress greeted us with a warm smile.

"There you two are. It's been a while." She pulled two menus from beneath the counter and led us to a booth in the back. "I'll give you a minute."

Corey hooked an arm around my shoulder. "You know, I haven't been here since the last time I came here with you."

Of course he hadn't. I kissed him softly, and as I settled into his embrace, in our spot, surrounded by memories and plans and so much love, the last piece of my heart snapped back into place.

The waitress cleared her throat as she placed glasses of water on the table. "So, what'll it be, lovebirds?"

We looked at each other, our mouths quirking into matching grins. "Fries."

Epilogue
Six months later
Corey

"**S**urprise."

I drop my pen as hands cover my eyes. As if I couldn't pick Andi's voice out of a sea of voices without effort. Her scent—sweet and floral—curls around me, and it feels like coming home. She lowers her hands and leans over my shoulder, her eyes traveling across the drawing I've been working on. It's Krystal's new house, one big enough for the soon-to-be family of four.

"That's coming along well." She kisses my cheek.

I push back from the desk and pull her onto my lap. "I thought you were coming tomorrow morning. Emily's out with Dustin and Delia."

"I know." She grins, and my body stirs like it always does in her presence.

"So that's why he offered to take them to the trampoline park on a Friday night." I tuck a strand of hair behind her ear and bring her lips to mine.

It's been five days since we've seen each other. Far too long. But with football season winding down, I couldn't get away, and while her boss is usually quite accommodating of her remote-working situation, their biggest trade show of the season is coming up, and she couldn't be spared.

Andi grins. "We *might* owe him a few weekday sleepovers."

"Only if he sleeps on the couch."

She laughs, and it's honestly one of my favorite sounds. "You're ridiculous."

"You love me."

Her hand slides under the top buttons of my shirt, and she places her hand over my heart. "That I do."

"So, what are we doing with our child-free Friday night?"

"Well, I think I found a place for us."

That's interesting. We've been house hunting for a few months—shifting through towns, looking at commutes, researching the best schools. There's a lot to consider and, at the same time, nothing at all because as long as I have Andi and Emily, I'm home. The rest is just a house. And I can build us a house anywhere.

"Really?"

She nods and hands me a sheet of paper. The house on it is beautiful and well designed. It has picture windows and a showcase chandelier, and if you look closely enough, you can spot the grand staircase. There's a little girl standing in front, her arms spread wide and a grin on her face on her first day in her new house. It's perfect, and I know everything Andi is giving up with this offer. Our eyes meet, and I study her, but there's no doubt in her eyes. She's rosy with happiness and comfort.

I lay the paper on my desk. "I wasn't aware that this house was on the market."

"I have it on good authority that the owner is looking for a roommate."

And she says *I'm* ridiculous. "Is he, now?"

She leans in, her lips brushing against mine. "Very good authority."

"Well," I say, pushing us to our feet. "Shall we check out the house? I hear the bedroom has a fabulous view."

She holds out an envelope. "One more thing."

I know what it is before I slip the typed letter out of the Scott and Johnson envelope. My fingers tremble a little against the sheet as I scan it, landing on Andi's signature next to mine and Ryan's. "Are you sure?"

She nods. "I already gave Steve my notice. A few more weeks, and I'm all yours."

My heart practically jumps out of my chest. On the nights I've spent alone in bed, as our schedules have kept her in the city and me in Fairford, this has been my private hope, especially after she accepted ownership of a quarter of the firm—Scott and Johnson Home Design with Andi Scott by my side. But I promised no pressure, and since handing her this paper six months ago, I haven't mentioned it once.

I fix my expression to as neutral as possible and keep my tone light, as if she hasn't given me my heart's desire like it was the easiest decision in the world. As if I'm not ready to ask her to spend her whole life with me this instant—if only the ring was ready. "So, when are you thinking about moving in?"

"Hold on. I believe you promised me a tour. I can't decide on a house sight unseen."

I link my fingers with hers and lead her out of my office and down the hall. "Here's a girl's bedroom, and this is a guest room, perfect for best-friend visits or in-laws or even, one day, a nursery."

She flushes. "That sounds nice."

Yes, it does. I never considered having more kids after Emily, but with Andi, I want it all.

We reach the last door in the hallway, and I push open the door to our bedroom. "Ah, and here we are, the master bedroom."

She tugs me inside and sits down on the edge of the bed, hooking her fingers through my belt loops. "Bed's comfy."

"And how's the view?"

She pulls me down by the shirt and locks her gaze on mine. "Best view in Fairford, hands down. I think I'll take it today."

I kiss along her jaw until my lips skim hers. I breathe her in. The woman of my dreams and the love of my life. "Welcome home, roomie."

Acknowledgments

F or a long time, I wasn't sure this book would ever be published. I wrote the opening scene in 2009 during my MFA program at Adelphi University. Per usual, I was squeezing in my homework wherever I could. In this case, I was sitting in my car, waiting to go into a job interview. That scene grew into the first true novel I would ever write. The twelve years since then have been a long and winding journey to its publication. *The Corey Effect* has been through many revisions, but its heart has always been Andi and Corey and their enduring love story. I'm so glad I have the chance to share it with readers.

So many people have played a part in getting *The Corey Effect* into the world that to try to name them all would mean I surely missed some. But know that whether you knew *The Corey Effect* as *Watch the Sky* or *Everything I Thought I Knew* or as a short story in a fiction writing workshop, I am grateful for you. Without my classmates, friends, family, and fellow writers, I may not have had the courage to write this story or the tenacity to keep trying to find it a home.

I would like to give a big thank you to my editors at Red Adept—Angie and Sarah—for helping me make Andi and Corey's story all it can be. A shout-out to Erica Lucke Dean for always calmly responding to my freak-outs no matter what time of day they arise. I couldn't imagine this journey without you. Thank you to Danielle Burby for believing in this book before anyone else. And of course, I'm so grateful to Lynn McNamee for continuing to believe in me and my novels.

To my readers, thank you for making the start of my publishing journey so special this past year. I wouldn't be writing this without you.

Lastly, none of this would be possible without the love and support of my husband, Tim, and daughter, Hailey. Thank you for believing in my dreams and living them with me. I love you more.

About the Author

Casey Dembowski loves to write stories that focus on the intricacies of relationships–whether romantic, familial, or platonic. Her novels focus on the inner workings of women and how everything in their lives leads them to exactly where they are, whether they like it or not.

The first story Casey remembers writing was in the second grade, though it wasn't until she turned twelve that she started carrying a battered composition notebook everywhere she went. Since then, there hasn't been a time when she isn't writing.

Casey lives in New Jersey with her family. She has an MFA in Fiction from Adelphi University, and currently works in corporate marketing communications. In her (limited) spare time, she enjoys reading, baking, and watching her favorite television shows on repeat.

Read more at https://caseydembowski.com/.

About the Publisher

Dear Reader,

We hope you enjoyed this book. Please consider leaving a review on your favorite book site.

Visit https://RedAdeptPublishing.com to see our entire catalogue.

Check out our app for short stories, articles, and interviews. You'll also be notified of future releases and special sales.

Printed in Great Britain
by Amazon

48197316R00169